STOP
THE TRAIN!

STOP
THE TRAIN!

A NOVEL BY
GERALDINE McCAUGHREAN

HarperCollinsPublishers

Stop the Train!
Copyright © 2001 by Geraldine McCaughrean
All rights reserved. No part of this book may be used or reproduced in
any manner whatsoever without written permission except in the case of
brief quotations embodied in critical articles and reviews.
Printed in the United States of America.
For information, address HarperCollins Children's Books,
a division of HarperCollins Publishers,
1350 Avenue of the Americas, New York, NY 10019.
www.harperchildrens.com

Library of Congress Cataloging-in-Publication Data
McCaughrean, Geraldine.
  Stop the train! / a novel by Geraldine McCaughrean.— 1st American
ed.
    p. cm.
  Summary: Despite the opposition of the owner of the Red Rock
Railroad in 1893, the new settlers of Florence, Oklahoma, are determined
to build a real town.
  ISBN 0-06-050749-7 — ISBN 0-06-050750-0 (lib. bdg.)
  1. Oklahoma—History—Land Rush, 1893—Juvenile fiction.
[1. Oklahoma—History—Land Rush, 1893—Fiction. 2. Frontier and
pioneer life—Oklahoma—Fiction.] I. Title.
PZ7.M1286 St 2003   2002027340
[Fic]—dc21   CIP
                                                               AC

Typography by Andrea Vandergrift
1 2 3 4 5 6 7 8 9 10
❖
First U.S. Edition, 2003
Published in the United Kingdom in 2001 by Oxford University Press

For the people of Enid, Oklahoma,
who did stop the train

CONTENTS

CAST OF CHARACTERS

Hulbert Sissney, a storekeeper
Hildy Sissney, his wife
Cissy Sissney, their daughter

Pickard Warboys, a telegrapher
Blosk Warboys, his wife
Their children: Amos, Ruth, Ezra, Esther,
Habakkuk (Kookie), Hosea, Nahum, and Haggai
Sue Warboys, Pickard's mother

Clifford T. Rimm,
chairman of the Red Rock Railroad Company
Nathaniel "Nate" Rimm, his son

Emile Klemme,
lawyer, sheriff, and doge of Florence

Jake Monterey,
a rancher who has lost his land
Fuller and Peatie, his sons

Gaff Boden,
rancher now occupying Jake Monterey's land
Tibbie, his daughter

Mrs. Loucien Shades,
a widow—"Miss Loucien" of Class Three

Sven and Lotte Lagerlöf, Swedish bakers
Harriet, Sven's second wife

Monday Morning,
a wheelwright and typesetter

Herman the Mormon,
a sign writer en route to Salt Lake City

Lloyd Lentz, an oculist and otologist

Charlie Quex, a barber

Samuel T. Guthrie, a banker

Virgil Hobbs, a boot maker

Jim Fudd, a toolmaker

Vokayatunga,
chief of the displaced Ponca tribe

Frank Tate, a cabinetmaker

Taffy Jones, an ex-miner

Children of Class Three,
including, Ollie West, Sarah Waters, Marlene Bell,
Barney Mackinley, Fred Stamp, and Honey

Everett Crew,
an actor with the traveling
Bright Lights Theater Company

1

THE RED ROCK RUNNER

Like a bad-tempered line jumper, the train rolled up against its buffers and gave a vicious jolt. Then it gave another in the opposite direction—a jerk that traveled from one coach to the next, tipping passengers back into their seats or forward out of them. Skillets and coffeepots clattered to the floor. Above Cissy's head, a pair of spurs scraped on the coach roof, and a saddle slithered past the window, flailing its stirrups. But still the train did not move off.

From end to end came the noise of men and children imitating the guard's whistle, but another ten minutes crawled by without the train making a move, and every second the passenger car became hotter and hotter.

"I paid for first-class tickets!" protested a latecomer, hopping up and down outside the coach door in a red-faced rage.

"All first-class on thissun," said the Negro guard, and he offered the latecomer a leg up onto the roof. "Make room. 'Nother one a-coming!" he announced cheerily, and there was a *crump* and an outburst of curses from over Cissy's head. She had never in her life heard so many curses as she had heard today.

She glanced sideways at the couple alongside her: a pasty pair, both shaped like loaves of bread whose dough was still rising as they cooked in the sweltering heat. She half expected their crusts to turn brown. When they had got in and plopped themselves down beside her, they had smelled of cinnamon and biscuits, but now they smelled more like old cheese.

Though she had been straining her ears for the sound all morning, Cissy never did hear the cannon, pistol shot, or whatever signal it was that set things moving. That was drowned out by the noise of the whistlers and the groaning old people and the crying babies and the quarreling children and the cries of ". . . bought a first-class ticket . . . !" The train simply gave another shuddering jerk, blew its own whistle, and set off.

A roar swept down the train—a roar of excitement and relief mixed with protests as those on the roof were enveloped in steam and cinders from the funnel. The faces and fluttering handkerchiefs of well-wishers fell away, and beyond the window views opened up of flat, unbroken prairies infested with moving figures.

The train, which called itself the Red Rock Runner, did not pick up speed, however. It settled instead into an ambling pace, so that the riders and wagons who had set off at the selfsame moment could keep pace with it. No one must be given an unfair advantage in this greatest of all races; the rules had stipulated twelve miles an hour for the train. A cowboy outside the train car window winked at Cissy's mother, who turned away, pretending not to see. But because the train was going no faster than the horse, the cowboy was still there an hour later, still leering in and winking.

The dawdling speed was not even enough to set up a draft through the crammed train. The passengers were simply jostled and rolled together by it, like cobs of corn boiling in a pot.

"How long before we get there?" asked Cissy, not remembering that she had asked seven times already. She got no answer.

Her father was making the acquaintance of the other passengers in the car. "How far you thinking of going?" he asked.

The Bread Loaves nodded at him, and a handful of words fell from their mouths like peanut shells: Swedish.

The black-haired woman with the spade clenched between her knees glared at Mr. Sissney as if he had asked to see her drawers, and Cissy's mother jabbed him in the ribs. It was not the done thing to ask where fellow "runners" were headed. Though the people on board the Red Rock Runner might all be united in a single historical journey, each harbored separate dreams of where it was taking him. They would not endanger that dream by confiding it to a stranger.

Oklahoma's northwest had been opened up to settlers by government decree, and tens of thousands of people—desperate, ambitious, hopeful, last-chance, stake-all, make-or-break, dare-all, nothing-to-lose people—had become, overnight, a colony of ants moving their nest. Each one was intent on grabbing his own particular patch of the patchwork earth and on staking his claim to a future.

"We're going to Florence," said Cissy, unhappy to see her father snubbed, hoping to smooth the scowl off the spade-wielding woman.

"All right, Cissy," snapped her mother. "The people don't want to know our business, thanking you kindly."

The Bread Loaves, though, had bulged forward in their seats, pop-eyed with glee. "Florence!" said the man, banging his chest with a blue-white hand.

"Florence, *ja, ja!* We go!" said his wife, and her cheeks, glistening with sweat, crimped like apple turnovers.

Though most of the land runners were dreaming of farms—of a future complete with a house and a barn and a cow and a harvest of wheat—there were some with different ambitions. Every forty or fifty miles, on their patchwork-quilt map of Oklahoma, the government had planned for a town—a center where those homestead farmers could go for their supplies, for their entertainment, for their hair to be cut and their cash banked, their lawsuits settled, their carts mended, their horses shod. Farmers' children needed schools, and farmers' wives needed to buy cloth, flour, and coffee.

These map-born towns even had names. The one where Cissy was going was called Florence. She could imagine it now—a clapboard church, a double-fronted shop, board-walks shaded by overhanging eaves, hitching rails, a school yard . . . It had to be better than the filthy roominghouse they had left behind in Arkansas, with its rats in the basement and its flies in the milk. For the next two hours, Cissy wearied her eyes squinting forward out the window, hoping for a first glimpse of the rooftops of Florence, Oklahoma. But she saw nothing but land runners, a moving sea of humanity on bicycles and buggies and horseback in such numbers that she was sure Oklahoma could not be big enough to absorb them all. How many would ride clear through to Texas without finding a vacant quarter section to claim? How many would be disappointed, like children left standing at the end of musical chairs? And would she be one of them?

"How long before we get there?" she asked, but her mother only pinched her eyebrows together as if the question caused her pain, and nobody answered.

Every time the train crossed a stream or stopped to replenish its water tanks, people would plop down from it like berries from a wilting stem of holly. When the train pulled away again, it left them behind, their belongings strewn around their feet. There were little family groups, lone young men, elderly couples gasping in the heat. . . . Their heads twitched—left-right, left-right—as they watched each separate carriage pass them by, while those left aboard the train showered them with good wishes and bad advice.

At every stop, children's voices could be heard asking, "Is this us? Is this where?" and the babies, woken by the lack of movement, bleated and squawked. But no one got down from Cissy's car. It remained as tight packed as a jar of plums.

By four o'clock, Cissy had been lifted into the luggage rack, to ease the cramped seating. The luggage of three families lay under and on top of her, and she drifted in and out of a nightmarish dream in which she arrived in Florence to be told, "No room! No room! No chairs left, but the baker says you can sleep in the bread oven!"

Drowsily she looked out the window for the millionth

time—then started so violently that a frying pan on her chest drove its handle into her chin. A huge black pyramid—like a haystack but for its color—was moving across the landscape, slow and stately, keeping pace with the train. She could not see the wagon that supported it, or the horses that pulled the wagon. The cargo alone was visible, now and then screened by oak trees but keeping a course parallel with the railroad tracks. It was an omen, a portent. Cissy was sure of it.

In the suffocating heat, oppressed by boxes, blankets, and bins, half awake and kept in virtual ignorance of her parents' plans, Cissy saw plainly now the dismal warning behind this gloomy sight. Coffins, stacked twelve high and twenty deep, swayed with the motion of the cart, and as they swayed, they listed toward the passengers on the Red Rock Runner, as if beckoning them all on toward early graves.

Then above her, spurs scraped again on the coach roof and someone shouted, *"Train stopping! Alight here for Florence and Bison Creek!"*

2

NOWHERE

As the train drew to a halt, Cissy peeped out and had a strong inclination to stay in the luggage rack.

But her mother and father were already hurling their few possessions out trackside. The door was chock-full of sunshine. It dazzled Cissy so completely that she had to jump down into nothingness, her eyes full of blue explosions. It was a relief to be out of the car.

The Bread Loaves, too, were getting down, emerging newly baked and crispy. They struggled to fit their tremendous hips through the narrowness of the door. From all along the train roof, faces looked down, sun-flushed, anxious faces full of unspoken questions: "Why did they choose here?" "Should we be getting down too?" "Will these ones survive?"

Cissy turned her back on the train and looked around her.

Florence did not exist.

How could it? Nothing yet existed in the territory that was northwest Oklahoma. It was a dream in the minds of fifty thousand hopefuls. The 160-acre plots that would one day be farms were still uncultivated scrubland, without farmhouses or corrals. Its towns were double plots of the same sun-baked land, their marker flags a different color, maybe, but their grass the same parched prairie yellow. A notice said:

FLORENCE TOWNSHIP
CLAIM NOS. 3048–9

but this was not Florence. This was Nowhere, in the Territory of Nowhere. An empty space waiting to be filled.

Others had got down out of other cars: more would-be citizens of Florence. One man, in a dark suit, had no luggage but for a flaccid carpetbag at his feet. What kind of man starts a new life in a good suit with nothing but a half-empty carpetbag? The newness was hardly scuffed off his city shoes, Cissy noticed.

There was a middle-aged man in overalls and a woman's broad-brimmed straw hat, his baggage packed in two burlap sacks. There was a pair of brothers with a box of tools, a storm door, and a bale of oilcloth. There was a widow in black, with a net purse swinging from her wrist, a knitting bag, and a goat.

One family descended from the roof like an avalanche of melting snow—a tattered couple, eight children, and a grandmother, along with a chair, a tent, and several baskets, all of which spilled.

The Negro guard blew his whistle. A roar of protest went up—"There's one not off yet!"—and Cissy's father went to join a crowd of men at the rear of the train trying to help a man off-load a large, black metal cube. "A stove?" Cissy wondered. As the train pulled away, fellow passengers threw the man's hat out as well, and he shouted his thanks.

"What was it?" asked Cissy's mother above the *clickety-clack* of the train wheels turning.

"A safe," said Mr. Sissney in a voice full of wonder. "Fancy that, though! A danged strongbox!"

"Language, Hulbert," said his wife tersely. "Hope you haven't hurt your back none. Last thing we need. You with a busted back."

The sun glared down with the same raging ferocity as Cissy's mother. Cissy's heart seemed to come to a boil inside her, bubbling up into her throat. She knew she should not cry—that it would do nothing to soften the anger of either mother or sun—but the tears leaked out like sap from a tree.

Hulbert Sissney squatted down in front of his daughter and looked into her face. "We're home, kitten," he said.

"But where is it, Poppy?" she sniffed. "Where's Florence?"

Her mother gave a short gasp of exasperation or triumph—Cissy could not tell which. "Well? Tell the child, Hulbert. Tell her where it is."

Her father continued to peep in under the brim of Cissy's bonnet, leaning for balance on the window pole he had brought from Arkansas. It was his sole (stolen) souvenir of his career in the grim little office where he had been browbeaten and overworked. "Can't you see it, kitten? Can't you? It's right here. Look." And straightening up, he grabbed a calico bag of clothes and strode off, wielding his window pole, throwing his rickety right leg out in front of him and counting the paces he took. "Here's where the sidewalk will

11

run, with the forge here, maybe." (Reaching into the bag, he dropped a pair of work trousers on the ground.) "And here's the seed merchant" (a pair of Sunday shoes). "And here's the haberdashery" (a petticoat in fetching pink).

He came hurrying back and tried to take the carpetbag from the young man, to pinpoint the barbershop, but the young man clutched it to him and the barbershop had to be a baby's crib instead, the baby asleep inside it. Taking the Swedish couple by the hands, Mr. Sissney urged them farther down the nonexistent sidewalk. "And here's the bakery!"

The Swede scowled and moved his wife twenty yards down, to what he judged a better position for a bakery.

"Here's where the Sissney General Store will be—*always the highest quality at the very lowest price!*" called Hulbert from a long way off. "And over there—the school!"

"Not near *my* store, thanking you kindly!" muttered his wife, but he was much too far away—being a fuel merchant and a doctor's office and a courthouse.

"*And over there—on that bit of higher ground, where the trees are?—that there'll be the church!*" he shouted. "*White clapboard with a weather vane and a little vestry out back for the sewing bee to meet in, Thursdays!*"

The newcomers eyed him, suspicious that Florence had already acquired its resident village idiot. Those who did not like his town planning moved down the nonexistent main street to positions they preferred.

But Cissy had begun to see them—those ghost buildings, materializing out of the heat-wrinkled air—storefronts and hitching rails, windows and shop signs, a school yard, a library, a stable. Her father climbed up on a wooden trunk eighty paces away, and she had a clear view, through the arch of his bandy legs, all the way to the nonexistent churchyard.

"And here's the municipal horse trough!" he declared, working his way back down the street.

"'Tain't so!" protested the mother of the eight children. "That there's Pickard's telegraph office. Cain't you see the Morse key?" She was laughing as she said it.

Cissy's mother hooked her lips between her teeth so that the last trace of color was lost from her pinched face. But her glare did not have the range to reach Hulbert and knock him over.

"What am *I*, Poppy?" called Cissy, feeling her heels rise off the ground with excitement. "What's going to be here, where I'm standing?"

"Well, you're the railroad station, nat'rally, kitten! Porters with handcarts. Buggies pulled up, waiting for folk off the train. Folks buying tickets. A newsstand. Mail sacks down the end of the platform. Crates stacked up ready for shipping in the freight cars. This here's a railway town, see? Kinda place is always jumping."

Behind her, though the train was already two miles down the line, the rails were still *wang-wang*ing with the sound of it: an odd kind of rhythmic music. The young man with the shiny shoes referred to some papers in his carpetbag and jotted down in his notebook the number of people present: some thirty souls.

The mirage faded. The town of Florence dissolved once again into parched prairie. Its various future citizens staked their claims to the rectangles of thistle and scrub, pitching tents or simply unrolling blankets on the crispy grass. By nightfall, a nearby thicket of trees had been so hacked about for firewood, for brushwood shelters, for claim posts, that it masked the slender rising moon no more than a threadbare blanket.

Out to the east and west, fires glimmered on parcels of land staked by sodbusters planning to plant some wheat, raise a few animals. One day they would bring their surplus produce into Florence, to trade for kerosene or beans or calico or a set of new horseshoes. One day music would trickle down the street from the bar. Now only a harmonica played jauntily somewhere in the dark, and the bugs whispered to each other of fallen bread crumbs, discarded apple cores, and soft, sleeping, succulent skin ripe for bloodsucking.

Cissy and her father sat watching the coffeepot heat over a brushwood fire while Mrs. Sissney stood, restless and anxious, wringing her hands, running critical eyes over the patch of darkness to which they had staked their claim.

"Shouldn't we be closer up to the railroad tracks?" she fretted. "Then we could take supplies directly off the train and no call for a cart. How are we ever going to afford a cart?"

"We shall get a wheelbarrow, my dear," said Hulbert Sissney soothingly. "Now stop plaguing yourself and set down. Railroad engines are great noisy beasts, and they churn out the dirt and shake everything around them. No point living so close we get no sleep, and get cinder burns in

14

our sheets and have the place fall down around our ears with the vibration. Didn't come all this way to sleep in a rail yard." He leaned back on his hands to admire the firefly stars. Cissy copied him, and the bigness of the starry sky made her feel better. At least it made Oklahoma feel a little smaller—not such an edgeless wasteland. Then a shape loomed out of the dark, and she gave a squeal of fright.

But it was only the good-looking young man with the carpetbag.

"Good evening, folks," he said, white teeth catching the firelight. He sat down beside Cissy, and she could smell the palm oil on his well-groomed hair. Something about him made her heart beat quicker.

"Nathaniel Rimm," said the young man. "Well? Not quite the paradise you envisaged, I imagine? Nothing but a patch of dirt, in fact." Hulbert Sissney sat more upright, whereas Hildy Sissney was finally persuaded to sit down. "You fine people deserve better, and I have a proposition for you! Have a candy." He produced a paper bag, its top already rolled back, and offered it around. Cissy was even more charmed by Nathaniel Rimm's speaking voice than by his bag of candy.

"Coffee, mister?" said Cissy's father.

"On behalf of the Red Rock Railroad Company, I am empowered to offer you fifty dollars—yes, fifty dollars—for your claim."

Out came the money, offered, like the candy, to one face at a time. Mrs. Sissney was a great deal more charmed by the money than by either sweets or speaking voice.

Hulbert lit his pipe. "You made this offer to any folks else?"

Nathaniel leaned eagerly forward. "This is just between you and me."

Hulbert took a suck on his pipe. "Cissy, be a good girl and go and ask next door. This young man been offering them fifty dollars the same?"

But Nathaniel Rimm threw an arm around Cissy, beaming cheerfully. "They all agree! Well, naturally they do. Seeing the hardship ahead. Feeling the heat. Show me that man who cannot profit from fifty dollars cash!"

Mrs. Sissney's anxiety erupted into a flurry of nervous movement. "You hear that, Hulbert? The rest are going. The rest can't see a future here, no more than I can!"

"I'm well enough suited, thank you," said Hulbert.

"Ah, but how much better prepared you could be to provide for your charming family with fifty dollars in your pocket! Somewhere the climate is more . . . amenable."

"If it's so bad, why do the railroad want it?" said Cissy.

Her mother was incensed. She came around the fire at Cissy, grabbing up a tin jug as she came, and Cissy could hear the anger crackling in the starch of her underwear. "I think we can manage without your smartness, thank you kindly, miss! Go and wash yourself at the creek and make ready for bed, if you please. And bring back water for the morning."

A washcloth flicked painfully in Cissy's face; the tin jug caught her a clout across the shoulder. She stumbled away into the unfamiliar darkness. But as she went, she could hear her father saying, "The child has a point, mister. Why d'you want to buy us out, if this place is so . . . unpromising?" Cissy hung back to hear the answer.

"Ah, Mr. Sissney! Shunting yards! Machine shops! Fuel piles. Locomotive sheds! These things don't feel the heat, Mr. Sissney. They don't feel the winter cold. They don't die at the first snakebite! Red Rock needs trackside facilities . . . whereas you, Mr. Sissney, you and your neighbors need fifty dollars. Look around you! The whole of Oklahoma Territory is open to you! More! The whole . . ."

The small babbling hiss of the creek smudged out Nathaniel Rimm's eloquence, and Cissy began to feel tree roots underfoot as she stumbled uncertainly down to the waterside, the empty jug banging against her knees. The moon had gone behind clouds. Bison Creek was hardly more than a trickle in the summer drought, and she could fill only one third of the jug by laying it on its side in the water. The insects were loud and biting. The dark was disorienting; she could feel her eyelids straining after more light.

And what eyes were watching her as she crouched down, afterward, to relieve herself? If the moon were to come out again, in this flat country, everyone from Texas to Missouri might see what she was doing. Waterside pebbles crunched against one another; she gave a squeal of alarm, lost her balance, and fell over onto her elbow. Something was moving around at the waterside—a mountain lion maybe, or Indians or Mormons or vaudeville actors or any of the other dangers her mother had warned her about. Cissy tried to disentangle her shoe heels from her skirt hem. *"Who's there?"*

"Habakkuk Zebediah Warboys!" came the whispered reply. "You a Indian?" It was a boy's voice, high and piping and scared.

Crossly, Cissy straightened her clothing, felt about for the jug, and stood up. "What's your mother do, buy names by the yard to sell by the letter?" But a part of her was pleased to hear another child's voice in this place invented by adults. "We're the general store. Came on the train. Cecelia Sissney."

"That's not a name. It's a sneeze," said Habakkuk, but he too moved toward the sound of a fellow child. "We're the telegraph office. But you're going, ain't you?"

"Going?"

"Grandma says your dad ain't got the sticking power of a monkey on a greased pole."

"Excuse me!" retorted Cissy. "I don't know that someone who ain't acquainted with some other person ought to go bandying monkeys—"

"But you took the railroad's money, didn't you?" the boy interrupted. "My paw's never seen fifty bucks but he says he wouldn't give up on the first day—not for five *hundred* bucks."

Cissy did not answer at once. "We didn't take it. You took it."

"Who took it? My maw says she didn't spend three weeks packing up her life and then have to do it all over again, just so the railroad can build shunting yards!"

"But Mr. Rimm said *everyone* took it. Mr. Rimm said—

Meet you back here tomorrow. 'Bye!"

Cissy picked up her skirts and ran. She ran all the way, forgetting the jug, forgetting her washcloth. Stumbling over the uneven ground, she lost her bearings and blundered into a strong smell of stewing apples and found herself on the baker's claim at the wrong end of "Main Street."

"Did the railroad man offer you fifty dollars?" she asked.

The Swedes smiled and nodded, nodded and smiled.

"Young man. Carpetbag. Fifty bucks," mouthed Cissy. "Did you say yes or no?"

"*Ja, ja,*" said the baker's wife, nodding and smiling and holding out a bowl of stewed apple. Cissy knew they had not understood one word.

In running to the next claim, she collided with a signboard wedged into the ground. The sign (which read "First Bank of Florence") fell over onto the ridge of a one-man tent and brought a man's face out into the firelight. "What'd you do that for?"

"The railroad man! The one with the carpetbag! Did he offer you fifty dollars for your claim?"

"Sure did," said the face. "Guess they want to own the trackside towns as well as the track. I told him no deal."

So Cissy ran on, along the passageway of darkness between a dozen campfires, and was just in time to see Nathaniel Rimm counting one-dollar bills into her father's open palm.

"...Others didn't...!" she panted, and found she hadn't the breath to say more. "...Others didn't..."

Hulbert Sissney closed his fist around the dollar bills, reached across, as though he were going to pat Rimm on the shoulder . . . and pushed the folded bills into his breast pocket. "In that case, Mr. Rimm, I believe I'll be staying too. Hildy, be so good as to pass Mr. Rimm his hat."

Nathaniel Rimm did not seem very put out. He dusted the tails of his jacket, snapped the fastening of his carpetbag. "Don't decide now. I shall return in a while—when you have become better acquainted with Oklahoma. Good night, sir . . . madam."

Hildy Sissney's eyes still rested longingly on the young man's breast pocket, her hopes dashed of ever again seeing so many bills back to back.

For the first time, Cissy realized something, and that something weighed like a stone on her stomach as she lay wrapped in her blanket that night. She had seen that her mother was journeying to Oklahoma with bad grace—but then Mrs. Sissney did everything with bad grace; it was just her way. What Cissy had not realized before was her mother's complete lack of faith in Florence, Oklahoma. She believed in none of those phantom stores and businesses. She did not believe a livelihood could be grubbed up out of this rectangle of balding earth. For Cissy it was a scary feeling, to think of her parents pulling against one another—as though the legs on one body had set off to walk in two different directions.

The question was: Which of them was right?

3

VILLAGERS

Nathaniel Rimm did not choose to wait in Florence for his answer. Though he staked a claim in his own name, close to the railroad track, he did not squat on it like his neighbors, eating beans out of a can. He boarded the Red Rock Runner as it returned north to its depot, saying that he would be back to buy up, on behalf of the railroad, whichever sites "proved unsuitable" to their owners.

"Don't hold your breath!" someone called after him, as the train pulled out.

"Don't trouble yourself!" called another. But there was a note of wavering doubt behind the bravado. Nobody had foreseen quite how hard life would be in Florence, Oklahoma.

"If we stand firm, the Red Rock Railroad can go shunt themselves," said Mr. Fudd. "The land rush was meant for individdles! Government never meant for big, rich companies to buy up the land."

"That's right," agreed Taffy Jones. "If they get their way, the railroad will turn this place into a 'company town'—decide who lives here, how much they get paid. . . . I was a miner in a company town. The company owns you body and soul in a place like that. You have to get their permission just to work for them. Then they own your house and the shop that sells you your food and the land you get buried in. They own the mine and the coal in it, and every drop of sweat you sweat, just so they can get a little bit richer. Never again, I swore. I'll never live in another company town. I came here to be my own man! Independent!"

"Like I said: individdle men and women! That's who Oklahoma was meant for!"

"Could do with a few more of the individdle women," someone muttered, and there was a groan of agreement from all the young men. (There was a great shortage of marriageable girls to be found roughing it out on the plains of the Cherokee Strip.)

This first meeting of the Florence Town Committee of Citizens was a democratic affair. It consisted of a chain of men off-loading supplies from the freight car of the Red Rock Runner, shouting their opinions above the noise of the locomotive. As yet, of course, there was no official station on the Glasstown–Guthrie line by the name of Florence, but the engineer always stopped at the creek to take on water. So Hulbert Sissney had felt safe to order two hundredweight of beans, a sack of coffee, and twenty pounds of nails, to stock the no-shelves of his nonexistent store. Other settlers were off-loading furniture or belongings sent on after them.

"The fact they want the land shows the land's worth having!" chirruped Lloyd Lentz.

"They'd go up as high as a hundred dollars, maybe," said

Angus Wright, a saddler from Nebraska.

There was no point in Hulbert Sissney's ordering anything more than coffee and nails and beans; there was no one in Florence who could afford to buy other wares. As it was, the investment had cost him his entire savings, all but ten dollars.

"The railroad's got one foot in the town already. I hear that man Rimm staked a claim for the railroad," said Monday Morning. "They are putting a grain silo on it. Big metal thing. So I hear tell."

"Well, that's a good thing, ain't it? Ain't that good? A silo is good. We want them in the town, don't we?" argued Hulbert peaceably. "This here's a railroad town, after all. You'd expect railway men."

"*Legally*, in fact, Rimm made the claim in his own name," Klemme pointed out. "*Legally* he could not stake a claim on behalf of a giant company like the railroad. As you said, Oklahoma was opened up for *individuals.*" Most of Emile Klemme's sentences began with "legally." He was a lawyer and was earning his keep by registering claims for the government and settling disputes between settlers. There were plenty of such disputes.

"Jake Monterey punched Gaff Boden outside the lawyer's tent!" Habakkuk confided in Cissy as they squatted together in the dust, watching the men work.

"Oh! Why?" Cissy was scandalized.

"Well, it's like this. The Montereys were 'Sooners.' They took a gamble and settled here last year, before the territory was 'ficially opened up to white men, see. Then in comes Gaff Boden and his family and overstakes his claim (along with four more empty ones), and Monterey says, '*What d'you think yer doing?*' and Boden says Monterey's got no right, in law, to be there, and they go along to the lawyer's office and the lawyer says Boden's right, Monterey's got to get off the land—him and his boys and his six cows—even though he's been there a year. And there's nothing Monterey can do, only swallow his cusses."

Cissy was hugely impressed. "Who else do you know, Kookie?"

Habakkuk Warboys sat back on his heels and narrowed his eyes into the sun. Flies landed and took off again from his bristly hair, like seagulls resting on a ship in midocean. "Well, him there, taking bags of nails from your paw, is Samuel T. Guthrie, the banker. That man next to him is my paw, of course: the government sends him a reg'lar paycheck just for being a telegrapher—leastways they will do, when there are some telegraph poles and a telegraph office. Ma says the Lord's gonna have to provide for us in the meantime, so I hope the Lord's feeling flush. The black man along from him—that's Monday Morning: he's a wheelwright 'mong other things. The Injun there, that's Vokayatunga. He's a Ponca, you know. That's the tribe around these parts— leastways it was till the government comes along and says it's Oklahoma Territory and the land runners can have it."

"You mean we overstaked him, kinda thing?"

"Kinda thing," said Habakkuk, "though the Poncas are past caring. They was only forced to live *here* so the whites could have their tribe lands. 'Fore that, they were up north. That there is Herman the Mormon—the one with the white face and the pea jacket and the hat like a chamber pot? I call him Herman the Milkman, 'cause he don't drink liquor: it's 'gainst his religion. He didn't mean to come here at all, but they throwed him off the train here, 'cause he only had a ticket as far as Hennessey, and no money. Herman don't believe in money, 'cause he's a Mormon and Mormons don't use it. Everything he wants, he has to get by doing swaps— and the only ticket he could get by swapping was one to Hennessey, when what he really wanted was to get north to Lincoln, then west to Salt Lake City, which Dad says is full of Mormons and empty of liquor."

Cissy gazed at her new friend—the boy she had met in the darkness by the creek. "How is it you know all these things, Kookie? I didn't even know where we was coming or why. My folks don't tell me a thing."

Habakkuk screwed up his face into an expression of intense wisdom. "Aw, when there's eleven of you sleeping in the one room, you can't hardly keep from catching on to the drift." He pointed at the line of people. "That's us Warboyses. From the boy with one ear—that's Amos—right along to the one with the yellow behind—Mam mended his dungarees with a dust rag: Amos, Ruth, Ezra, Esther, Hosea, and Nahum. Mam has a Bible, see. She's kinda working her way through it. Nehemiah, he died of strawberry tongue, and the baby, well, she shouldn't rightly be called Haggai, but Mam thought it was a girl's name and by the time she found out, it was set. She's a fright, Haggai, but how can you be pretty with a name like that?"

"What's your grandma called?" asked Cissy.

"Sue. I guess her folks didn't have a Bible. How come yours have only got you?"

"Don't know," said Cissy, who had never thought about it before.

"They got a double bed?"

"Y-e-e-es." Cissy was cautious, not seeing the relevance of this.

"Ah! My paw says he bought a single bed to save on money and space, but it was a false economy, 'cause look where it got him."

The children regarded each other for a moment, then shrugged. Neither of them could make any sense of that.

Cissy sat back on her heels in a way that mirrored Kookie exactly, but she knew that if she lived to be a hundred, she would only ever be a pale reflection of this wonderful boy who could talk and talk and never run out of words. If words were nails (or beans), she thought, Kookie Warboys could make his fortune overnight in Florence.

Kookie went back to identifying the people in the off-loading line. "Lloyd Lentz, he's an eye man."

"An *eye* man?" gasped Cissy. "You mean he sells eyes?"

"Well, that's what Mam calls him. The eye man. Though Paw says he does ears, too."

"*Ears too?!* Maybe he could make one for your brother."

"And that's Frank Tate. He's the coffin man, of course."

"Oh yes. I know *him*," said Cissy hastily. "He's come to bury us all as we die."

She had woken, on only the second morning, to the sound of her stomach grumbling. It was a familiar feeling. Hunger was an old friend. Before opening her eyes, she had tried to remember where she was, and when memories of the train journey and Florence and the prairie came flooding back, she was too afraid to open them. Where was the food to come from that would ease the pangs in her stomach? Poppy always said that God would provide, but God (it seemed to Cissy) had a very erratic delivery system.

The sun shining in her face was already turning her eyelids purple. She bit her lip, opened one eye.

What she saw made her whisper aloud: *"Manna!"* God had dropped manna from heaven to feed the land runners of Florence! Thousands of tall, thin black plants topped by slender, twin, translucent leaves seemed to have sprung from the ground during the night. Then she sat up—and the hundreds of rabbits sitting bolt upright in the morning sun moved off in a great dusty flutter, disappearing within seconds as completely as water into the cracked, parched ground. Rabbits! At least there would be meat once in a while. Rabbits were a kind of manna, after all, Cissy supposed.

And then, over a prairie wavering in the early heat, came that same omen she had seen from the train: a square, dark shape, growing as it came closer, into a huge, teetering tower of glossy caskets; shiny brass handles like ladder rungs; a small fluttering tarpaulin draped over the top. . . .

"Poppy! Poppy!" shrieked Cissy, and her father reached for his window pole in the very moment of waking and

kicked his way out of his blanket.

"What is it, Injuns?" he breathed. "Mountain lion?" His eyes followed her pointing finger.

The horses were visible this time, black as oil, blinkered, and with high plumes of black ostrich feathers fountaining from their brow bands. Black pall cloths had been draped across their backs. And perched up on the buckboard of the hearse, like a nightmare perched on a headboard, was a spider-thin youth in his shirtsleeves. A dead man appeared to be swinging, lynched, from one of the brass coffin handles. Cissy stifled a second scream.

As it came closer, she could see that the hanged man was in fact a suit of black clothes on a clothes hanger, and that the driver was standing up on the buckboard, peering toward her. Perhaps he was looking for people to fill his coffins. . . .

"Am I too late?" His voice came, reedy, out of the distance. "Are all the claims gone? Had to keep stopping to straighten up the cargo. Real slidy, caskets are. Then one of the horses went lame. . . . Am I too late?"

"You aggercultural or city?" Hulbert Sissney called back. "All the quarters along the creek are gone, but there's still plenty of sites in town."

"Hallelujah!" cried the young man, so loudly that the horses tossed their black plumes. "Point me the way, will you? Pardon my manners, mister, but can I be sociable another time? I been driving two days and nights solid, thinking the sites might all be gone." And shaking the reins, he urged his horses on down "Main Street" in the direction Hulbert pointed, calling apologies to those whose claim poles he knocked out of the ground.

"He's drunk," said Mrs. Sissney. "Look at him swaying to and fro."

"He's been awake sixty hours," said her husband. "He's entitled to waver a mite."

"Come to bury us all as we die," said Cissy's mother with heart-chilling gloom.

"Hush up, woman. You'll frighten the child," Hulbert said, but her mother had spoken no more than Cissy already believed. The coffin man had come to bury the citizens of Florence as they dropped down dead of heat and thirst and starvation.

"No, he ain't!" said Kookie with a hoot of laughter. "His uncle was an undertaker in Denver and he was apprenticed in carpentry work. Well, the uncle up and died, with nothing in the bank. But he did have this great stock of coffins. All best oak and yew. All grade-A work. So that's what Frank Tate inherited, and that's what he brought with him. You don't leave stock like that to go to waste! He's setting up as cabinetmaker. Got himself the only satin-lined cabin in Florence—made o' coffins stacked up this ways and that. Says when coffins are all you got in the world, coffins have to serve. Says he'll make my paw a telegraph desk out a one, just as soon as Paw's got a telegraph office to put it in. Desk with a satin-lined kneehole! The real business!"

Cissy was enchanted, and not only by the idea of a telegraph desk with a satin-lined kneehole. For the first time in days, she thought, she might be able to get to sleep when night rolled in over the prairie like a stampede of bison. She would not have to lie awake listening for the coffin man to drive up in his hearse and summon her away to her death. Only one thing she did not understand. "What does a cabinetmaker make?"

Kookie shrugged. "Teensy little cabins, I guess."

Apart from Frank Tate's coffin cabin, and the shining metal silo that the railroad put up on their claim, the tents and shacks that represented the town of Florence were mostly built of packing cases or canvas, of suitcases and branches, or sacking and turf. Most were dug out to a depth of four feet, so as to use less material above ground, and some were excavated completely out of the hard earth—earthen caves more suited to badgers than human beings. The ferocious sun made the pots and pans hung up outside *ping* and *tink*. It made the flames of the cooking fires invisible. It made the dogs lie on their sides gasping. It made the livestock sudsy with sweat. It made Bison Creek—what there was of it—steam and fume.

Settlers who had come with nothing in the world survived on rabbit, prairie dog, and pack rat meat.

The first time Cissy ate pack rat, she thought she was eating her father's old work boots, complete with the dirt caked on them.

"This what you call providing for your family?" enquired Hildy Sissney, sharp as any mosquito.

Her husband drew his head down between his bony shoulders. "Won't always be like this," he said. But he soon put his fork down and, a moment later, walked out of doors

30

onto the prairie to draw on a pipe empty of tobacco.

"Can I go play with Kookie Warboys?" asked Cissy cautiously of her mother.

"You can go and join the Ninth Cavalry for all I care," snapped Hildy. "No use to me, are you?"

So Cissy slipped away, the pack rat writhing so hard in her stomach that she thought it must still be alive.

The children of Florence tended to gravitate toward the creek while their parents slept away the noonday heat. Kookie had set up a throwing field, where they competed to knock stones off other stones by throwing stones at them. He called the game Stones. He also organized turtle hunts and beetle races, using hairpins for the betting. The Monterey boys, Fuller and Peatie, mostly just rolled around on the ground fighting and tearing their clothes. But Kookie seemed to be able to think of a different game to play every day. He had even incorporated a bunch of Ponca children into the group. Fuller Monterey said they ought to tie the Ponca kids up and throw stones at them, but Kookie pointed out, quite accurately, that it would be more fun to ask them where and how they caught fish out of the river and then see who could catch the most.

Not surprisingly, the Ponca Pirates (as Kookie dubbed them) won the competition, but since all the fish caught were cooked together in one bonfire, everyone profited equally from the game.

Cissy noticed that Kookie pocketed half his food to take home to the telegraph office.

Roaming about in this pack of miscellaneous children, Cissy Sissney felt like a wild bronco mare, with little Kookie

Warboys leading the herd and nothing to stop them from galloping all the way to Texas and the sea. It put out of her mind the bad atmosphere that filled her family shack blacker than the swarming flies did.

Their aimless straying took them onto the Boden claim, which bordered on the Florence town site. They saw, in the distance, a round-faced girl with long blond braids, sitting on a pony, watching them with wistful, wishful eyes. Cissy longed to see that hair close up, to discover whether there was a secret to growing hair that long and in that color. But when the Monterey boys saw the rider, they just shouted, "That's Gaff Boden's girl! Let's get her!" and began throwing stones at the distant, mounted figure. She drew her pony's head around and trotted away, and Cissy felt an oddly familiar pain in her chest—as if one of the stones had hit her, not Tibbie Boden.

"We went clear out to Golden Ridge!" she told her parents that night at supper. "And Kookie showed us how to blow reveille on a blade of grass!"

"Very improving, I must say," said Mrs. Sissney acidly. "And I'll thank you not to tear about barefoot like one of those *savages.*"

"The Ponca Pirates, you mean?" said Cissy, eager to explain their usefulness in the business of fishing.

"Any of 'em!" retorted her mother. "They're all savages. Specially that rabble at the so-called telegraph office. Them and those louts who go about with sticks and bowie knives."

Hulbert Sissney gave a soft laugh from behind last week's

newspaper. "And who are we, then, to be so high and mighty? Close kin to the tsar?"

His wife glared at the newspaper. "I just don't want her mixing with that kind," she hissed.

"What kind? The girl has to have friends."

"Not here. Not in this place." Hildy Sissney grated her spoon around the bottom of the bean pan. "We won't be staying long enough."

The newspaper gave a kind of quiver. So did the braid of hair down Cissy's back. The only noise, for the rest of the meal, was the scraping of spoons on tin plates. Then Hulbert Sissney folded his paper, laid it down beside his plate, and suggested, "Walk, Cissy?"

They walked down Main Street to where the ridge tent stood with the placard beside it reading:

First Bank of Florence
Proprietor Samuel T. Guthrie, Esq.
"IN THE DAY OF PROSPERITY BE JOYFUL" *ECCLESIASTES 7:14*

"Mr. Guthrie? You open, Mr. Guthrie?"

The small head emerged that Cissy had already met once before—though in the darkness she had not appreciated the redness of the hair or the size of the ears. Even now, in the declining daylight, the banker was puce with the heat.

"Good evening to you, Mr. Sissney," said Mr. Guthrie. "Hot, isn't it?"

"You done much business?" asked Hulbert.

A long, pale finger on a long, pale hand emerged from the

tent to push Mr. Guthrie's half glasses up his nose. "Made a fair few loans. My rate's five percent a month if you're interested."

"Don't want a loan," said Hulbert succinctly. "You open for deposits?"

"I am, Mr. Sissney. One percent a month."

Hulbert reached into his pocket. "There's ten dollars, then."

Mr. Guthrie looked at the crumpled bill in his hand. Cissy was half afraid, half hoping he was going to reject it for being too dog-eared. Then the hand withdrew inside the tent, and the head followed it. "I'll get you a receipt, Mr. Sissney." The voice sounded oddly deep throated, as if something momentous had just taken place and Mr. Guthrie was only narrowly in control of his emotions. Cissy's scalp prickled as her hair detected something Cissy herself could not understand.

Ten minutes later they returned to the shack with its three walls of crate plywood and fourth of blanket propped up with the stolen window pole. Cissy had taken her father's arm for the walk downtown, but now she walked five paces behind him, partly out of awe and partly out of fear of the ructions to come. Heat was welling up out of the very ground, as if the earth were retaliating after a day under the sun's relentless whip. Every one of her garments was sticking to her. Her father stopped in front of the shack to peel his shirt out of his armpits. Then he ducked inside.

"Hildy," he announced, "I just banked ten dollars." It was a boast, a taunt and a dare, all rolled up in one.

His wife was slow to answer. When she did, Cissy (even from outside) knew that her hands were on her hips and her lips rolled back off her teeth in that way that made her look ugly. "You gave ten dollars of our money to a total stranger? You're even more of a fool than I took you for! You seriously think you'll ever get it back?"

Cissy looked down at the slip of paper her father had given her to carry.

It said:

Received from H. B. Sissney . . . $10.
First Bank of Florence, Oklahoma Territory
Account Number 0000001.

"It's a matter of trust," said Hulbert. "If you believe in a thing, you have to take risks. You have to trust it to happen."

"He'll be gone in the morning, and our money with him."

"Won't get far with ten dollars."

Cissy peeked inside. Flies as black as hatred buzzed between the two faces: Hulbert and Hildy. Others flew in angular, everlasting circuits, staking their claims to the incandescent air. Cissy felt her heart blackening, too, like something strangled. At first, she heard nothing of the commotion behind her.

Then Kookie's brother Nahum came tearing along the street, panting and hollering and waving his arms. "Come quick! It's the baker's wife! She's down on the ground and she ain't breathing! Come quick, everyone! Anyone!"

Wrapped in her great pastry shell of flesh, Lotte Lagerlöf had succumbed to the heat of the Oklahoma summer. She had strained uncomplainingly under the great weight of sunshine, but it had pressed down on her, like the grain in a silo, and squeezed the very beat out of her heart.

Sven Lagerlöf stood now at her head, his flour-dusty boots to either side of her coils of netted hair. Lloyd Lentz, a dark little man in high-waisted trousers and suspenders, planted his small hands on Lotte's great bosom and lunged down on her heart. "I'm an oculist!" he said, over and over again. "I'm not a doctor, I'm only an oculist! I have no experience!" Great circles of sweat spread out from the armpits of his clean white shirt.

It was Pickard Warboys who finally laid a restraining hand on the oculist's shoulder and told him, "You've done your best, Lloyd. Leave her be. Let the dead lie peaceful, Lloyd. It was this infernal place killed her."

Cissy saw a look pass from her mother to her father—a triumphant look that said: "And *this* is the place you chose to bring us!"

The baker stood, his mouth a little ajar, his round eyes glistening like raisins in a bun. He knew too few words of English to express his thoughts, and so he said nothing; nothing in answer to the words of sympathy, nothing to Lloyd Lentz, nothing to the woman who brought him a glass of water or the man who offered him a swig of whiskey; nothing during the impromptu speaking of the Lord's Prayer; nothing while they carried his wife indoors. Only then, when she was laid on the makeshift table where, a few hours before, she had pounded and pummeled dough, did Sven Lagerlöf sniff the air and say softly, "Bread is burning, I think. Your bread, Lotte. It burns."

There was no church bell to toll Lotte Lagerlöf to her grave, but halfway through the funeral, the Red Rock Runner came around the bend in the tracks, clanging out its signal to clear the track.

When it pulled up, who should get down but Nathaniel Rimm, his carpetbag under one arm. Faces at the coach windows saw him hesitate, then pick his way between the tents and shacks and up the shallow gradient to a church not yet built.

Everyone was gathered there, standing around an open grave. The ground had proved so rocky that a spade head lay nearby, bent out of shape and snapped from its handle—a serious loss to its owner.

Frank Tate had provided the biggest coffin he owned—one that had been ordered and never collected, so that the name on its lid read JOHN GRUBER, DIED 1870 RIP. But someone with a can of red paint had daubed LOTTY LAGERLÖF along the lid. The faces of the people of Florence, already famished by hunger and shriveled by the sun, were pinched by a new kind of suffering.

But as Nathaniel Rimm approached, the men separated off from their womenfolk and stepped toward him as with a single mind.

"You come to gloat?" said someone.

"No, sir," said Rimm. "Whom did you lose? I'm deeply sorry for it." He set the carpetbag down at his feet. "I'll wait for you down by the tracks."

"State your business," said Lloyd Lentz, his feet still dancing a little with nervous strain.

The railroad man looked embarrassed. "In that case . . . I imagine life here must have proven harder than any of you expected. My fa— I mean, the railroad has sent me here to renew my offer. Fifty dollars for any claim signed over to them today"—he glanced toward the grave and modified his deadline—"tomorrow."

The women and children were watching too now, big eyed and sorrowful. Sven Lagerlöf raised his eyes from his wife's coffin and fanned himself with his hat.

When, after a minute, no one spoke, Hulbert Sissney said, "I think you came too late, young man."

"Too late?"

"Well, I don't rightly see how we could go now, Mr. Rimm. We just put one of our number underground, and now we owe it to her to stay close by. Seems to me it wouldn't be neighborly to move out on Mrs. Lagerlöf." There was a rumble of agreement from the other men.

Nathaniel Rimm lifted his face and his voice, too. "Is that your feeling, Mr. Lagerlöf? Will you be staying?"

"*Ja, ja.* Florence for me," replied the baker in his deep bass. "We come. Lotte and me. I do not go."

The rancher Gaff Boden took a step forward, in case the railroad executive needed persuading to leave. He was confronted by Nathaniel Rimm's outstretched hand. "Then I wish you all the good fortune in the world," Rimm said. "You people have my undying admiration and my prayers. I shall tell the railroad company that Florence Town is already spoken for—that you were unanimous in your decision. Now, if you will let me apologize for imposing on your grief, I shall return to the train before it finishes taking on water. I cannot see any good reason for me to stay here." And bowing courteously in the direction of the widowed baker, he turned and walked back down toward the noisy clanking and hissing of the train.

Angus Wright scurried furtively after the young man and caught up with him at the trackside.

"I'll take it! I don't mind going!" he yelped. "I'll take your fifty bucks, mister! You can have my site and welcome. 'Tain't fit for hogs, this place."

To his astonishment, the young railway executive passed him the money with such a look of contempt that Wright quailed and drew the bank notes in against his chest.

"Sign here," said Rimm. "Then get off your claim in the next three days." And boarding the train, he slammed the door behind him, saying something that sounded like "They're better off without you."

4

NO GO

The memory of Angus Wright the saddler did not fare well after he had gone.

"Judas," said Monday Morning.

"From Nebraska. Never liked Nebraska. It's full of his kind," said the toolmaker.

"Call himself a saddler?" said Gaff Boden. "Wouldn't put one of his saddles near a horse of mine."

"No, you'd sooner steal another man's horse, already saddled," snarled Jake Monterey, who poked a jibe at the rancher whenever the chance came up.

They fenced off Angus Wright's claim. Now, if the railroad came looking for its piece of land, they would find no way onto it but by pole-vaulting.

"Used to wall up vestal virgins like that in ancient Greece," said Monday Morning.

The FTCC pondered this for a moment. "What a waste," said the young men. They would have liked to wall up Angus Wright himself, for betraying Florence, but settled for spitting over the fence onto the plot of land he had abandoned.

The fence was only one of the plank structures now

going up in Florence. Lumber was in much more plentiful supply. Every day it arrived by cart or train, so that Florence could start to take shape. Wood-framed two-room shacks took the place of the dugouts and some of the tents. Their inside walls were papered with pages from the *Watonga Republican* and the *New York Tribune*, which arrived by stagecoach, six whole copies at a time. In the back room of the general store, Cissy Sissney could now lie in her home-made hammock and read of robberies in Cincinnati, legislation in Washington, plays in New York. At least, she could read them once her father had read them out loud to her, because Cissy had a good memory. Before it grew too dark to see, she would run her eyes over the lines of dots, strokes, and curves and remember what her father had said, so when she was sleepy enough, she half believed herself able to read.

"Ten years old and can't read nor write," she heard her mother say, blaming her husband. "What's going to become of her? Who's gonna want her?"

"I wanted you, didn't I, honey?" Hulbert would reply mildly. "Don't rush me. I'll get around to teaching her. Just let me get the store straight. . . . Anyways, there'll be a school here soon enough."

Cissy was not alone; many of the adults in Florence could not read, let alone the children. All the more surprising, then, that Florence sported so many signs. Almost every business had a sign. Even if the premises consisted only of a cart with a man asleep in it, there would usually be a sign out front, immaculately scripted, and underneath, the proprietor's name and an apt quotation from the Bible:

EMILE KLEMME

LAWYER, RECORDER OF OATHS,
WILL MAKER, CLAIMS ARBITRAITOR
TO THE OKLAHOMA TERRITORY.

"MIGHTY IN DEED AND WORD"
LUKE 24:19

WM. T. BOLTON
BUILDER

"I will build him a sure house"
[1 Samuel 2:35]

GENERAL STORE

"ALWAYS THE HIGHEST QUOLLITY AT THE VERY LOWEST PRISE!"
PROPS: H & H SISSNEY
"take food for the famine"
GEN. 42:33

L. LENTZ
M. S. O. P., M. S. O. M.
OCULIST & OTOLLOGIST

(leg irons also made)

"The hearing ear, and the seeing eye,
the LORD hath made even them both."
Proverbs 20:12

LAGERLÖF'S
BREAD, COOKIES, PASTRYS
"GIVE US THIS DAY OUR DAILY BREAD"
Matthew 6:11
MR. S & L LAGERLÖF

TELEGRAPH OFFICE
Prop: PICKARD WARBOYS
TELEGRAFIST & AGENT FOR OSAGE STAGE CO.
"SEND THY MESSENGERS FAR OFF"
ISAIAH 57:9

CHARLIE QUEX
BARBER
"THY HAIR IS AS A FLOCK OF GOATS"
SONG OF SOLOMON 4:1

VIRGIL HOBBS: BOOTMAKER
"my feet were almost gone"
Psalm 73:2

TOOLS & REPAIRS
Mr. & Mrs. Fudd
"He hath made me a polished shaft."
Isaiah 49:2

At the crossroads there were even street signs, where the dusty lanes between the ramshackle buildings crossed each other:

MAIN STREET: "Wisdom crieth in the streets."
EAST ROAD: "Many shall come from the east."

It was Herman the Mormon they had to thank for these. A sign writer by trade, he painted in return for payment in kind (owing to his moral objections to money). Quite often his offer was turned down by men who thought they could get by nicely without the luxury of a sign. But Herman would go ahead and paint one anyway, and he was such a craftsman that the business owner was usually won over and paid for it with a can of beans or a free haircut or the removal of wax from Herman's large ears. One day, he believed, he would make the ultimate swap, and earn himself a train ticket to Salt Lake City. That is why, though he accounted himself only a temporary citizen of Florence, he looked forward as much as anyone to the day the town would have its very own railroad station.

Probably the greatest service Herman did people was to interrupt the boredom of day-to-day survival. From one day to the next, the hardships never changed, and that kind of routine suffering makes for a purgatory of boredom.

The rabbit hunt had more to do with killing boredom than killing rabbits. Even so, by September, everyone in Florence had eaten quite enough prairie dog and pack rat to last them a lifetime. They needed to taste edible meat. So one day the whole town turned out, armed with sticks or hammers or rocks, to do war on the rabbits of the Cherokee Strip.

Hildy Sissney was the most eager for the slaughter. Having planted out the yard behind the store with little squash plants, lettuces, and sunflowers, she had gone down to the creek for water to give them a soaking, only to come back to find the garden a seething mat of rabbit fur, as three score mouths devoured her tender shoots.

"My ma says God didn't invent rabbits," said Cissy, recounting this disaster to Kookie as they traipsed out onto the prairie, dragging lengths of sacking. They and all the other children had been sent as "beaters" to stir up the rabbit population and drive them in the direction of the adults. "She says rabbits are the devil's revenge after he was cast out of heaven. Says there couldn't have been rabbits in the Garden of Eden, or there wouldn't have been no Garden of Eden."

Kookie nodded shrewdly. "Same with weevils and roaches. And lice," he added as an afterthought, scratching his scalp vigorously.

On the other hand, the children *had* discovered God's secret intention for turtles. Kookie, with the help of the Ponca Pirates, had managed to collect upward of fifty turtles and held regular race meets on the far side of the creek. The children bet with the buttons off their clothing, with the result that Kookie had enough buttons to hold up the Brooklyn Bridge, and everyone else had to keep tight hold of their waistbands and dungaree straps. He was willing to sell the buttons back, a penny apiece, but only Tibbie Boden had so far been able to take him up on the offer.

At the sound of the signal—a gunshot—the rabbits started into motion, running the wrong way because the shot had scared them. Confronted by this tidal wave of rabbits, the children froze, thinking to be overrun. Then Ezra and Hosea began whirling their sacks, and the rest joined in, stamping their feet and roaring.

Peat and Fuller Monterey saw their chance and moved around behind Tibbie Boden, so when they began whirling their sacks, the burlap caught her across the back, sending her blond braids flying.

"You quit that, Peat Monterey!" said Kookie.

"Stop it!" shouted Cissy. "Don't!" But the Monterey brothers were intent on their bullying. All the hatred their father felt for Tibbie's father they had decided to feel for his pretty, blond-haired daughter. She gave a shriek and ran forward, just at the moment the rabbits saw the sacks, turned, and scuttled back toward the adults. The whites of their tails wrote a kind of musical notation from one side of the field to the other. Some darted away at a tangent, and the men with shotguns took potshots at them, with little success. Most rushed in a headlong panic, like land runners racing each other for territory. Their burrow entrances had been filled in, though, and they were obliged to charge on, trampling over each other. Women whirling jackets funneled them in toward the rabbit hunters of Florence. Some, blind with panic, ran directly in among the clubs, and furry little bodies flew off to right and left, while the clubbers cursed each other for the blows they caught by accident. Some of the rabbits doubled back time and time again, but there was no escaping once they were in the wire run. Both hunters and beaters closed in on the squirming multitude of rabbits—a plague of rabbits—hundreds upon hundreds, leaping straight up, high as a man's head.

And in among the rabbits came Tibbie Boden, the rancher's daughter. Her persecutors had dropped back, but Tibbie had no way of knowing it, since now she was being buffeted and bombarded by wounded and leaping rabbits. Her hands were over her head, her eyes shut, her screams blotted out by the noise of rabbit Armageddon.

When the adults finally saw her, their clubbing faltered and came to a halt. Her father ran forward—"Tibs?"—uncertain what was going on.

Parents shouted questions and threats up the field at the children who advanced, dervish mad, kicking up dirt, whirling their sacking and howling like savages. A handful of rabbits seized the moment to sprint between legs and reach open prairie. Cissy caught up with Tibbie, but Gaff Boden pushed her roughly away and put comforting arms around his daughter.

"What you children need is a whipping!" he raged.

"What those children need is taming," said someone, picking up a brace of dead rabbits.

"What them children need is *schooling*," said another, shouldering a club ragged with bits of bloody rabbit fur. "They's turning into ruffians!"

They asked Herman the Mormon if he would put off his journey to Salt Lake City and fill in until Florence could get hold of a schoolteacher. He said no: He would be leaving any day now for Salt Lake City.

So it was decided to advertise for a teacher in the *New York Tribune*, which was widely read throughout the frontier as well as on the East Coast. Everyone chipped in ten cents toward the cost of the notice:

> **God-fearing schoolteacher wanted for growing school, Florence, Cherokee Strip, Oklahoma Territory. Salary by mutual arrangement.**

The piece about the salary was Emile Klemme's idea. No one else could think how to phrase the fact that Florence had no money to spare just then, for a teacher or even for a schoolhouse to put one in.

Kookie's father took solemn charge of the brown paper bag on which this advertisement had been drawn up. Not that he could actually send any telegrams as yet, owing to the lack of any telegraph poles or wires within a hundred miles. But since he took his responsibilities very seriously, he did the next best thing. He rode once a week to Fort Goodridge, where the collection of mail was a regular and reliable affair.

The service was greatly in demand, for many of the men in Florence had left families outside the territory, waiting to be sent for when a home had been built and there was a living wage coming in. For those who could not write, or did not know what to write, Mr. Warboys even wrote the letters.

"How do their kin read it at the other end, if they can't read?" Cissy asked Kookie, as they waved Mr. Warboys off one day.

"There's always someone around who can read it to them," said Kookie. "Growing fad, this reading and writing. My folks been doing it for years."

"My paw can read the Bible. And the newspapers," said Cissy tentatively, since it sounded as if Kookie disapproved of the fad.

"Mmm," said Kookie. "Just so long as they keep it to theirselves and don't get us to doing it. Hey! Did you hear about Mr. Lagerlöf advertising for a new wife?"

"*No?!*"

The baker had come into the telegraph office with his shoulders hunched high around his ears, waggling a copy of the *Tribune* and jabbing his fingers at the advertising pages.

"You want I place a notice for you?" said Pickard Warboys. "'Bout your poor wife?" He drew the Swede's finger across the page in the direction of the black-rimmed death notices.

"Wife! *Ja! Ja!*" said Lagerlöf and pointed obstinately back among the advertisements for ramrods, store managers, and traveling salesmen. "Alone is no good. Wife I need. You put in notice, *ja*? Good strong woman. Big!" He drew in the air, with pale, floury hands, a shape close to that of his dead wife. Then, remembering how Lotte's size had been her undoing, narrowed the gauge by five or six inches.

Warboys's face must have shown how much the idea

shocked and offended him. There was Lotte Lagerlöf, hardly cold in her grave, and her husband was advertising for a replacement!

"Business no good with one. Must have two!" cried the baker, his big throat swelling with all the unspoken words of Swedish he needed to explain himself properly.

Warboys nodded, took his money, and agreed to place the notice. It seemed an immense relief to the big man, who shrank down visibly, emptied of bluster and aggression. "I thank you, Pickard Warboys," he said, and ducked his way cautiously out of the shop for fear of dislodging the doorposts.

Blosk Warboys slapped her husband's arm. "That's plain indecent! Why did you agree to a thing like that? Indecent, that is! Plain un-American!"

"Times and circumstances, honey," Pickard said, putting an arm around his wife and holding her close against his side. "No room for sentiment in a place like this and in times like these."

"So he wrote an advertising notice for this big healthy wife!" Kookie recounted. "Paw says lotsa men on the prairies do that, but I'm danged if I would!"

"Who would you marry, then, Kookie?" asked Cissy, deliciously shocked by the awful news.

"Oh, that's easy," he said, in his most matter-of-fact voice. "I'm going to marry Tibbie Boden."

Even though Florence sprawled over six square miles, the daily passage of the train had a way of drawing men and children from all over, just to watch its great barrel-bellied bulk bluster into sight, with billowing steam, and slide to a cacophonous halt beside the creek. It was a break from the boredom of toil. The Ponca children were still terrified of it, believing it to be the Cannibal Giant of their fairy stories, and they ran in the opposite direction.

One day, when the Red Rock Runner stopped to take on water, a passenger got down from the car festooned with baggage and called for help to lift down a heavy crate from the baggage car.

Men broke off from what they were doing to stare, but they did not go to his aid. He and the guard had to man-handle the crate onto the ground between them, and then only after he had slipped the guard a whole dollar.

It was Nathaniel Rimm.

"What you doing here, Mr. Rimm?" called Hulbert Sissney, descending a ladder from his roof and hurrying down the street. "You come to up your offer?"

"No. No, I—"

"'Cause we still ain't interested. No more than we were last time. You keep your money in your pocket."

"I intend to," said the young man, and there was something about him that was different from before—less shiny, less slick.

"The railroad and us, we can get along just fine. We need each other, that's plain and obvious," said Emile Klemme from his office doorway, "just so long as we all know where we stand."

Nathaniel Rimm gave a weary laugh that barely reached the corners of his mouth. He looked down at his feet and said to himself, "And where's that, I wonder?"

When he looked up, he was speaking to them all.

"My father . . ." he said, taking off his hat, "my father, Clifford T. Rimm, is chairman of the railroad. He sent me down here to get a first taste of business. Only it was a taste I did not care for. It was a taste like a bad smell."

"That'll be the pack rat stew," said a voice somewhere in the crowd.

"My father was not best pleased when I came back empty-handed. He said that I lacked the 'killer instinct.'" Rimm broke off, head lowered like a man at prayer.

"You come to prove him wrong?" called Monterey through a mouthful of chewing tobacco.

The young man looked up again and, with a shudder that shook his whole frame, squared his shoulders and placed his hat back on his head. "I'm here to throw in my lot with you people. Since I find more here to admire than I did in my own back parlor."

The men looked at one another, each checking with his neighbor whether they had just been paid a compliment.

"The claim I staked was meant for the railroad. But I made it in my own name."

"Told you so," said Klemme smugly.

". . . so I reckon it's mine in law. I can hardly take down the railroad's silo—you wouldn't thank me for it anyhow—but there's room alongside it. And I mean to use it to start up a printing office. It's the profession I would have chosen if my father had not . . . chosen otherwise."

The crowd murmured its approval and began to turn

away, some excited by the prospect of Florence having its own newspaper, others by the notion of the railroad chairman's son preferring their little town to Glasstown. Most of all they appreciated Rimm for giving them something to talk about for the next few days.

"Wait!" said Rimm. "There's more. You may not think I've done you any favor when I'm done telling you."

The crowd turned back. Women who had been listening from inside the shacks showed themselves for the first time. Nathaniel Rimm jumped up onto the wheel rim of a cart. "My father is a petty, vindictive man!" (The women sucked in their breath. It was against the teachings of the Bible, after all, for a son to speak ill of his father.) "My father says (and I quote): 'If I can't have Florence, then Florence can go to hell!'" There was a gasp at the profanity, as well as the venom behind it. "He says that if you are too good to take his money, he'll be damned if you get rich thanks to his railroad!"

They were staring at him now, mouths open, as if he were the father and not the son.

"He says there will be no Florence station on the Red Rock Railroad Line. He says it and he means it. From here on out . . . the trains won't be stopping at Florence. Ever."

5

BRIDES AND GREASE

"Not stop?"

"We're busted, then."

"Done for."

"Finished."

The news struck the people of Florence like a runaway locomotive plowing into their midst. Men sat down on the ground where they were. Blosk Warboys looked around for her children and hugged her ugly baby close. Hildy Sissney gave her husband a shove on the shoulder. "Thanking you *very* kindly, Hulbert Sissney. Didn't I say we should have sold while we had the chance?"

"You figure he's open to negotiation?" asked Emile Klemme of the young man on the cart.

Nathaniel shook his head. " 'Red Rock' Rimm? My father is incapable of changing his mind. Once he has said a thing, it is carved in stone."

"Like the law of the Medes and Persians," said Monday Morning under his breath.

"In that case, I say we shoot his boy!" suggested Virgil Hobbs, pulling out a pistol and waving it in the general direction of Nathaniel Rimm.

Emile Klemme, who had appointed himself temporary sheriff, waded in between and cautioned against it. "You never want to shoot a man whose kin can afford lawyers," he said.

"So what's the great tragedy?" croaked Jake Monterey. "We still got the stage, don't we? I got by for a year here without the help of him and his danged train. It took a bigger rogue than 'Red Rock' Rimm to ruin me!" And he glowered at Gaff Boden.

But hardly anyone else saw it from his point of view. They had come to Florence because Florence had been created as a railroad town—a stop on a journey between cities, a place for ranchers to load their cattle, farmers their grain, craftsmen their wares. It was supposed to be a living organ connected to the heart of America by arteries of wood and steel and steam. Without the railroad, Florence would wither and die—become a dead town for children to point at out the windows of a speeding train: "What's that place, Mommy?"

"Lord knows, precious. Just some place where the people moved out and the dust blew in."

"Who needs railroads anyhow?" asked Jim Fudd. "One day soon there'll be wind-driven carts. I read about it in the *Tribune*! This guy's invented wind-driven carts!" The citizens of Florence looked at him with undisguised disgust. Some glanced up at a sky set steel hard for want of a breath of wind.

Kookie watched the tears crawl out between his mother's tightly shut lids, tears that, despite hunger and heat and hardship, had not run since the death of Nehemiah. "Then we'll just have to *make* it stop!" he piped up.

Cissy felt her heart flex back into shape, like a bouquet pulled from a magician's sleeve. "That's right! We'll *make* it stop!" she repeated.

Waspish, her mother gave her a push from behind. "Oh yes? And how you gonna do that, if you please, miss? Stand on the tracks and wave your hankie? Do it! And take your father with you! Dreamers, the both of you!"

But Kookie's father had taken heart from his son's outburst. He looked almost shamed by it. "The children are right!" he declared. "We can change the railroad's mind! The train's gonna stop here in the long run. Heck, it pulls up every day to take on water! And the railroad's put up a silo, ain't it? All we got to do is make ourselves undispensable!"

The mood of the crowd visibly brightened. Of course the train would stop at Florence. It needed Florence as much as Florence needed it. "I say we put up a water tower—proper carpentry water tower. A kinda peace offering to 'Red Rock' Rimm. What do you say?" There was a buzz of enthusiasm for the idea. People began chattering tongue-and-groove to each other about timber and plans and ladders and artesian wells.

Nathaniel Rimm was left alone and unmolested, in the middle of Main Street, loosening his string tie and using it to tie back his long, disheveled hair.

"Except that you don't believe it, do you?" Monday Morning emerged from noonday shadows so black that they

56

had hidden his very presence.

Nathaniel took the measure of the man's face. "My father said he wouldn't touch Florence now at one cent an acre."

"Sour grapes. Like the fox in the fable. . . . You want a hand with that crate of yours?"

"Like the fox in the fable," Rimm agreed with a weary smile. "Yes, please."

The whole town gathered next day to see whether the Red Rock Runner would stop, as usual, to take on water. Their teeth rattled in their heads as it tore through at forty miles an hour, whistling like a frenzied demon and clanging its bell. The Ponca Pirates scattered screaming with terror and were not seen in town again for days. The engineer in the locomotive wore such a malevolent grin that his false teeth stuck out of his mouth, crooked and overlapping, and even the settler children were unnerved by that.

Cissy's father, having ordered up a ten-gallon drum of lard and ten sacks of beans, was obliged to rent Frank Tate's hearse and drive all the way up to Glasstown to collect them. By the time he got back, the lard had turned to rancid slime.

People traveling to Glasstown were obliged to go by stage, and a journey on the Osage stagecoach was, as Monday Morning put it, "about as comfortable as Orpheus's descent into the Underworld."

People who got off the stagecoach in Florence did look like ghosts escaped from the Infernal Regions. They were white from head to foot, for one thing, either from the dust or because they were wearing white duster coats to protect their clothing. Stepping down off the folding stair, they staggered from motion sickness, their faces green, their hats crushed from being bounced up against the roof. The luggage, which might have started the journey neatly stacked on the stage floor, cascaded out the door ahead of and behind them, dented, burst open, upside down. A man who had been bombarded by it throughout the trip kicked a hatbox thirty feet down the road as he climbed down.

Generally, the stage only stopped in Florence to drop off the papers and for the horses to be watered; and everybody climbed back in after stretching their legs. But today, when driver and passengers trailed unwillingly back to their seats, two ladies stayed behind.

"You missed two!" called Kookie, who was helping his brother to sink the base of the new horse trough into the rock-hard street.

"Nope. They come here voluntary!" called the driver, and he whipped up the horses to a gallop, shaking a roar of anguish from the passengers beneath him. Brother Amos took off his hat—a remarkable occurrence, in Kookie's experience.

One of the ladies was a slim needle of a woman with plump, pink cheeks, wearing a crushed bonnet and net gloves. The other wore a bright-yellow underskirt, her iris-blue overdress caught up here and there so that it resembled the sea receding from a golden beach. A pair of old scarlet leather riding gloves was tucked into her waistband, and her hair was hardly less red.

58

"Oh my," breathed Amos Warboys. "Who's that?"

Charlie the barber (while he waited for people in Florence to afford the luxury of a haircut) had gone into the business of making lemonade. The stuff he sold had never seen a lemon and brought nobody any aid, but whatever he added clouded the water enough to *look* like lemonade in the glass. He brought some now—a tumbler in each hand: "Refreshment, ladies?" Then his sharp little eyes spotted that each was holding a copy of the *New York Tribune* open at the appointments section. "You ladies after teaching school for us?" he asked in a voice as cracked as his porcelain barber's bowl.

Up and down the street, children felt a thundercloud gather over their heads; they took off for the creek, to discuss the catastrophe. Not Kookie. He stayed, because he liked always to be in full command of the facts.

The women smiled, not at the barber but at each other, as if to say, "Is *that* who you are? I was afraid you might be . . ."

"I am not," said the thin one, swiveling her body shyly to and fro and blushing and folding her netted hands one over the other. "I am here at the behest of a Mr. Lagerlöf, who I believe resides here'bouts."

Kookie gave a low quiet gasp of relief. "That makes the other one the teacher!" he whispered to his brother. "Wait till I tell Cissy!"

The barber looked expectantly at the woman in yellow and blue, trying to keep his eyes on her face rather than the huge outthrust of her chest or the pistol strapped just underneath it. He was waiting for her to say what business had

59

brought her to Florence, but she simply said, "You direct this lady the way, and I'll tag along." She did, her yellow underskirt flicking up behind a pair of block-heeled boots, her strides longer than the barber's.

"Under that there stripy dress there's a *whalebone corset*, betya a dollar," whispered Amos, as if he had just sighted a rare species of whale. "Saw one in a newspaper one time."

Up and down the street, work on rope splicing, house roofing, rabbit skinning, and wood whittling came to a halt, and men sauntered in the direction of the bakery, all taken with a sudden desire for one of Mr. Lagerlöf's malt cookies.

The big man stood behind his trestle table, an apple pie balanced on his fingertips, while he trimmed around the pastry lid with a knife. He looked up to find his shop crowded with people. He understood in an instant—almost as if his wooden pan rack and all his cooking pans had fallen over on top of him—that not just one but *two* women had come in answer to his advertisement for a wife.

They had not posted him their details. They had not waited to be invited. They had not written first to tell him they were coming. They had just come. Sven wiped his hands on his shirtfront and said something in Swedish. A dozen faces looked on to see what he would do.

The two women stood side by side, their faces turned a little away from each other. Lagerlöf came around the table, hands outstretched. "I am Sven Lagerlöf. Have! Please!"

"Harriet Pim," said the slim needle in the net gloves.

"Loucien Shades—widow," said the other, and they took the iced buns he was offering.

Sven, his vocabulary used up, turned on his heel, went back, stuck his head in the oven, and began raking out the ashes. Mrs. Shades took a large bite out of her bun.

Hulbert went and pretended to help Sven with the oven. He whispered, "You can't keep your head in the oven all day. 'Tain't American, this, Sven. Not a genteel situation at all. Someone stands to get their feelings hurt bad. Well, say something to them, at least!"

Sven looked at him with desperate spaniel eyes. "I think, 'Letter.' I think woman send letter. Photograph! I read. I choose. I write. She come. *One* come. You get me?"

The woman in yellow and blue cleared her throat so loudly that Sven banged his head on the inside of the oven. "You'll want to get acquainted, Mr. Lagerlöf!" she called. "A man don't buy a horse just by looking."

"Yes, yes," said Miss Pim weakly. "Is there a hotel, per-haps? Somewhere?" but her voice was tremulous. This was not how she had imagined meeting her prospective husband. She seemed just to have noticed Loucien Shades's pistol and to be unable to look away.

"Come on, sister," said Mrs. Shades. "We are embarrassing the man. He ain't gonna choose by dipping, is he? Or tossing a coin? Why don't we have dinner here tonight, Sven Lagerlöf, so's one of us can sway you." She turned to go, her skirts sweeping pastry trimmings across the plank floor, her arm around Miss Pim's waist.

"No!"

There was another clang as Sven again cracked his head on the inside of the oven. Then he emerged, soot smeared and sweating, a desperation in his eyes that made the crowd draw back a pace.

"No," said Sven again. "I know! I can know this!"

The men smiled to themselves; it was not hard to guess which of the two women any man would pick, especially presented with them both together, like bookends. The townswomen knew which one would make the more *respectable* wife.

Sven advanced on his mail-order brides wild-eyed, his hands in his hair, so he appeared to have turned white with the strain. But when he was face-to-face with Miss Pim, he offered her his two hands. It took a moment for her to dispose of the bun he had given her before; then she put her two hands in his, doing her best to smile. He kept hold for a long moment, looking deep into her eyes.

Next he did the same with Mrs. Shades, though as he held her hands, his eyes strayed over the black ribbon tied around her upper arm, the Choctaw bead choker that circled her throat. Even so, he saw the irises of her eyes shrink down to pinpricks when he said, "Very sorry, missis."

Turning to Miss Pim, Sven took a hold of her wrist. "This is wife. Cold hands, see? Hands cold for pastry must be."

No one was more surprised than Harriet Pim.

There was a surge of congratulation and cheering. The first wedding in the history of Florence! For a moment, all eyes turned on the rejected bride, to see if she would draw her pistol and shoot the baker dead on the spot. When she did not, they were content to disperse, abuzz with gossip, back to their work. If they had a kind thought to spare for the surplus woman, it was that such a handsome, statuesque, *characterful* woman would have been wasted on a man whose first priority was his pastry.

Hulbert watched Mrs. Shades move away down the street and stand intently reading the WANTED notices pasted to the only fence in town. She rolled and lit a cigarette, using a big patent tin lighter. One of Jake Monterey's evicted cows came and stood beside her; it too seemed to be studying the notices.

"Cissy," Hulbert said, finding his daughter close to hand, "run and show the lady to the hotel, will you? She's come a long way to no good purpose. She must be wore out."

But Loucien Shades shook her head when Cissy suggested it. "It's a very nice hotel!" Cissy urged. "No bugs yet! Went up last week. Best canvas. Got roll-up mattresses an' every-thing!"

But the lady still declined. "Guess I'll just wait here for the next stage, honey."

"That'll be the day after tomorrow!" said Cissy.

Mrs. Shades examined her large, warm hands. They appeared to anger her so much that she pulled her red leather riding gloves on. Cissy noticed that every fingertip was coming unstitched. "And then there's the problem of money. Hey-di-day."

"Why? Are you a Mormon, like Herman?"

Mrs. Shades laughed sharply. "No, child. A Mormon I ain't. Just down to my last button. Lacking the means. Stone-broke. On my beam-ends. Your bakerman could at least have put off choosing until he had fed us both supper."

Cissy felt awkward. She knew she ought to invite the lady home—that was what Poppy would have done. She equally knew that her mother would glower at her for two weeks if she did; another place to set, another mouth to feed.

"Kookie's brother Amos says you're from Wales."

"Then Kookie's brother is mistaken. I'm half Choctaw, half Minneapolis. That's Choceapolis. Sounds good enough to drink, my husband used to say. Hey-di-day," said Mrs. Shades, rubbing her knuckles in her eye sockets.

"Kookie says you drank down all of Charlie Quex's lemonade—every drop! No one ever did that before!"

"Child, after eighteen hours on that stage, I'da drunk cuckoo spit. You got to take hospitality when you can find it."

Cissy was floundering. Any moment now she would invite Mrs. Shades to supper, and then there would be heck to pay from her mother. "Kookie says you must be our new schoolteacher, come to teach school."

"Your friend Kookie sure does do a lot of thinking, don't he?" Then Mrs. Shades started, as if a fly had buzzed in her ear. Her eyes widened. She stood for a moment, one hand and its lit cigarette resting absently on Monterey's cow. Then her mouth widened into a smile. "Well, you know, he's a pretty smart Kookie at that. Do you people have a schoolhouse?"

"We have a tent we call church on Sundays," Cissy offered.

"Then you know what? Kookie is absolutely right! That's what I am! Your new schoolmarm!"

"*But you smoke!*" Cissy had said it before she could help herself.

64

Loucien Shades looked down at the cigarette between her fingers as if startled to find it there. "Oh, this? I was just minding it for a friend." And she flicked the cigarette away into the dirt. Never again did Cissy see her smoke.

Sent out on their daily mission to gather cow chips, the children of Florence bemoaned the fact that their freedom was at an end. Some of the older children had been to school for a while, before their families decided on staking a claim in Oklahoma. Some of the Ponca Pirates attended a school of their own, beyond Chimney Rock.

"What do folk do all day who go to school?" asked Peatie.

"Oh, spelling, 'rithmetic, geography," said Ezra, urbane man-of-the-world. "Speaking sometimes."

"*Speaking?*" snorted Kookie disgustedly. "I can do that already!"

"You have to take your own water in a bucket—to scrub down the latrine seat—and if you want to 'go' during lessons, you have to put your hand up—so." Ezra held up two fingers in a V shape. They all practiced asking to leave the classroom.

"What else?" demanded Kookie, desperate for all the facts.

"Well, you can't talk."

"But you said . . ."

"And you can't fool around. And you can't go out by way of the window."

"Schoolhouse ain't got a window."

"And the teacher can hit you with anything that comes to hand. Kill you and bury you under the floor, far as I can see, and nobody turns a hair."

Gloom settled on the children thicker than prairie dust. They toiled along, hauling behind them zinc washtubs on lengths of rope. (All the firewood was gone now, the landscape stripped bare by settlers. There was nothing left to fuel the cooking fires except dried cow dung, so it was everyone's duty, whenever and wherever they walked out, to chip the dry pats off the grass.)

"Our one has a gun!" said Kookie.

"Oh Lord!" groaned Fuller Monterey. "She'll probably shoot us all inside of a week!"

The Florence Town Committee of Citizens had also convened to discuss Loucien Shades.

"Perhaps we shouldn't hurry this manner of thing?" said Lloyd Lentz. "There may be other applicants. Maybe we should hold off until—"

The others silenced him with a look.

"Question is," said Klemme, "how we are going to pay her? Can we, in point of fact, *afford* her at this stage in our . . . er . . . civic plan?"

Pickard Warboys hated to speak in public, but he did now, hoisting himself to his feet, his voice trembling with nervousness and strength of feeling. "Seems to me we've given the children hardships enough already, bringing them here. It would be a crime to leave them ignorant and wild and unlettered now, for want of a teacher." There was a groan of assent.

The baker sat holding his kneecaps and sweating profusely. Even though he understood very little of the proceedings, Sven religiously attended the meetings of the FTCC. This evening he knew that his advertisement was the cause of the day's dilemma, and he was mortified. The ladies of Florence had let him know, in no uncertain terms, that he had behaved disgracefully, whether or not he had meant to. Sven ached to put things right.

"Well, let's have her in, then, and find out what she expects to be paid," said Klemme. "Does anyone know the going rate?" Nobody did.

Charlie the barber lifted the tent flap and ushered in their candidate for the post of schoolmistress.

It was as if he had brought in an enormous bouquet of flowers.

Seven men offered Loucien Shades a chair, but she chose to remain standing. "I'd sooner wait till I know my fate," she said gruffly.

"I am certain you will be admirable!"

"Sure!"

"Fine!"

"Perfect," said a chorus of voices.

Some of the tension left Mrs. Shades's face, and she risked a smile.

"It is just a question of money," said Emile Klemme, like a man picking his way through blackberry brambles.

There was a pause.

"And who knows the answer to this question?" she enquired, looking from face to face.

"Thing is," said Virgil Hobbs brutally, "we ain't got none."

There was so long a pause this time that it seemed likely no one would ever speak again. The candidate herself had to come to their rescue.

"I admit, I *am* partial to eating," she said. "And to having a blanket over me at night. Bullets in my pistol. Coffee to wake me up. You think you can manage those things? You folk with kids?" The FTCC realized that she was outlining her salary.

"Are you a Latter-day Saint, by any chance?" asked Herman.

Unable to believe their own luck, they quickly appointed Mrs. Loucien Shades headmistress of the Florence Academy for the Education of Young People—before she could change her mind. Lloyd Lentz called for a vote of thanks to appear in the minutes of the meeting, and then, with rising spirits, the committee moved on to discuss the latest progress on building the water tower.

Loucien Shades pulled out an empty chair and sat down. The FTCC (which was made up entirely of men) stared at her in surprise.

"Well? I'm a citizen too now, ain't I?" she said.

The water tower was complete—a work of immaculate woodwork that had taken all the timber destined for the building of the church. It was a thing almost as beautiful as a church, its bleached white planks sleeving a lead tank capable of holding five hundred gallons. It had a siphon pipe to dip into the creek, and a canvas hose hung down from its base, like the trunk of an albino elephant. Printed around the tower, in foot-high letters, were the words:

A spring of water welling up to eternal life!
FLORENCE TOWN STATION

It was styled exactly on the water tower down the line at Merlin, and it was generally said that even "Red Rock" Rimm himself would not be able to find fault with such a piece of work.

There it stood now, homemade bunting stretching from its white brink across the railroad track to the roof of Nathaniel Rimm's printing office. Gaff Boden, who had eight veal calves ready to ship out, had brought them down to the trackside. Pickard Warboys clutched the mail. The townspeople gathered to see what would happen when the Red Rock Runner rounded the bend and its engineer glimpsed this magnificent landmark steaming like a churn of fresh milk in the noonday sun.

The tracks began to *wang-wang* ahead of the distant train; the crowd craned their necks. The locomotive rounded the bend, its bell already clanging. The clanging stopped as the engineer saw the water tower. The crowd surged forward, waving neckerchiefs and newspapers.

"Look cheery, now!" enjoined Emile Klemme. "Look cheery, not hostile!"

Then the clanging started up again. They could see the engineer leaning out of his cab, grinning like a loon. He sounded the whistle in the very second he passed by, deafening them all and sending the calves skittering in every direction.

And as the locomotive went through, it gathered up the bunting around its funnel and carried it away—a snaking, flapping hair ribbon of red and blue and green among the long tresses of gray steam.

"Maybe tomorrow," said Kookie's grandmother. "After he's told them 'bout our lovely tower. . . ."

But the breaking of that bunting had declared open war between Florence Town and the Red Rock Railroad Company. The smiles on the faces of the adults hardened into snarls. If the train would not stop of its own accord, then it must be made to stop.

Nathaniel Rimm only now came out of his shack. The day had held no surprises for him. All along he had known the train would not stop, that water and bunting would not soften the malice of his father.

Hildy Sissney's anger was reserved entirely for her husband. It was him she blamed for marooning her here, in a nowhere town, bypassed by civilization. Her voice, viciously sarcastic in her sorrow, berated him loudly: *"Better find a good use for rancid lard, hadn't you, Hulbert Sissney? There won't be any other kind from now on!"*

Cissy was mortified—first that her father should be blamed so unfairly, secondly that her mother should tear into him in public—humiliate Poppy in public—not even save her savagery for suppertime. Suddenly Cissy could not bear to have all these people believe Hulbert Sissney was as stupid as his own wife said.

"He has got a use for it!" she protested. *"Poppy's planning to spread that lard on the rails so the train cain't grip!"* She shouted it out, as if her noise might obliterate the insult and hurt.

Hulbert's head snapped upright. "Now, Cissy girl, don't you talk—" But he found himself looking directly at Nate Rimm. Here was the railroad owner's son . . . and yet there seemed to be a glint in his eye, as if someone had just told him a splendid joke.

"How much lard does your paw have, child?" asked Rimm, though his eyes stayed on Hulbert and Hulbert's stayed on him.

"Ten gallon, sir."

"And not fit for eating, you said?"

"Rancid as the milk in a dead cat," said Cissy feelingly.

"Then I think he should go ahead and do it," said Rimm.

6

SITTIN' ON SATIN

They larded the railroad tracks for fifty feet, the stench setting their heads spinning, the flies of fifteen towns rattling around their heads and hands as they daubed the rails an inch thick. But on the hot metal, the grease turned instantly to liquid and flowed down to blacken the ground round about.

Up to the very last minute, Hulbert Sissney worked, scooping out gobbets from the base of the ten-gallon tub, daubing it on the rails, squinting along the length of track looking for any bare inch that would give the train wheels traction. As the RRR came clamoring around the bend, Cissy ran over and stretched his suspenders, trying to haul him away. "Leave it, Poppy! It'll work! Leave it! Please don't get squished!"

"Leave it, Hulbert! That's enough!" the others shouted, flailing their arms to pull him off the tracks.

Hulbert was finally persuaded to move. He picked up his daughter and ran, flicking out his rickety legs sideways and forward, like a scuttling gecko.

The Runner began clanging its bell. Its cowcatcher caught the empty lard can and sent it spinning in among the onlookers. The engineer, thinking it had been put there as an obstacle to stop him, put back his head and laughed. Then the front set of wheels began to spin—and the second—and the third.

A shock wave of deceleration ran down the train, making the cars buffet into each other. Then all the driving wheels were over the grease and slipping.

Impetus drove the locomotive forward five more, ten more, fifteen more feet. The look on the engineer's face was remembered long after in Florence. He yelled for the fireman to throw more coal into the furnace. He hung over the side of his cab and watched the huge wheels spinning and helpless to drive the train forward. *"What you done, you bunch of renegades!?"*

"Stop the train!" the crowd called back.

"Not for all the bugs in the jam! What you done to my engine?"

As its wheels spun, the train gave off a noise like a cow in labor, spurting steam from odd parts of its anatomy. The crowd ventured forward until they were virtually standing alongside; the only reason they needed to shout was the hysterical hissing of the boiler.

"Stop the train! We wanna talk!"

"See the water tower we put up?"

"Why don't you stop and take on water?"

The engineer's only response was to open the throttle as far as it would go.

"We'll make it worth your while, Peter," said Rimm, speaking just loud enough to be heard.

For the first time, the engineer was listening. "How much?"

"Three dollars every time you stop."

"Ten," said the engineer.

"Four," said Rimm.

"Eight." They might have struck a deal, too, but for the flammable nature of lard.

Whole minutes seemed to have passed, and yet it was only seconds before the spinning wheels cut through to the metal beneath the film of lard. With the throttle wide open, the meeting of metal and metal was enough to strike sparks. The sparks ignited the lard, and with a thump barely audible above the steam jets, fifty feet of track and grass burst spontaneously into flame.

"*What you done, you loons?*" screamed the engineer, convinced they were trying to burn him alive in his cab. The train, suddenly finding friction, lurched forward, jostling the cars and the passengers who had their heads out the windows and were screaming, "*We're on fire!*"

Then they were away down the line, flames licking out from under the carriages, until the last of the lard spatter was burned off.

The people at the trackside ran around, jumping on patches of fire for fear it might spread through the tinder-dry grass to their tents and shacks.

When the excitement was over, Hulbert Sissney stood looking down at the empty lard tub, its sides staved in as deeply as the hopes of Florence.

"Shoulda used molasses," said Virgil Hobbs sourly.

"We don't have no molasses, Virgil."

"Naw. But molasses wouldn'ta burned."

A coffin, if you drop one side down, makes a very passable pew.

Frank Tate had meant to wait until the church was built before revealing the work he had done. But when the Sunday-church tent also became the schoolhouse, and there were no desks for the children to sit at, he shyly drove his handiwork around to the school tent thinking to install it before anyone was about. That way he could save himself the embarrassment of being thanked.

To his surprise, he lifted the tent flap to find Loucien Shades, wrapped in a pair of blankets on the floor, newly awake and pointing a pistol at his head. "What's your business, son?" she said.

Frank Tate named his business, and Mrs. Shades, still wearing her blankets, came outside to look over the pews on his cart. "Dan-*dee*," she breathed. "You are some kind of carpenter, Mr. Tate. Ain't this going to be the fanciest little schoolhouse on the whole wide prairie? Quilted satin and everything. Give me a minute to put my clothes on and I'll give y'a hand down with them."

"Oh, truly—I can manage!" protested Frank, but she was gone, back into the tent, and he could only wait meekly outside until she returned fully dressed.

"Forgive me, Mrs. Shades, ma'am," he said falteringly as they carried the last pew inside, "but I had no idea you was *living* in the schoolhouse."

"Nowhere else for me to live right now, son."

"Didn't no one offer you a place to board?"

"Mrs. Warboys did—and her with eight kiddies and a mother-in-law. Gaff Boden did, but a schoolmistress has a reputation to think of. Nope. I'm fine. I've known better days and I've known worse."

They set the pews in lines, all exactly parallel to one another, all an exact distance apart.

"Forgive me saying, Mrs. Shades, ma'am . . ."

"You apologize too much, son. What is it?"

"Well, I couldn't help noticing how you don't have a bed to sleep in, and I thought . . . I mean, if you'd allow me . . . I could maybe make you . . ."

"Haven't got a penny, Mr. Tate."

Frank Tate blushed to the roots of his hair. "Oh, Mrs. Shades!" he protested. "A school's the heart and soul of a town! I wouldn't ask a red cent! I figure it's everyone's duty to oblige where they can!"

Loucien Shades put her hands on her hips and regarded him warmly. "Then you'll be on the skids before you're forty, Mr. Tate. And the skids will be all the sunnier for having you."

The children arrived, in fear and trepidation, for their first day at school. They hovered outside the tent, hoping that someone would say the project—like stopping the train—had failed. Some had been brought by their mothers, tenderly, coaxingly. Some had been turned out of doors at six in the morning and told to walk the several miles into Florence on their own.

The worst of the weather had passed, and eddies of wind

chased little worried tufts of dust in among their feet. There were Cissy and Kookie, Tibbie Boden, Peat and Fuller Monterey, Ruth, Ezra, Esther, Hosea, and Nahum Warboys, and six thin-shanked individuals off the various prairie farms with their heads all shaved, on account of lice— it was hard to tell if they were boys or girls. And there was a pretty little girl with hair like spun sugar whose parents bellowed at her like percussionists taking turns to strike a gong.

The children's awe was increased when they saw the seats they were to sit in: black, shining, and plushly cushioned in cream satin.

"They's Frank Tate's coffins, ma'am!" breathed Nahum.

Mrs. Shades, though she had not realized this before, hid her surprise completely. "Ought to make you extra glad to be alive in 'em," she responded briskly. "No, that's no good. I can't see you all like that. You big ones move to the back and the little ones to the front. Then I want you each to stand up on your hind legs and tell us who you are—all supposing you know."

A kind of disbelieving laugh ran round the tent. Could it be that school was not, after all, going to be a nightmare of canes and shootings and grammar?

When it came to the turn of the little girl with the honey hair, nothing would coax her either to stand up or to speak her name. "Then I shall call you Honey, honey," said Mrs. Shades, "and we will assume you fell outa some angel's knapsack as she was flying over. . . . What you got your hand up for, boy, like you're signaling a bet at the Kentucky races?"

"Asking to go to the latrines, ma'am!" said Peatie, scowling at his hand as if it must have given the signal wrong.

"Well, don't sit there waving at me! Git! Sweet Mikey, boy, that's satin you're sittin' on. And next time, you just holler out and run! For Frank Tate's sake."

So that is what they did. And if Frank Tate ever found out that he had become a password for going to the toilet—*"For Frank Tate's sake, ma'am!"*—he never said he minded.

Meanwhile, the FTCC convened to discuss how Florence could survive despite Clifford T. Rimm and the Red Rock Railroad Company.

"In Athens they named the city after the god who granted the most useful gift to the town," said Monday Morning. For a moment everyone was silenced, wondering how it would be to live in a town called Lentzville or Fuddtown or Lagerlöf City.

"That'd be the man who thinks up how to stop that danged train," said Charlie Quex. "Should we try and bribe the engineer again, maybe? He looked pretty willing."

"I know Peter Bull," said Nate Rimm. "We might have bribed him. But he'll be dead set against us, now he thinks we tried to kill him." The opinion of the meeting was split between those who thought this was a pity and those who thought Peter Bull deserved killing if he was not prepared to stop his train for four dollars a time.

"It's my fault," said Hulbert, his hat clutched abjectly between his knees. "I never thought of it catching fire."

"Nor us," came a chorus of comforting voices.

Emile Klemme rose to his feet, one hand on his coat

lapel. "Charlie Quex is right. I propose a reward to the man who thinks up a way to stop the train. Some position of public influence, perhaps . . ."

A dozen fists banged on the trestle table in agreement.

"I'd make that man mayor!" joked someone, but the joke was seized on by a dozen others.

"Yeah! The guy who makes the train stop gets to be mayor of Florence!"

Two sheets of paper were folded up and torn into sixteen segments, which were passed around the table for anyone to write their ideas on. Gaff Boden put his Stetson on the table to hold the slips. Monterey immediately spat in it.

"Shouldn't it be 'doge'?" asked Monday Morning softly, to himself, but was obliged to explain. "It's just that in Venice and Florence and suchlike Italian places, they have doges, not mayors."

Nate Rimm gave a chortle of delight. "Yes! We could have the only dogedom in America! I'll vote for that!

"Then I submit," said Klemme, clasping both lapels now, "I submit that we set up a grade crossing barrier and charge a toll to lift it. Legally we would be within our rights."

"Hey! I wanted a chance to be doge!" protested Charlie Quex. But the rest had already turned over their slips and were sketching their idea of a grade crossing built of planks, of railroad tracks, of piled-up boxes.

Monday Morning pointed out that two carts, placed either side of the track with their shafts facing each other, could easily be run forward to block the line and backward to clear it.

"Yeah! Herman can paint us a sign, 'ficial like," said Jim

Fudd. "He did a swell job on my storefront."

And then they were gone, like a nest of ants on the day they get their wings, leaving only Nate Rimm and the black man sitting across the table from one another.

". . . except it won't work," said Monday.

"He'll drive straight through," said Nate, nodding gloomily.

"Waste of two carts, really."

The tent flapped around them, noisy and agitated in the rising wind. Nate drummed his fingertips on the table's edge. "Er . . . don't take this amiss, Mr. Morning, but you seem to me a remarkably *lettered* man."

"For a nigger, you mean?"

"For a Florence wheelwright, it was in my mind to say. Would it be an impertinence to ask after your spelling?"

"My spelling?"

"Yes. How's your spelling?"

Monday Morning glanced defensively at Rimm out of the side of his eyes. "We generally agree, the dictionary and I."

"Yes, and how is that? I mean, a man's background is his own, naturally, but would you mind telling me how you come to be in such accord with the dictionary?"

Monday Morning had never confided his story to anyone in Florence. Then again, he had never been asked it. A small frown puckered his forehead, like that of a man contemplating whether to share his last quid of tobacco with a stranger. Then he said: "My last employer, she owned my grandparents as slaves. She freed my parents, and I grew up into employment, so to speak. Well, she grew to be an old,

old lady. Her eyes were whited over, like a pond under ice. Stone-blind. So she had me read to her come day, go day. On and on. Reading. I was none too good at first, but you can't do a thing for seven years without improving somewhat. And Mrs. Martha, she had a ferocious hunger for all manner of books. She had a library the size of Zanzibar. American history, philosophy, politics, memoirs, travel books, diaries, plays, journals from England, classics, schoolbooks, poetry, novels . . . I was like Sinbad in his treasure cave: rich past all expressing. No way of spending the riches, of course—but at least you can't lose that kind of wealth in a card game. The bailiffs can't come and repossess your brain, can they?"

Nate Rimm played a short adagio on the edge of the table. "And do you find yourself suited, making wagon wheels? I mean, please tell me if I am giving offense."

Monday Morning at last turned face-on to Nate. "I have a wife and children, Mr. Rimm. If I had a job that paid enough, I would have sent for them to join me before now."

"Ah. Mmmm," said Rimm, trying not to show his surprise at this piece of news. "It is just that I need a . . . typesetter. And I wondered if you would care to join me in the newspaper business."

The black man picked out C major chord on the edge of the table with a pair of hands twice the size of Rimm's. "Books too?"

"Books, pamphlets, plays, verse—whatever the public can be persuaded to buy."

"Then I'm your man, Mr. Rimm."

"You are *nobody's* man, Mr. Morning. That's why I want

81

you." And they shook hands across a trestle table that leaped and jumped at the vibration of the noon train rattling through.

Sven Lagerlöf could not rest for thinking about the bride he had rejected. The women of Florence would not let him rest, for one thing, glowering at him as they bought his bread, sniffing sharply as they passed him in the street.

"You've got nothing to reproach yourself with, my dear," said his cool-handed wife, stretching silken pastry over a pecan pie.

But Sven knew that his conscience would not be clear until he had baked a score of doughnuts, dredged them in sugar, and asked Amos Warboys (who was passing) to take them down to the schoolhouse, as a gift for the schoolmistress.

Amos, when he got there, was hesitant about lifting the tent-flap door. There was a strange noise beyond it—a squealing of metal, the thump of leather against flesh. He had been to school, and all his memories of it were bad.

"*Now give him a jab in his ribs, 'cause he's blowing himself out to fool you!*" said the schoolteacher's voice. Amos swallowed hard and ventured in.

He was confronted by the back end of a horse.

"Now the back end of a horse you treat like the loaded end of a cannon, and make it a rule in life never to go near!" the teacher was saying. Amos took this advice and edged around to stand with the horse between him and the children. The horse smelled the doughnuts and tried to turn around.

"Can I do something for you, young man?" enquired Mrs. Shades. "There's learning going on here."

"That's our Amos," said Nahum.

"Well, Amos, do you have something to say? Because we had just got to fastening the cinch."

Amos looked around, only to be unnerved again by the sight of his brothers and sisters sitting in converted coffins. He tore his eyes away and held out the doughnuts with such a jerk that one rolled onto the floor. The horse swiftly ate it.

Told who they came from, Loucien Shades regarded the tray of doughnuts like a basket of rotten eggs. There was a pause so long that into it fitted all of Miss Loucien's recent life.

They were memories of a husband's death; of bailiffs clamoring at the door; of furniture seized before the funeral guests could sit on it; of a borrowed carpetbag big enough to take her pride (if she crushed it down real small); of a four-hundred-mile journey through bandit country, bounced between floor and roof and dredged in dust; of the humiliation of offering herself to a man she was not acquainted with and who did not speak her language; of warm finger ends protruding shamefully through unstitched red leather gloves.

And Sven Lagerlöf wished to make amends with twenty sugar-coated doughnuts.

"You may tell Mr. Lagerlöf, I'd like to take his doughnuts and . . ."

The creak of polished oak, satin-quilted pews made her

look around at seventeen figures tilting forward to catch her words. Their ears were listening; their eyes, though, were on the doughnuts—those plump, oil-glistening, white-spangled, sweet-smelling doughnuts.

Miss Loucien pursed her lips and shut her eyes. "You may tell Mr. Lagerlöf I would like to take his doughnuts . . . on behalf of the children of Florence Academy, on this our opening day. Please thank him warmly for his kindness *to the children.*"

They ate their doughnuts out of cupped hands, as if the delight were alive and might escape between their fingers at any moment. "Today Swedish doughnuts," said the teacher in a voice of intoxicating sweetness. "Someday, children, it will be oysters on the half shell, straight off the train from Houston!"

If, after that, Loucien Shades had sent her class out to collect the stings from scorpions, the eggs from marmots, or the eyes from Mississippi, there was not one of those children who would not have died sooner than disappoint "Miss Loucien." She christened them "Class Three," rather than Class One, "because here in the Oklahoma Territory, none of us is right at the beginning," she said. "We've all come from somewhere, fellers, even if we do have a ways to go, now we're here."

Herman painted a notice for the grade crossing, and since he was nicely off for beans and socks, the FTCC gave him a laying chicken for the excellent job he made of it. The chicken laid six fertile eggs within the week, and he incubated them in a straw bale, on Angus Wright's empty plot.

The notice, which hung on chains between the two carts, read:

FLORENCE TOWN GRADE CROSSING

APPLY BREAKS AND SYGNALL FOR ASSISTENCE

"Enter ye in at the strait gate;
for wide is the gate, and broad the way,
that leadeth to destruction."

The carts were placed so that their shafts projected across the lines, almost, but not quite, touching. A big red circle was also strung under the notice, so that Peter Bull could not fail to see that the barrier was there.

The only legal way (said Emile Klemme) to stop the train in this way was if traffic was actually crossing the tracks at the time the RRR came down the line. So it was decided that Frank Tate should drive his hearse to and fro across the tracks as soon as the train was due.

"Can't promise to make a regular thing of this," Frank said warily, wishing someone else had been asked to do it. "Some days I'll be busy with work." But the crowd just told him to get a move on, waving their hats in a way that made the mares skittish and nervy.

By this stage, all the carts in Florence had sprouted wings—flat shelves of wood jutting out above the wheels, which could be used for carrying cow chips. Every outing was viewed as an opportunity to gather fuel. (Such a heap had been accumulated in Florence, in time for winter, that Taffy said it reminded him of the slag heaps of Wales.) So it was a strange-looking procession, a winged hearse, surrounded by excited well-wishers, that wound its way down to the railroad track. Once there, it began taking practice runs across the tracks. The new schoolteacher even brought her class outside, in the hope of watching the RRR forced to a halt.

Frank Tate had put wooden chocks against the tracks to make a ramp for the wheels, and the hearse crossed over with a jaunty bobbing motion that put heart into everyone who saw it.

Then the train came into earshot, sending its unmistakable sob ahead of it through the rails. The crowd on either side of the hearse moved away, and Frank Tate felt vulnerable and alone, perched up on his buckboard.

The vibration made the grass shiver between the tracks. It made the pigeons take off from the house roofs and flap like bunting across the line. It made the wooden chocks by the rails move too; they bobbled away across the gravel and fell over.

So when the rim of Tate's back wheel hit the track, it could not get over it. The horses pulled, but the hearse just rocked to and fro, trying to lift its rear end over the rail but only managing to straddle the track. Amos Warboys, armed with a red flag, ran to the barrier and made elegant figure-eight signals with it. But Peter Bull had plenty of reasons to keep the throttle wide open going around the bend. These losers had tried to burn his train. His boss, Clifford T. Rimm, in handing him a nickel-plated watch, had called him "a credit to the railroad," then, within the same puff of exhaled cigar smoke, had told him, "Your job here with the railroad is absolutely secure, Bull—*just as long as the RRR never stops at Florence.*" Praised and threatened within the same breath, Peter Bull had left the chairman's office and mounted his platform like the cavalry mounting up for war. They could have felled a forest across the track that day, and Peter Bull would not have stopped.

"*Get off the line, Tate! He ain't stopping!*"

Frank Tate, driving his uncle's best hearse, stood up on the footboard, cracked the reins, and screamed at the horses to *PULL!* But the more they pulled, the more the back wheels spun against the smooth metal of the rail.

"*Jump off, Tate! He's not fooling!*"

In the corner of his vision, the locomotive grew from a dark blob to a fire-breathing monster, but Frank Tate continued to roll to and fro, front wheels on one side of the track, rear wheels on the other.

"*Tate!!*" bawled the crowd.

Loucien Shades placed herself in front of the children, but they wormed to either side of her, eager to see what would happen. Loucien drew her pistol and fired a shot to spur on the horses. It was a puny sound against the train's roar.

Though blinkered from seeing it, the horses heard the

train's noise grow from a fire-breathing monster to a stampede of bison. They stopped straining and they bolted, jumping forward into their harnesses as if they were jumping out of their skins. The wedged wheels hopped over the first rail, then the second, launching Frank Tate a yard into the air and shortening his spine a whole inch.

At the same instant, the RRR hit the carts barricading the line and shunted them both a hundred yards down the track, gradually reducing them—by wheel and wing and axle and brake paddle and plank—into a skidding flotsam of splintered firewood.

"I think we have something to report in our first edition," said Rimm to his typesetter, when the last of the debris had rattled down around their ears.

7

STRONG LANGUAGE

Class Three learned how to light wet kindling and how to splice rope. They learned how to find north with the help of a pocket watch and how to recognize warble fly on a horse. Kookie had to bring in Haggai so they could all practice changing a diaper. When Fuller Monterey said that was "girls' work," Miss Loucien said that unchanged babies smelled just as bad whichever way you wore your bloomers. While Haggai was on hand, they also learned how to christen a baby if it looked like dying before a preacher could be fetched.

In art, they drew pictures of their various ideas for stopping the train. They discussed whether they would vote Republican or Democrat when they got old enough, and how best to pluck a prairie falcon. They painted a mural entitled *Florence in the Future* on the piece of fence around Angus Wright's claim—a jolly notion of how Florence might look in twenty-five years' time: 1918. They learned how to say, in Choctaw, "I am lost. Please give me some wampum and a drink," and they learned all the words to

> *Way down yonder on the reservation,*
> *A cowboy is my occupation.*

They learned not to shelter under trees in a lightning storm, because a feller of Miss Loucien's acquaintance had once done it and the lightning had traveled clean down from the dollar coins in his hatband to the spurs on his boots, and left his kidneys cooked to a turn.

Loucien Shades appeared to have known any number of unfortunate people, and every so often she would introduce them, as a cautionary example. There was Slim Decker, for instance, who, being unable to count past four, had produced a fifth ace from his cuff while playing poker on a Mississippi paddle wheel and been thrown overboard. There was Cora "Bow-Front" Dinsdale, who had been unable to tell a toadstool from a mushroom and poisoned her husband the morning after their wedding. There was Sylvester Lefanu, who had shot seventy-five marmots and still starved to death because he had not waited for them to step clear of their holes, and each one had dropped back down its burrow, which everyone knows is deeper than the average well.

Every day she opened their eyes to some new piece of knowledge, and the children of Florence Academy wondered how they had ever lived without knowing it. By November, there was not a child in Florence who could not tell iron pyrite from real gold, and how to recognize if a claim had been "salted" with a shotgun full of gold dust, to mislead some gullible sap.

They played the roughest games of lacrosse imaginable, girls against boys, and they ended each day with the Cowboy's Prayer.

"Yeah, but can she read and do number work?" asked Hildy Sissney when her daughter brought home a bowl woven from willow leaves.

"Read to your mother, Cissy," said Hulbert, pointing to the wall with his empty pipe. So Cissy stood up and ran her finger along the lines of yellowing newsprint that papered the wall behind her father's chair.

"Paris: A traveler's first Impressions. Straddling the River Seine like a tapestry draped upon a silver washline, the city of gay Paris appears at first sight as must the Celestial City appear to the righteous Pilgrim. Everywhere are avenues wide as shipping lanes, and parks as expansive and grand as the Great Lakes themselves. Everywhere cathedrals rise in snowy marble, to catch the sun's rays in nets of stained glass, while down the little alleyways of the Quartier Lateen tumble the sounds of sweet music and the sensuous smells of culinary joy. . . ."

"Aw, quit it," said Hildy Sissney, banging her pots together and refilling the bowl on the counter with quids of chewing tobacco. "Pride goeth before a fall, my girl. That's what the Good Book says, and I'm perfectly sure it had you in mind. You just watch your step, missy. I don't hear much talk of the Ten Commandments from that school of yours."

Hulbert did not comment at all on Cissy's reading until, at bedtime, he came to poke his stubbly chin over the edge of her hammock and kiss her good night. "Mighty fine reading," he said, in a low whisper that would not carry as far as

91

the next room. "Pity I papered over Paris last week."

Cissy rose up on her elbows. "You papered over Paris, Poppy? But that was my favorite."

"Don't really matter, do it? Since you've got it word perfect in your head. Still, it would be nice if that Miss Loucien taught you your alphabet one of these days."

Cissy had to admit that she herself had wondered when the school curriculum would tackle reading and writing. She needed to be able to read. If Kookie were to marry Tibbie Boden, then she (Cissy) would undoubtedly have to scour the *New York Tribune* small ads in search of a husband. (She could never bring herself to marry Peat or Fuller Monterey, and all Kookie's brothers were much too old.) She supposed there must be other advantages to reading, too.

It would be good to read the *Florence Morning Star*, for instance, with its splendid editorials calling on Congress to consider the plight of poor persecuted Florence. But just so long as the president was reading the *Florence Morning Star*, she supposed it did not matter if she was not.

It would be good to be able to read one of the books Nate Rimm and Monday Morning were promising to print: the poetry of Alfred, Lord Tennyson, the novels of J. Fenimore Cooper, the cookery books of Mrs. Beeton, the wit of Oscar Wilde. . . . But her mother insisted the Bible was the only book worth reading, and most of that seemed to be written up on Herman's signs, in one place or another. (Cissy had memorized all of them.) Apparently, you did not need to know your alphabet anyway, to read the Bible. To judge from her mother, all you had to do was to keep one in your apron pocket all day every day. Maybe words were able to soak through calico and the wall of the stomach and get into you that way. So for ten days, Cissy wrapped a double-page spread of the *Watonga Republican* around her body before getting dressed. But the only effect was that her underwear turned black with newsprint. Nothing in the way of reading rubbed off.

She dared Kookie to ask Miss Loucien to teach them some reading, but he pulled a face and said he liked school well enough the way it was.

In the end, to everyone's surprise, it was Tibbie Boden who brought the subject up. Timidly, her hand raised on a wilting, skinny arm, Tibbie said in a terrified whisper, "Dadda says are we gonna do reading sometime ever?"

Miss Loucien abruptly turned her back, and the Monterey boys seized their chance to throw a handful of broken cow chips at Tibbie that lodged brownly in her glistening yellow hair.

Miss Loucien went to her bed, which doubled as a desk. It was one of Frank Tate's coffins (converted, of course), raised up on a chest of assorted drawers and cubbyholes—a masterpiece of carpentry that housed everything Miss Loucien owned in the world. Out of this magician's chest had come the bowie knife she used to demonstrate skinning a rabbit and bleeding a cactus. Out of this had come a dried scorpion and a lava bomb, an assortment of fishing lures she had made herself, and a dog whistle no one could hear. Somewhere inside was the potassium permanganate she used for treating their injuries. Under her pillow she kept a photograph of the late, great Mr. Shades and of her grandfather—a chief of the Choctaw Nation who wore drooping eagle feathers over his ears and the selfsame choker his grand-daughter now wore around her throat.

Now, from out of the chest of drawers, she fetched a bullwhip and laid it on the nearest desk, her breast rising and falling like a neap-tide sea. Seventeen pairs of eyes widened. Seventeen pairs of hands slid under seventeen pairs of thighs. Tibbie Boden bit her lip and trembled so hard that the cow chips slid out of her golden hair.

"What's the hurry?" Miss Loucien wanted to know. "Could Adam read? Or Eve? Could Abraham? Or the Virgin Mary? *Could Jesus read?*"

No one ventured to suppose that Jesus could read—after all, there had been no *Watonga Republican* in Nazareth— until recklessly, insanely, Kookie Warboys cheeped, "The Ten Commandments, maybe?" Sixteen pairs of eyes turned on him: they had never seen a boy flayed alive with a bull-whip before.

"Aw, *them*," said Miss Loucien. "Sweet Mikey, you don't need to read to know *them*. Everyone knows *them*, don't they?"

Her lilac eyes appraised the class. No longer arranged in serried rows, it had ended up in a kind of polished oak heptagon, with everyone facing in toward the center. Tibbie Boden was shaking her head. She did not know her Ten Commandments. The motion was catching. One by one, all the heads began to shake.

"Thou shalt not kill?" said Ezra, still looking at the bull-whip.

"Right!" Miss Loucien congratulated him. "Thou shalt not kill. Thou shalt not steal another man's horse. Thou shalt not lie, nor cuss, nor fall down and worship gray imaginings. Thou shalt not play suzyfandangle with your neighbor's wife, nor play poker on a Sunday, nor cheat at cards. . . . 'Part from that, you have to love God as fierce as you love your aunt Matilda who gives you a dollar coin every Thanksgiving. There again, you have to love that cantankerous old curmudgeon Uncle Willie, who don't. Well, now that we've done the Ten Commandments, why don't we move on to whip cracking? Unless anyone has a powerful objection?" And she set up a row of ten empty bean cans on the hitching rail outside, and they learned to dislodge them with three yards of bull hide. Meanwhile, she told them about Bill Pickett, who could wrestle a running steer to the ground without use of his hands, just by sinking his teeth into its nose.

The newspaper piece about Paris preyed on Hulbert Sissney's mind often that day, and not just because he marveled at Cissy's being able to remember it, word perfect, when it wasn't there. What power that passage had to bring a foreign place to life! Why, he felt almost under the spell of Paris and its stained-glass cathedrals smelling of pain au chocolat.

Finding the slip of paper from the FTCC meeting, Hulbert wrote a few words on it and walked around to the offices of the *Florence Morning Star.* There he found Nate Rimm in heated argument with the Ponca chief, Vokayatunga, in front of the building.

95

"Yes, but why newspaper say my name and I not in it?" asked Vokayatunga.

The editor, clearly bewildered and exasperated, shook the latest issue in front of the Ponca's face. "But *where* does it say your name?"

Vokayatunga jabbed with a forefinger. "There! There!"

"Where? Where?"

"Pardon me," said Hulbert quietly, "but I believe that 'Morning Star' is the meaning of the gentleman's name: Morning Star: Vokayatunga. People can be touchy about their names."

"And why shouldn't they?" muttered Monday Morning, on the far side of the storm window. "It's the handle folk take hold of you by."

"*But I not in it!*" protested Vokayatunga in a melancholy roar.

Nate Rimm put his head back around the door and appealed for Monday's help. "What does he want? Paying? Does he want paying? I can't afford to pay him!"

"I think he'd just like to be in the paper," said Hulbert mildly.

Monday Morning emerged carrying another copy of the *Morning Star.* Alongside the banner he had sketched the head of a warrior chieftain in full warbonnet. The editor was not slow to catch on.

"Well, naturally, Vokayatunga, we wanted to call our paper the best name we could think of, and that's why we chose yours. . . . How would it be with you if we were to carry your portrait right here—beside the title—as our *heraldry*. You would of course receive a free copy of the paper each week, by way of our thanks!"

Vokayatunga scowled. He threw the newspaper on the ground—but only because he was farsighted and could not see the sketch close to. He found fault with the kind of feathers in Monday's drawing, but the delight behind his carping was plain to see. He went away with a spring in his stride, to tell his relations that the town paper had indeed been named after him, just as he had said all along.

"Respectability," murmured Hulbert, watching him go. "That's the thing about newspapers. Fame and respectability." And he thrust his note into Rimm's hand, being too shy to make his suggestion in person.

Nate Rimm read the scrap of paper in his palm and gave a little skip of excitement. "Monday!" he called. "Hold the front page! We're just about to test the power of the press!"

HARMONY ON THE PLAINS

A cross section of every race and color, where tolerance goes hand in hand with Christian brotherhood, the little town of Florence has been called "a model town blessed with all the human riches America possesses." The president himself has vowed to visit Florence whenever he is next summoned to Oklahoma Territory.

GATEWAY TO PROSPERITY

Equipped with banking facilities of the highest order, and the financial confidence of government

itself, Florence is the place to grow rich. Where else is real estate free to the ordinary man? Where else is the climate so reliable? Where else is the railroad so close at hand? This is indeed the geographical and business crossroads of the mighty United States.

"HEALTHFUL RESORT" IS HAILED BY DOCTORS
Doctors have congratulated the people of Florence on the healthsome environment of their newly founded city. "The dry air hereabouts," says Doctor Isaiah Witherspoon of San Francisco Teaching Hospital, "is perfect for those afflicted with rheumatics, dropsy, or a weak chest, while every kind of recreation is available to benefit body and soul."

OPERA HOUSE OPENS TO CRITICAL ACCLAIM!
Florence Opera House opened to another triumphant season, with plays, addresses, slide shows, and concerts planned between now and Christmas.

Laugh! Weep! Tremble! Edify your children with the works of Shakespeare, Ibsen, and Aristophanes!

A few tickets still available.

FLORENCE ACADEMY HAS VACANCIES
Florence Academy for the Education of Young People, renowned for its high standards of

teaching and moral discipline, invites new pupils to partake of its wide-ranging and stimulating curriculum. Enquiries should be addressed to Mrs. Loucien Shades, Florence Academy, Florence, Oklahoma Territory. *"Decorum et sapientia."*

A CREATIVE WONDERLAND

For persons artistic or scholarly, there is no place on the prairies the equal of Florence, Oklahoma! With its publishing house, libraries, local crafts, and thriving church community, Florence has everything to enrich the life of all sensate beings.

Musicians! Hearken to the music of the spheres!

Poets! Discover your muses among the beautiful women of Florence!

Artists! Witness the color of the changing prairie seasons!

Every night sees concerts or drama, social or church events.

NATURALIST HAILS ABUNDANCE OF WILDLIFE

"Such interesting flora and fauna abound in Florence, Oklahoma," said New York naturalist Miss F. B. Peasemore last week, to members of the Botanical Society of America. "Why, within ten steps of my hotel room, I encountered twelve different species of invertebrate!"

Huntsmen, too, are flocking to this new center of excellence. Crown Prince Alexander of Minsk, whose train passed by the small, trackside town while he was hunting bison in the Oklahoma Panhandle, was heard to remark to his entourage, "I think this must be the perfect place for a young family!"

The piece about the opera house was a complete lie when it was written—Florence had nothing remotely resembling an opera house—but it did not stay untrue for long. A company of actors touring the prairie came across a copy of the *Florence Morning Star* while working in Glasstown and at once decided to favor the town with a visit.

"You see?" said Nate Rimm, watching them unload from an old frontier-style covered wagon. "Say a thing and it becomes true! That's the power of the press!

There was no unpleasantness when the actors found they had no stage to perform on. "We of the acting profession understand the need for . . . exaggeration," said the actor-manager graciously. "We have acted in barns and coach houses, under the stars, and in saloons and gambling dens! Show us a space twenty paces by thirty, a couple of dozen chairs, and we will show you *theater*!"

Some of the more virtuous citizens asked whether traveling players were a wholesome influence on the young—asked whether plays might not lead to gambling and strong drink, looseness and strong language. Hildy Sissney, for example, said that vaudeville actors were agents of the devil. But the actor-manager, one Cyril Crew, disarmed them all when he and his actors turned up at Sunday service wearing somber clothes and spit-shined shoes. At the end of the service he stood up and made a speech:

"Strong language we shall bring you! For we bring you the language of Shakespeare and the poets, the language of great literature! We will subvert the minds of your youth, for we shall make them ask, 'What a piece of work is a man? How infinite in faculties!' Sin? Yes, we shall bring you sin, for we shall show you injustice righted, crime punished, tyranny brought low, pride humbled!"

The mouths of the congregation gaped wide at this fancy talking. Many there had never seen a theater, never watched acting but for a nativity play or a puppet show at a fair. From the moment the Bright Lights company of actors—all six of them—rose from its pew and bowed to the congregation, it held Florence in thrall.

Nate Rimm licked his pencil, ready to review the play. Young men raided the general store for hair oil, already in love with the leading actress. The Waldorf Hotel invested in three of Frank Tate's coffin-beds, so as to offer bug-free accommodation to the manager and his two leading ladies. And the school closed early, so that it could be transformed into a theater.

"Be sure and go to the show tonight," Miss Loucien told her pupils. "It's a window on the world, a good play, and a thing to treasure in your rememberings."

Memorable it certainly was.

The Bright Lights Theater Company did not, in fact, choose to perform Shakespeare or Ibsen. They looked their audience over and judged *The Perils of Nancy* might go down better. It was a racy melodrama about a young orphan girl pestered by her villainous landlord for rent money she did not have. The girl was played by the theater manager's daughter, her secret admirer by Cyril Crew himself, and the villainous landlord by Everett Crew, his brother.

Everett Crew sported a mustache like a purple martin's nest, and a low-crowned hat with silver-tipped cords that hung down his back. Before ten minutes had passed, his villainy was obvious to every member of the audience, and the Monterey boys were standing on their benches hissing and throwing peanut shells every time he came on. Those behind stood up to see over the boys' heads, and soon the whole audience had risen to its feet or climbed onto the seating. The noise level rose, as men speculated on what would happen and women told each other it was a crying shame. Jake Monterey, who had himself been evicted from his house, took so extreme a dislike to the landlord that he had to be restrained from climbing onto the stage. To counter the noise, the actors spoke louder and louder, Nancy's sweetheart bawling his secret admission of love at the top of his voice, and Nancy's mother whispering her deathbed speech double fortissimo. By the time the landlord told the heroine to marry him or starve, he was largely relying on mime.

"Shame!" shouted Amos. "Get your hands off her!"

"Marry you? Never! I would sooner die!" cried the heroine, her voice hoarse from shouting. A stem of goldenrod, thrown by an admirer in the audience, skidded across the stage and lodged in the hem of her dress.

"Goldarn it! The very flowers of the prairie run to her aid!" said the villain (who prided himself on being able to keep going come what may), and he broke the goldenrod across his knee.

That ad lib broke down the last barrier between audience and actor. If anyone could still recall paying ten cents to watch make-believe, in that instant they forgot. They were there, helpless witnesses to a cruel injustice. A silence fell as disturbing as the noise had been before.

The black-hearted landlord was able to lower his voice to a menacing hiss. *"But I shall soon change your mind, my beauty! Aha!"* And binding young Nancy hand and foot with washline, he tied her to a railroad track painted on the hardboard stage.

Cissy buried her face in her father's lap. Frank Tate, remembering the RRR locomotive bearing down on him when he could not move, suddenly turned green and covered his mouth. Tibbie Boden ran out of the tent, sobbing, *"Stop him! Stop him, somebody!"* and, finding herself alone on the empty prairie, ran back inside. Hildy Sissney dug her husband in the ribs and said, "This is what will happen to us, you see if it don't!"

"Don't you hear the train, my beauty?" sneered the vile landlord. "Submit or die!"

So Virgil Hobbs took out his Colt .45 and shot him.

At such close range, the impact threw the actor against the back wall of the stage.

"Holy Moses," said Nancy, and got up smartly from the railroad line.

Someone offstage screamed, "They shot Everett!" and the flat front of Nancy's shack fell forward with a smack as loud as a second gunshot. The actor-manager strode into the middle of the stage, arms over his head, appealing for calm. "Now please, folks, this is just a play."

Everett Crew lay clutching his thigh with both hands and, to keep from swearing, recited something Shakespearean and banged his forehead so hard against the scenery that it quaked and rumbled thunderously.

Amid these scenes of chaos, the northbound RRR raced through Florence sounding its whistle and clanging its bell. It was the noise of derision. It was the noise of civilization thumbing its nose at Florence, Oklahoma.

Next day, the Osage stage dropped off a string-bound parcel of the *Glasstown Daybreak*. The driver said he had read it, and it was a wonder the string had not burned through, "what with all the acid writ there."

THE DAYBREAK'S EDITOR WRITES:
Having my attention brought to certain libelous remarks concerning our fine city of Glasstown, your editor made it his business to investigate an odious rag entitled the *Florence Morning Star*. I

found it full of enough falsehoods to make a cat laugh.

Of the town of origin, my dear reader, you will not have heard, so let me depict for you Florence. It is a place fit only for grazing pigs and burying felons. So putrid are its streets that the excellent Red Rock Railroad will not stop there on any account, for fear of disease or violence befalling its passengers.

Its citizens are such heathens that they find no need of a church. Such a notorious crew of ne'er-do-wells roam the streets that the children go armed for their own protection. The Florentines are so devoted to strong liquor that they believe coffee to be an invention for the creosoting of fences. In short, it is Sodom and Gomorrah called by a prettier name.

Cockroach capital of the Territory, Florence boasts a hotel so lively with bedbugs that every morning, the blankets walk out the doors of their own accord.

As for the so-called newspaper, I would not use it to line my parrot's cage, for fear it offend the bird's good taste. It is a lying rag and I am perplexed to know why good paper and ink are wasted on it, for no citizen of Florence is clever enough to read. It must be bought only to swat the flies that hang in clouds over this pestilential

den of iniquity. I have it on good authority that the editor is an anarchist by persuasion and a villain by nature, and I fully expect his newspaper to report soon that he has been hanged for the villain he is.

Hulbert Sissney did not read aloud the editorial from the *Glasstown Daybreak* to his wife. He did not think she would find it comical. Nate Rimm said that this kind of thing happened all over—this lobbing of insults like hand grenades. He said that certain journalists saw it as an art form. "The editor of the *Daybreak* is a friend of my father's. That's who put him up to it, I daresay. It's good publicity, Hulbert! No one will believe it, and people will say it's proof that Glasstown's jealous of Florence."

But Hulbert Sissney did not think that his wife would see it quite like that, so he did not read it out loud to her.

Hildy Sissney heard it anyway. She was passing by the Waldorf Hotel just when Cyril Crew read the editorial out to his injured brother. Hildy stood transfixed to the spot, listening.

And she believed every word. It was no more than she had said all along about this clutch of hovels squatting on the soulless prairie.

When he finished reading, Cyril Crew noticed Hildy standing beyond the rolled-up tent flap and raised his hat to her. A vaudeville actor saluting her in the street! It was not to be endured. Hildy Sissney went home and packed the laundry bag full of belongings. At supper she said, "We are leaving, Hulbert." Cissy looked up, her soupspoon halfway between bowl and mouth. "We shall catch the northbound stage tomorrow. Go and stay with my mother."

"What brought this on?" asked Hulbert.

"Well? Have you seen what people are saying about this place? I won't be tarred with it, thank you kindly!"

"It's just the papers, Hildy! You don't want to believe what you read in the papers."

But Hildy Sissney was adamant. She had heard it with her own ears: the infamy, the slights, the written word. Hulbert put down his spoon and clasped both of his rickety knees, as he always did when he meant to be forceful. Cissy, unable to bear another quarrel, slid under the table and sat with her hands over her ears.

"I am going nowhere, Hildy."

"Then I'll go without you. I'll take the child, and you can come on and find us when you're busted—penniless. This is no fit place to raise a child. This is Sodom and Gomorrah. Says so in the paper." And she went through to the other room and climbed into Cissy's hammock, because there was nowhere else she could escape the vexation of looking at her husband.

Under the table, Cissy wrapped herself around her father's shins—they were thin as chair legs and trembling. One of his hands searched out the top of her head, and his fingers tangled themselves in her hair. The other took the pencil from behind his ear and gouged shapeless whorls on the newspaper in front of him. There was a bitter cold draft blowing in under the wall of the shack. "I don't want to go, Poppy! I don't want to go without you!"

But Hulbert's thoughts were still shackled by the long chain of events that had led him here, to this unhappy, bitter evening. "See what's happened?" he said. "That's the power of the word, that is. That's the power of the almighty, cussed, blue-blamed, stinkin' *word.*"

8

QUICK, QUICK, SNOW

True to her word, and despite a day of pouring rain, Hildy Sissney went to meet the northbound Osage stage the next day and, since Cissy was nowhere to be found, went alone. She made a lonely figure, her long thin body strung like a longbow into a rigid curve. The words came twanging out of her like arrows.

"Cissy always stickered up to you in a crisis," she told her husband resentfully. "Well, you can tell her she's welcome to the cooking and cleaning and the making something outa nothing. You deserve each other, tell her. You won't last, neither of you. Don't think it. She'll find out. Weak in the legs, weak in the head, that's you, Hulbert Sissney."

"Good-bye, Hildy. I'll write you," said Hulbert.

"Why? Cain't read, can I?"

"You're getting soaked through. And it's cold. Best get on the stage, Hildy. I'll write you."

Watching from the hayloft of the livery stable, Cissy clutched so hard at a rafter that the imprint of the nail heads marked her wrists all day, looking like shirt buttons.

Across the street, the Bright Lights Theater Company

was also packing up. "There's snow coming. If we don't get out of here today, Everett, we might get stuck here for the duration. We'll backtrack as far as Glasstown, then head off east—write you from wherever we hole up." Cyril Crew was loath to leave his brother in some penny-ante prairie settlement with a hole in his leg, but Florence was barely capable of supporting its own citizens, let alone six traveling players. Everyone needs to eat.

"I shall be entirely comfortable here," Everett Crew assured his brother, supporting himself on a pair of crutches made for him by the local oculist. "I shall join you as soon as I am fit." The villainous mustache was gone from under his nose. Without it he looked more like the old pictures of Washington Irving than a dastardly storybook villain. He wore a blanket draped over his shoulders for warmth; rain poured off the brim of his hat.

Stage and wagon set off at the selfsame time, the drivers finding comfort in each other's presence. But for Hildy Sissney the indignity was complete. Now she would be escorted all the way to Glasstown by a crew of vaudeville actors, and that made her feel dirty all over, long before the mud of the prairies splashed its way into the stagecoach.

"I say we shoot the buzzards to a standstill!" said Virgil Hobbs, his big old Colt .45 trembling in his hands.

"Don't talk so corn cracked, Virgil. How's shooting at 'em gonna make 'em stop?" And the FTCC rejected the suggestion, unanimous but for Jake Monterey, who liked to shoot at anything that moved.

Somehow, Emile Klemme had become doge of Florence despite the failure of his plan to stop the train. There was something about his square head and white cuffs, his swelling stomach and his tiepin that implied authority, respectability. He took command of the town committee meetings as though he had been elected to do so at birth. Already this afternoon he had declined Vokayatunga's suggestion that they should all perform a ritual dance to stop the train by magic.

Virgil, however, was no democrat. Raised in the foothills of the Rockies, he had seen the bullet settle everything: unpaid debts, lovers' tiffs, competition for business, overcrowding at a hotel bar. So he took his ancient Colt and climbed up the water tower—the beautiful, superfluous water tower—to wait for the four-o'clock train.

Herman (who had not been at the meeting) was gleaning worms and beetles from the trackside, to feed his chickens. (Vibration made the soil looser there.) For a time, the track edge had fluttered with Herman's posters enjoining the RRR to stop:

> "WHOSO IS SIMPLE,
> LET HIM TURN IN HITHER!"

> "COME, EAT OF MY BREAD
> AND DRINK OF THE WINE
> WHICH I HAVE MINGLED!"

He had made them from brown paper pasted to split-wood placards.

"COME UNTO ME, ALL YE
THAT ARE HEAVY LADEN . . ."

Tattered by the passing of trains, they had survived for a time, but townspeople desperate for fuel had uprooted the placards one by one and burned them to heat their shacks or cook their food. (Pickard Warboys had only narrowly persuaded them against uprooting the new, bare, unstrung telegraph poles and chopping them into firewood.)

Not liking to see someone past sixty go up a ladder, Herman asked charitably if Virgil needed any help.

"Ken still pull a trigger, boy," retorted Virgil, jamming a leg behind the ladder and one arm through a rung.

Herman dropped a palmful of insects into an empty tobacco tin. "You fixing to shoot up the train, Mr. Hobbs, sir? You can't do that. Not when it's full of God's children."

"Won't be shootin' at God's children," came the reply. "Next one along is a freight train. I'll just be shootin' that devil's spawn Peter Bull. Always drives the cattle freighter on a Thursday."

Herman wrestled with the last of his placards, uprooted it, and placing himself between the tower and the track, held it out sideways like a baseball bat. "Can't let you do that, Mr. Hobbs, sir."

"Git out of the way, boy! You're in my line of fire!"

"And that's where I'm staying," said Herman, his knees

visibly knocking, perhaps from cold, but more probably from righteous indignation. "You shoot at the train and you'll have to shoot through me!"

This was not strictly true. Even holding his placard, Herman could not shield single-handedly a seven-boxcar train and its locomotive, caboose, and tender. But there he stood, protecting (as best he could) Virgil's soul from the sin of murder and Peter Bull from meeting his Maker ahead of schedule.

Bull, when he rounded the bend, saw Herman waving his torn placard:

> "... AND I WILL GIVE YOU REST ..."

The engineer bared his loose false teeth in a malevolent grin.

Then a .45 slug bounced off the shiny paintwork of his platform, and another smashed a lump of coal in the tender.

"*You crazy sons of rattlesnakes!*" screamed Peter Bull, and stopped clanging the bell and blowing the whistle to crouch on the floor, while the fireman, similarly hunkered down, flung coal into the furnace with his bare hands.

All Virgil's other shots went wide. Most people in Florence never even heard them above the noise of the train.

Day after day, Hobbs climbed the water tower and Herman placed himself between Virgil and the train. It became a little ritual. Day after day, the cast of this melodrama grew bigger, with some people gathering around the foot of the tower to shout up at Virgil and others gathering (at a safe distance) to plead with Herman.

"Come down, you old fool! You'll be hanged like a turkey if you kill someone!"

But Virgil only spat.

"Don't you know what a terrible shot he is, boy? Could aim at Wyoming and still hit Utah!"

But Herman only began to sing, to keep his spirits up: a popular Mormon song entitled "The Iron Horse" that warned against all the sins and sinners that the railroads would bring to the lives of good Christian Americans.

> ". . . Saints will come, sinners too.
> We'll have all that we can do,
> For this great Union Railroad
> Will fetch the Devil through!"

Virgil was determined and Herman was immovable. When, to foil Virgil, they took the ladder off the water tower, he simply shifted ground to the railroad's empty wheat silo, and Herman shifted ground to the other side of the track, where he would again be in the direct line of fire.

It was a sad, useless building, the silo; if Florence survived long enough to harvest a crop, there would not be a train to ship out the grain. Its cavernous emptiness gaping beneath him, the sound of Herman singing down below, only fueled Virgil's rage and made him more determined than ever to shoot the train to a halt.

Soon afterward, Jake Monterey joined him. He was a man full of spleen, and shooting at a thing as big and fast and

114

impersonal as a steam train eased his pain.

Now that the town was taking shape, Monterey's home-less cows were seen as more and more of a nuisance roaming loose around the streets. They shoved their big heads in at people's windows, chewed through tent guy ropes, dropped their pats outside the bakery. "Can't you find somewhere to graze them beasts, Monterey?" people complained.

Evicted too late from his land to find himself another, unoccupied agricultural quarter, Jake Monterey had had to settle for a town site. He had gone into business butchering sick livestock and worn-out old horses, scraping a living from their bones and hooves and horns. But there was no room for his cows—the cows he had spent a year lovingly raising, before Boden came and cheated him out of his land.

"Can't you butcher them and be done with it?" people asked. "Can't you sell 'em?"

"Who to?" he would retort.

It all came back to the train, the lifeline that was not there for the use of Florentines. It all came back to the train and to Peter Bull. And Boden, of course.

Jake Monterey passed on his anxious, chafing rage to his sons, Peat and Fuller. One wet autumn day, they lay in wait for Tibbie Boden, who rode her pony to school. They pulled her out of the saddle and rolled her in the mud.

Kookie, who waited each day to hobble Tibbie's pony for her and to carry her lunch box inside, saw what was happening and ran to help her. But the Monterey boys were bigger than he was, and they knocked him down every time he came at them.

"Quick! Quick!" Kookie burst into the half-built school-church. Its tarpaulin roof billowed and rattled above him like thunderclouds. His eyebrow was bleeding and one cheek was swollen, and there was mud in his hair. Miss Loucien looked around from banging nails into the wall for coat hooks, the children from warming themselves around the stove. *"Quick, somebody! Quick! Anybody! The Montereys are killing Tibbie!"* But by the time the class had slithered through the slick, black mud, Peat and Fuller were nowhere to be seen, and Tibbie Boden was on hands and knees, gathering up clumps of her yellow hair out of the glutinous mud. They had even hacked off her bangs.

"I'll kill 'em," said Kookie Warboys.

"Thou shalt not," said the teacher, gathering Tibbie into her arms. "Not if I catch up to them first."

But the morning passed, and still Fuller and Peat did not show their faces in school. In the lunch break, Loucien Shades walked down to Monterey's yard to look for them herself. It was deserted, except for three of his cows, which greeted her with big anxious eyes and moved restlessly between a half-scraped horsehide and dangling clusters of cattle hooves. Horsetails gushed down from the roof like leaks of water.

"Jake? Jake Monterey?"

But Jake Monterey was not there. He had gone to join Virgil in the silo, ready to shoot up the midday passenger train.

Aboard the RRR, the car attendant tugged down his maroon vest and picked up his tray. Sinuously he moved down the train. He prided himself on knowing the track so well that no bend or jolt ever caused him to stagger.

"Comin' to Florence, ladies and gentlemen. Best git down on the floor and mind yourselves!"

There were always some, making the journey for the first time, who did not understand what he was saying. But the car attendant never stopped to explain; it would have halted his stylish glide through the coaches, lowering blinds, wiping slops of coffee off the polished wood fittings, moving on along.

"Comin' to Florence, ladies and gentlemen. Best git down on the floor and cover your heads!"

Behind him, regular passengers explained to newcomers how Florence was full of ruffians who took potshots at the train whenever it passed. The words were always greeted with little panicky squeaks or gruff oaths. The car attendant glided on, unflappable. "Comin' to Florence, ladies—gentlemen—best git down on the floor and cover your heads!"

Those crouching on the floor invariably toppled over into the aisle as the train rounded that last sharp bend before Florence. It amused the car attendant almost as much as the lousy, ineffectual marksmen of Florence. Reaching his cubbyhole at the front of the passenger cars, he sat down with a bottle of Mexican tequila. The moment the town flashed past the window, he would lean into the aisle and hoot down the train in a voice as big as Colorado, "Ladies and gentlemen, you may now resume your seats! Florence is passed!"

Today, a bullet from a Smith & Wesson came clean

through the wall and smashed the tequila bottle into shards the size of green peppercorns. The car attendant opened the door of his cubbyhole and leaned his head out. His knees, jumping like dice on a craps table, did not seem to want to take his weight. His hands fluttered like butterflies. His eyebrows seemed to be tangled in his hairline. One eyelid twitched involuntarily. He opened his mouth and called, "Laymen and gentlies, you can reseat your crooms. Fourpence's post."

Fortunately, no one heard him, because his nose and windpipe were full of tequila.

"Jake Monterey? You up there?" Miss Loucien called. Her voice was huge in the echoing, empty silo. She could hear the two men cackling with hysteria, like children who have worked each other up to devilment. In the quiet after the passage of the train, rain prickled against the metal silo. "Jake Monterey! You got your boys up there with you? You training them up to be hoodlums same as you?"

"I ain't got 'em." Monterey's face appeared over the rim of the loft hatch, his nose blue with cold. "Why ain't you got 'em in school?"

"They run off," said the teacher, hands on hips. "Thought maybe they fancied shooting up a train full of innocent people or some such clever stunt."

Jake Monterey was worried. The excitable grin of a boy with a peashooter faded from his face, and he forgot his gun as he climbed down the wall ladder. He could be heard calling out to his boys as he trudged back up the street toward his yard—"Peatie? Fuller! Where you hiding yourselves?"—and only Virgil was left crowing like a rooster on the roof of its barn, jeering at Herman the Mormon, forlorn and shivering on the trackside. "Hit her today, didn't we? Couldn't block us today, could you, boy?"

As Miss Loucien walked back to the schoolhouse, the sky overhead was the same black pall as the tarpaulin rattling over the schoolroom. Perhaps they were both straining at their moorings, ready to break free. She stood in the center of the heptagon of benches, turning around slowly so as to meet the eye of every child. She came to rest at last looking at Tibbie Boden, tearstained, grubby, shorn.

"You know something, fellers?" said Miss Loucien. "We got a town breaking itself apart here. We got adults behaving like children. We got children behaving like animals. Now I want to ask you: Is there any chance that you people can fill in for them, while their wits are straying? Is there the smallest chance I can ask you to do something mighty grown-up, for me and for the town?"

That night, when Tib Boden returned home, clean clothed, but with her hair clipped close to her scalp, her father reached for his gun: *Who did it?* Quickly Tibbie explained how Miss Loucien had been checking the class for lice and had found her scalp a-crawl, and nothing for it but to cut off the lot and scrub it with carbolic soap.

No rumors reached Boden to make him disbelieve her. The same was being said by every other child, returning home with stories of scissors and tears and Tibbie Boden looking like a prairie dog without her curls. Even Kookie, accused by his mother of fighting in the school yard, did not defend himself with the noble truth. His brothers said he had been picked on; beyond that nothing else was said. For Miss Loucien had charged them with holding the town together, plastering over its cracks with their silence. She had made them guardians of the peace, and as guardians, they dutifully held their peace.

Only Peat and Fuller Monterey, hiding out in the livery stable from the repercussions of what they had done, did not know that they had got off scot-free.

That was where Cissy came across Peat, occupying the same hay bale where she came to cry about her missing mother. "This is my place," she told him peevishly. Then she saw that Peatie, too, was crying—heartbrokenly, uncontrollably, gulping for breath, driving the heels of his hands up his face as if he could push the tears back into his eyes and nose.

"Miss Loucien covered for you," said Cissy. "She didn't want Tibbie's paw to shoot your paw."

Peatie was slow to take this in. His face went on twitching, out of control. "Don't make no difference. Paw'll wind up dead anyways." Tears got the better of him again, and he screwed his face into the hay bale.

"How d'you mean?" said Cissy, standing sideways to him, feeling a traitor to her friends just by being there, talking to him.

"Well, pretty soon he'll kill someone on that train. Or he'll shoot that fool Herman who keeps standing in his way. And then Sheriff Klemme will come and arrest him and hang him, and then where'll Fuller and me be, with nothing but a bunch of cows and some horse bones and what-all?" His voice ended in a howl of desolation imitated by the wind that had been scouring Florence all day for no-hopers just like Peat.

Next day that same wind brought in snow—a blizzard, a white whirling wall of lumpy flakes, dizzying, drifting. There was no sound after it fell, so it was like being struck deaf.

The mud-caked hems of trouser legs and skirts froze into rigid, scratchy hoops. The water kept by the latrines bulged, frozen, out of its buckets. Quail and prairie chickens froze, too—whole flocks lying dead and rigid. Their feathers came off in a single sheet, crackling, like the shell off a hard-boiled egg.

No Osage stage galloped out of the wheeling whiteness. The winged carts and wagons stood axle deep, their fuel shelves piled high with snow. The long slag heap of cow chips was hidden by a blanket of soft whiteness. It was Thanksgiving, but an outbreak of influenza kept people indoors, frightened of contact with neighbors who might pass them germs and yet another excuse to die before Christmas.

"Nothing to be grateful for, anyways," said Jake Monterey, boiling up the hooves of a dead mule for the glue. It was like some dreadful parody of a Thanksgiving feast, that cauldron full of stinking hocks.

So nothing happened. Nothing could happen. A leprous paralysis seized on the people of Florence. There was no horizon to their white world; it blended imperceptibly into the sky. Their sordid, shored-up shacks were masked over with prettiness; each tent's guy rope carried its own mane of snow. But it might as well have been a magic spell of sleep, for no one could stir, nothing could be achieved. Only Jake Monterey's straying cows scooped halfheartedly with one hoof, in search of grass where none grew.

Climbing down from their perch in the silo, Virgil and Monterey found their hands sticking to the metal ladders with the cold. The oil in their revolvers froze.

At night sometimes, Cissy thought that she must be the cause of the cold—that it emanated from the place inside her chest that groaned like pack ice, from the empty hole in the air where her mother ought to be.

Each day, Doge Emile Klemme called at the school-church to escort the teacher home to take tea, holding her elbow lest she slip on a patch of ice.

Every evening, Mr. Fudd cooked a quail for his supper by resting it on the top of the glass chimney of a lamp and turning up the flame.

Only a handful of children were able to reach school, where they found Miss Loucien wearing a horse blanket and a hat made from a marmot she had shot herself. They had to bend double beneath the low swag of the ceiling. The tarpaulin roof had filled with snow and bulged downward, filling the classroom as if some fat giant were using it for a hammock. Hulbert Sissney came with his window pole, and Frank Tate with a plank of wood, and they tried to push the tarpaulin upward, to empty out its burden of snow. But suddenly it burst its guy ropes and slumped down, loosing an avalanche of snow into Miss Loucien's bed and the white satin pews and the stove. In her red leather gloves, Miss Loucien scrabbled to unearth the photographs of her husband and grandfather. Then turning to the children, she told them, "Go explore the possibilities of snow, fellers. I got my hands full here."

Naturally, the children looked to Kookie to tell them what to do with their freedom amid the great wealth of whiteness—what games would relieve the blue pain in their hands and feet, what pleasure was to be got from snowdrifts. But Kookie was silent, withdrawn, sealed shut like the latrine buckets by their little lids of ice. Cissy thought it must be the loss of Tibbie's hair, his failure to save it from the shears. "It will grow back, you know," she said, resting a hand on his sleeve.

"What will?"

"Tibbie's hair."

Kookie looked at her blankly, snow catching on his lashes in big clumps, skidding down his face. "My gran died last night," he said. "The cold took her. I hate this place." The snow danced and tumbled, so light that the smallest breeze sent it spilling upward again. Gravity had ceased to exist. "Frank Tate says the ground's too hard to bury her, and to wait till a thaw comes." Snow creaked under their boots as if the earth itself were cracking open.

"Let's go track hares," said his brother Amos. "I feel like killing something."

"No," said Cissy. "Let's go stop the train."

They moved snow on spades and in buckets. They rolled up great boulders of snow and carried it in armfuls like phantom babies. They worked till their coats were encrusted with ice and their marmot-skin mittens hung from their wrists like dead, wet rats. They shoveled with skillets and saucepans and planks of wood. They moved the snow on a sheet of canvas that had once been the First Bank of Florence. (Samuel T. Guthrie had moved into warmer premises.)

It was numbing, mindless work. They felt like the stupid giants in fairy tales, tricked into braiding sand or baling out the sea. But what with the cold and the hard labor, it was impossible to think while they worked, and that was all they wanted. The railroad tracks were not even visible—a scar across the prairie that had miraculously healed. It was hard to believe that an iron locomotive had ever hurtled through the same air as now supported solid blizzard.

When their parents saw what they were doing, they too came, with spades and trowels, Sven Lagerlöf with his bread paddle. But the children stood on their tumulus of snow, red faced and savage, like primeval druids, and said, "It's ours. We can do it ourselves."

They did. They blocked the track with a snowdrift.

And then no train came.

Of course it didn't. Every one of the routes south had been rubbed out, and the locomotives of the RRR stayed in their engine sheds as snug as the bullets in the chamber of a gun. No passenger trains, no freight or cattle trains, no flatcars stacked with lumber, no Peter Bull, no movement. As night fell, the compacted barrier of snow showed up as

124

nothing more than a grayer, dirtier tumor on the leprous landscape.

That night, Agnes Bentley's goat froze to death. Still upright, it stood like a riderless rocking horse outside her door, and Thomas Grigg, in trying to carry it home to butcher into joints for her, slipped and broke a hip. Blosk Warboys took it upon herself to nurse him better. "See how Grandma's bed came free to some purpose," she told her husband in that quiet, contented voice of hers.

The following night, the snow on the roofs swagged, crazed, and began to slurry down wetly into the roadway. The icicles along the eaves wept themselves away. The railroad track, like a geographical fault line, emerged through the melting snow.

But the mound, built of compacted snow, survived, as the stumps of snowmen persist on a green lawn. Ten yards long and as high as a man's head, it crouched across the line, shining with melted snow but as solid as rock salt.

"Bring out your mail, Pickard," Hulbert Sissney told his neighbor. "I really think the train will stop today."

Suddenly, Florence woke from its torpor and stirred out of doors. Mrs. Warboys stacked up pillows behind Mr. Grigg's head so that he could see out the window and down the road. The bruised black sky was gone, and instead, a bright, pale sun slid across the sky like a new penny. The children's snow mound began to sweat and stream with water, but there was not long to wait now—only an hour or so.

By eleven, the day was mild, with slush turning Main

Street into a quagmire and setting the roofs steaming. The barricade of snow was steaming, too—steaming and shrinking like a knob of lard in a frying pan. When they patted it, to keep it solid, the water splashed in their faces. But it was still huge—as big as an albino elephant sitting on the track. The RRR would just have to stop.

Noises like ticking watches and breaking twigs came from inside the barricade, noises like groans and whimpers. A great lake of water circled the base, and little by little the elephant was changing shape, its spine flattening, its flanks sinking.

"Only a while longer to wait," said Miss Loucien, joining hands with the children on either side of her. It was noon. It was twelve thirty. It was quarter to one. Remnants of snow on the tracks had made Peter Bull late.

At one o'clock, the train approached. Vibration shook the hillock of dirty snow, shivering ice into granules, lumps into beads. The ice elephant sprawled in its puddle of sweat, its spine only as high as Cissy's shoulder.

Herman, remembering his daily duty, looked in the direction of the silo and wondered whether he needed to take up his place in the line of fire. But then he saw Virgil Hobbs and Jake Monterey among the trackside crowd and did not bother. Perhaps hatred had thawed, along with the snow.

The RRR, its blinds drawn down, came around the bend slowly, still nervous of ice patches and of losing her footing. This hesitancy put hope into the people waiting by the track. They could not hear the nasal crooning of the car attendant warning people to "git down on the floor."

"Stop the train!" they shouted, waving scarves and hats. "Stop the train, won't you? We don't wanna fight! We just want a train!" Peter Bull, hat tied on with a tartan muffler, saw the barricade and turned his false teeth sideways in his mouth. His mittened hands muffled the clang of the bell, and he fumbled the cord of the whistle. To the fireman's annoyance, as he threw a double shovelful of fuel into the furnace, one of his gloves went with it. To Bull's far greater annoyance, he was not sure whether he could get through the snow wall. Taking shelter from any sharpshooters, he opened up the throttle, cussing the engine for its sluggishness.

It did not seem sluggish from the trackside. The RRR plowed into the snow barrier at twenty miles an hour, lifting into the air half a ton of freezing slush. Ice glancing off the engine barrel turned to steam with a noise like ripping canvas. For the rest, it exploded into a thousand fistfuls of dirty shrapnel, flying upward, outward, and falling from the sky in bruising, drenching pats of cold, soaking the Florentines through three layers of clothing, knocking children down like bowling pins to roll breathless in the deep puddles of melting mush.

Cooled by its collision with the blockade, the locomotive slowed, like a man walking into ground elder. Then it was kicking itself free and picking up speed, its pistons elbowing Florence aside, its cowcatcher crammed with blocks of snow, so it appeared to be baring white teeth in a beamish grin.

9

ONE-WAY TICKET

"Remarkable, how well the children dance," said Everett Crew, sitting on the sidelines of the Christmas dance. "I am almost glad to have an excuse to keep from dancing alongside them. The comparison would be odious."

"It must be that teacher of theirs who taught them how," said Nate Rimm, tapping his foot to the music of Lloyd Lentz's fiddle. "She follows a most unusual syllabus."

The children of Florence Academy stripped the willow, do-si-doed, and swung each other around as if they had been square-dancing for years. Little by little, the smiles fixed to their faces by Miss Loucien's strict orders gave way to genuine enjoyment as they realized they were dancing the socks off their elders and betters.

Everett Crew the actor was a very different figure of a man when he was not tying distressed maidens to railway tracks. He sported a long velvet smoking jacket and yellow cravat, along with heeled boots, shoulder-length gray hair, and a large dried sunflower pinned to his lapel. His injured leg was propped up on a second chair, so he reclined like some antique Roman accepting the salutations of his gladiators. As each person entered the finished schoolroom, he greeted them:

"Good evening, Mrs. Warboys—how's that patient of yours doing? Sir! How are you? Young man, what an excellent suit of clothes; are you courting? Miss Cissy, how is your imagination? Will it stretch to dancing an imaginary waltz with me? Doge Klemme! Any scandalous lawsuits to enliven the evening? Season's greetings, Mr. Morning. What a masterpiece of typesetting the Christmas issue is!"

At every wave, Nate Rimm would spin around in his chair, thinking to see some celebrity guest of honor arriving, for Crew's face would be alight with pleasure, as if his greatest hero or dearest friend had just entered the room. And yet they were just Florentines—people who had known the actor barely a month.

"Virgil, you old rogue! Do you go armed tonight? Mr. Fudd, I do declare, you've trimmed your wick especially for the occasion! You look like a well-pruned hedge! Don't lurk out there, Herman, my boy! I promise not to breathe alcohol in your direction, and I'm sure the Swedish catering runs to a glass of milk!"

The guests, in turn, lit up like paper lanterns. The men grinned, the women giggled, the children ran over to see if Everett had any toffees. "You been electioneering, Everett?" said Nate when the fifteenth guest had greeted Crew like a long-lost brother. "If you ran for president now, I reckon you could be in Washington by the weekend."

"Me, Nate? I'm just basking in good company. Cakes and ale, my old comrade, cakes and ale. I love a party. As I said to Oscar Wilde—"

At this, Nate, who had been tilting his chair backward,

fell off it with a clatter. "Oscar Wilde? You met Oscar Wilde? The playwright?"

"I most certainly did! On his triumphant tour of the frontier. I was privileged to hear him give his talk on Aesthetics in the Home and Workplace, in Cincinnati. Can you not see the impact he made upon my person?" he added in self-mockery, gesturing at his clothes and lowering his nose in the direction of the desiccated sunflower, big as a dinner plate on his chest.

Gentle amusement on Nate's part gave way to awe and envy. "Would you write a piece about him for the *Morning Star*?"

"Gladly; I'd be hono—" For the first time that evening, the actor made an effort to stand up—a clumsy, unsuccessful struggle that ended with him knocking over his ginger ale. "Mrs. Shades!—Miss Loucien, I mean. How very—are you? How? Delightful. Your pupils' dancing, I mean. You must have had them practicing since Easter."

"Mr. Crew, didn't you know? Last Easter this part of the world was Not. Didn't exist. God was still parting light and dark and dry from wet. There was none of this Garden of Eden you see in front of you." Miss Loucien was wearing a skirt made from Indian weaving, and dark, cartoon-style stick figures ran up the front pleat, in pursuit of a bison on her hip. She had polished her cracked boots to a cherry shine, and her red hair, which was normally worn in a French twist, hung to a prodigious length down her back. "In actual fact, Mr. Crew, I would relish your advice."

"Ah! Mrs.—Miss . . ." (The easy compliments did not

seem to flow so easily now, Rimm noticed.) Everett Crew stood, his hands on two chair backs, his hurt leg bent so that only the toe of his boot rested on the floor, pretending not to be in pain. For her part, Miss Loucien seemed unwilling to speak in front of the newspaper editor.

"Forgive us, Rimm," said the actor, swaying his great head in Nate's direction like a dinosaur clearing brushwood.

Nate Rimm made himself scarce, much as he would have liked to stay and discuss Oscar Wilde. As he left, he heard the teacher say: "Mr. Crew, may I confide a great secret to you? You being from out of town, kinda . . ."

After the influenza, a lightning strike had burned down three shacks at the north end of the town. Two families who had come to Florence simply in search of employment found none, ran out of savings, and had to ride the stage south into Texas, destitute and frostbitten. The newspaper war raged on, with the *Glasstown Daybreak* becoming more and more abusive about Florence:

> **. . . that stinking louse-infested hole-up for bandits and desperados, loose women, and fatherless children, polluting the prairie like an oil spring and giving Oklahoma such a bad name that skunks are swimming in droves over the Red River to keep from breathing the same pestilential air.**

One of Jake Monterey's cows died, falling into the foundations of the only brick building in town, Sam Guthrie's bank. The town bought the carcass from him, but after the snow thawed realized that it would not keep until Christmas.

So somewhere between Thanksgiving and Christmas, they were celebrating. They were celebrating having survived as long as they had: It was the only good fortune anyone could call to mind.

And yet somehow they were having a good time despite themselves, despite the train's refusal to stop, despite the sleet outside, despite the dark, pungent taste of the iffy meat.

Emile Klemme, for instance, turned quite pink with pleasure when, during the evening, the teacher asked him to come and talk to the children about being a sheriff. "Mr. Crew says he will come and teach us the Declaration of Independence," she said encouragingly, though Emile Klemme needed no encouragement at all.

Herman the Mormon was full of zeal, because Miss Loucien had invited him to tell the children about the Church of Jesus Christ of Latter-day Saints; also about raising chickens. Vokayatunga was telling everyone that Miss Loucien had invited him to relate the sad history of the Ponca tribe and show them a dance or two. Mrs. Warboys had offered to teach crochet, and how to set a leg with plaster of paris.

When Kookie caught wind of these visits, he volunteered his father, too. "Paw could teach the Morse code!" And Monday Morning offered to recount the Legend of Odysseus. Nate Rimm, without even realizing it, found he had offered to lecture on freedom of the press.

"What an exciting semester we have ahead of us!" said Miss Loucien, completing her circuit of the room back to where she had started, beside Everett Crew. "I am indebted to you, Mr. Crew. I truly am. There wasn't one person who minded me asking!"

"Ah, that's the lure of the footlights, Mrs. Shades," said Everett Crew confidingly. "Everyone likes to perform. . . . Perhaps after the Declaration of Independence, I might . . . if you don't object, I mean . . . I could tackle the wonders of Shakespeare? And the theories of Oscar Wilde on art?"

"Why, Mr. Crew!" cried the teacher, pressing his arm warmly. "With such a richness, there will hardly be a moment free for me to teach them everyday knowledge!"

The noise in the carpetless building rose to a happy din. The music to which the children danced was barely audible any longer above the clatter of feet on the board floor, and that was no louder than the chatter of neighbors commiserating about the flu, about the railroad, about the weather. Then Pickard Warboys burst in with news that the wiremen were even now stringing telegraph wires on the posts alongside the railroad track—at least they would be, when it stopped sleeting. And Mrs. Warboys told him not to leave the wiremen outside, poor things, but to bring them in to get warm and join in the party.

"Is this venison we're eating?" asked someone about Jake Monterey's beef.

"I wish," said Tibbie Boden, starry-eyed and red cheeked from dancing, "I wish the people in Glasstown could see what a swell place this is."

Then Emile Klemme raised a toast to the church, and everyone headed for the punch bowl, to scoop up a cupful of something concocted by the oculist. It could hardly be strong liquor, they told themselves—not something mixed by such a mild-mannered man.

"To Florence church!" "God bless it!" "To Florence Academy!" "To Florence!" "To Christmas!" "To Thanksgiving!" "To the president!" "To Republicans!" "To democracy!" "To Florence Opera House!" "To Oklahoma!" "To oysters on the half shell, all the way from Houston!" "To the doge!" "To the *Morning Star.*" "To the telegraph company and every one of its poles!" "To the *Glasstown Daybreak,* may night fall on it!" "To the penkas of the pople! . . . I mean, to the people of the Poncas! What's in this punch?"

The sleet rattled in vain on the new tin roof.

"To William Shakespeare!" "To Abraham Lincoln!" "To Sweden!" "To Wales!" "To the Old Country!" "To the New World!" "To the planet!" "To the universe!" "To us!" "To *us!*"

Mr. Fudd had climbed onto the teacher's coffin-bed-desk. His Christmas haircut bristled like the mane of a jackal and he grinned a jackal's grin. "And I say . . . *let's derail the train!*"

The Christmas crowd grinned back. Someone opened the door, and a wind full of villainy blew in.

"Perchance . . ." said a voice practiced in quelling riots. "Perchance," said Everett Crew, lowering himself casually onto a length of satin-quilted bench. "Perchance . . ." he said, casting aside his crutches. "Perchance . . . we need to bring to the problem a little more . . . *subtlety.* You heard what the child said: 'I wish the people in Glasstown could see what a swell place Florence is!' Well? Let us tell them! Let us tell people what kind of a town it is that we've got here!"

The Florence Town Committee of Citizens met in Sheriff Klemme's office. All eyes rested on Herman and Frank Tate: volunteers for the job at hand. The two sat opposite each other on hard chairs, blushing, embarrassed, silent.

"What do you think?" asked Emile Klemme, turning to Crew.

"We-e-e-ll . . . they both have suits that fit them," replied the actor. "Who else volunteered?"

"No one."

"Ah! Then I say these two are perfect," said Crew. "They'll be a triumph."

"I volunteered too!" Kookie Warboys wriggled himself around the office door. "I volunteered! I could do it!"

"Habakkuk Warboys!" His teacher cut him short. "Don't make us have to tell you again. This is a job for grown-up folk. You just git back to the schoolhouse, you hear?"

". . . I just wish you'd wait until I'm fit, and let me do it," said Everett Crew.

"But why would you want to trouble yourself, Mr. Crew?" said the lawyer suspiciously. "You are not even a Florentine."

"Oh, you know us thespians. Any excuse to play to an audience. . . . And Herman there isn't a Florentine either, for

135

that matter. He would be a Salt Lake City man if he had his way."

"We are *paying* Herman," the oculist explained.

"A pig!" Herman pointed out, in case Everett thought he had sinned by accepting money. "A weaner."

"And what's in it for Frank?" the actor asked forthrightly, but Frank Tate only shrugged and blushed to the roots of his melancholy hair. "I do wish you people would wait and let me do it," Crew said again.

"Just how difficult can it be?" said Klemme, puzzled. "They only have to give out a few handbills and be pleasant to folk."

"And stay alive after," said Everett, but only to himself.

The handbills read:

GREETINGS FROM THE PEOPLE OF FLORENCE!
COME SEE US SOMETIME IN '94
FLORENCE!
IT'S THE BEST LITTLE PLACE IN THE WORLD!

On the back was a list of all the businesses already operating in Florence. And on the border around the edge were pictures, hand drawn and colored in by the children during schooltime.

Now it was the job of Frank Tate and Herman to hand out these pretty handbills to the passengers of the RRR, and to be ready to talk glowingly about Florence. It was a salesman's job—a foot-in-the-door-can-I-interest-you-madam-in-a-twenty-one-volume-gold-tooled-treasure-of-a-town sort of job. But Florence had no salesmen. It had only Frank and Herman. And there was, of course, the slight danger the two would be spotted by a railroad official.

Pickard Warboys drove Frank and Herman north to Glasstown. (Someone had to drive the hearse back to Florence, once the lads had boarded the train.) "You sure you wanna do this, boys?" asked Pickard.

The undertaker's nephew looked a sickly green, his deep-sunk eyes ringed with shadows, his unruly hair oiled flat to his head so every bump and ledge of his skull was visible. "Could wish I was a better talker," he admitted guiltily. "I confess, I do let other folk do the talking, generally."

Herman said gloomily, *"He that openeth wide his lips shall have destruction."*

It was strange to see the RRR standing still in the station—stationary—this train they had tried so often to stop. Warboys shook hands with the two and watched them climb aboard. "Best of luck, boys!"

Then he lifted down from the buckboard fifty copies of the *Florence Morning Star*, which he delivered to the barbershop, general store, saloon, and station waiting room. How much longer could Nate Rimm afford to go on publishing for free? he wondered. It was a marvel he had not run through his savings already.

On board the train, Herman and Frank appeared so uneasy that the car attendant looked them over like a fishmonger checking herring. "Where you going?" he asked Herman, though it was plainly written on the tickets.

"Bewick," said Frank.

"You're in second class," said the car attendant contemptuously, though they were already sitting down in a second-class coach with its hard plank benches. "You *stay* in second, you hear?" And giving a dandyish tug at his maroon vest, he moved on to insult a better class of passenger.

The RRR was almost empty in comparison with the day of the land rush. Its passengers were mostly Texans, homeward bound. They talked in loud voices across several rows of seats, chewing on their vowel sounds like men chewing tobacco. They talked about horses and cattle feed, about Glasstown and cheese and fleas and the government. Frank and Herman, however, sat opposite each other and wondered when to begin talking. The more they wondered, the less they said, their eyes drifting toward the window. Once, Frank began to ask Herman about his plans, about Salt Lake City. But then he thought better of it. Herman would probably start praising Salt Lake City instead of Florence.

A shoe-shine boy came through, telling the passengers he gave the best shoe shine since God invented shoes. But no one could afford a shoe shine. Some of them could not even afford shoes. Herman and Frank examined their boots. The train pulled out of Glasstown, slow and jolting over the points, then settled into a swaying, rhythmic rattle. The prairie opened up on either side of the train.

"You know that place Florence?" said Frank at last. He said it so softly that Herman did not catch the words.

"Pardon?" He had been sunk deep in thought.

Frank coughed and said it louder. "You know that place Florence? I hear it's getting to be a mighty fine place."

"Mmm," said Herman, a hunted look in his eye.

"Yeah! I hear they got a bank and everything. A real comfortable hotel."

The look in Herman's eyes changed to panic. He tried to signal, by wriggling his eyebrows, that lying—actual *lying*—was not in him. Instead, he took a Bible out of his pocket and began to read it. Frank Tate shrank back into his seat and drew with his finger on the dirty window. None of their words had been loud enough to carry, in any case. Two ghosts would have made more noise between them.

"Did you say 'Florence'?" A small razed head, like a coconut, appeared over the back of Herman's seat, making him drop his Bible. It was Kookie Warboys. "I heard that too. Mighty fine town! Lots of prosperity! A whole tubful!" bawled Kookie. "I read about it in the newspaper. They reckon the president hisself goes there sometimes for a holiday! There's rodeos and circuses every Saturday, and that dandy silo thing just bustin' with wheat!"

The two shy young men stared at the little boy, shoulders rising around their ears. Herman put on his hat.

"How did you get here, Kookie?" whispered Frank.

Kookie beamed back at him, delighted with himself. "Been right there behind you in the buckboard all the way! Under the canvas. Snuck aboard the train while the attendant was polishing his buttons. Figured I could help. You got the handbills? We ought to get started."

"You shouldn't have come, Kookie," said Frank Tate. "It might not be safe."

After sneaking his way onto the train, however, Kookie felt indestructible. He grabbed a bundle of handbills and headed off along the train. Frank and Herman had no choice but to follow.

Most of the passengers in second class took the sheets without an argument, but soon after, they tore the pages into halves and quarters. (Toilet paper was always hard to come by on the prairie.) One woman slipped Kookie a quarter, thinking that he was collecting for charity.

A few passengers put their hands over their pockets and asked if they were expected to pay for the handbills. But the really bad behavior was confined to the front cars.

"Ain't interested. Go chase yourself."

Herman blushed and turned away, his hand on the Bible in his pocket.

"I didn't pay first class to be pestered by hoboes," said an elegant gentleman in a Stetson to his elegant wife in a flowered bonnet. They looked straight ahead, ignoring the handbill Frank held out to them. He slipped it into the lady's basket, and she gave him a look as if he had just hidden a rat among her possessions.

But by the time they caught up with Kookie, he was talking as fast and as loud as a cattle-market auctioneer, thrusting the fliers in people's faces and singing the praises of Florence. ". . . Why, I even heard they found gold when they was digging out the rabbit warrens. And what with the park they're laying out and the big factory, it's fixing to be bigger than Houston pretty soon! Oysters on the half shell, that's what folk ate in Florence on Thanksgiving!"

"Come, come, Habakkuk," said Herman, under his breath, clutching his wad of handbills to his chest as if to dissociate himself from the lies.

"Don't take my word for it! Read all about it! Buy the *Florence Morning Star*, why don't you?" Kookie exhorted a florid man in a fringed leather coat.

"Just let the fliers speak for themselves, Kookie," urged Frank, giving the boy a little shove. "Don't vex the good people with your chatter." But Kookie was into his stride now.

"Pretty soon there'll be timber coming in on one train and chairs and tables going out on the next—whole houses, even! There's this cabinetmaker I know can hammer you up a little cabin in half a day . . . and mansions! There's gonna be mansions with lawns outside and trees all down the road and—"

"Ain't that the place where they shoot up the train?" a grain salesman in a pony-skin vest pulled himself halfway out of his seat to call. "All desperadoes out of the Panhandle, that's who lives there!"

"Oh come now . . ." Even Herman felt moved to protest.

"No, no! Not anymore!" said Frank. "That was a mistake . . ."

"No one will shoot today!" shouted Kookie. "Bet you a dollar!"

Just then, the car attendant emerged from his cubbyhole. He stooped to pick up a handbill off the floor and read it through. His vest strained its silver buttons as his belly filled up with pleasure. "We been expectin' you," he said from under a flaring top lip.

Frank Tate grabbed Kookie by the collar, snorted, "Leave off!" and pulled him back down the train. Herman loped along ahead of them, steadying himself from seat to seat like a white-faced lemur swinging from tree to tree. "What did he mean, 'We been expecting you'?" To their relief, when they looked back, the attendant was not hard on their heels.

He came five minutes later.

He had stayed to enlist every man on the train who owned a gun.

Bristling like a porcupine with shotguns and carbines, the posse squeezed through the cars, gathering behind it a following of nosy spectators hoping to catch sight of a real live outlaw. They saw instead two pale young men, awash with paper, sandwiching a ten-year-old into his seat while one menaced him with a Bible open at the Ten Commandments.

At the sight of the posse, Frank Tate got to his feet and banged his head on the luggage rack.

"You're some of them assassins outa Florence," stated the car attendant.

"We are not assassins, sir," said Herman, milk white under his brown bowler hat.

"Come to shoot up the train on the inside, now, have you?" said the car attendant, raising a roar of alarm and anger from the mob behind him. Someone jabbed Tate in the chest with the barrel of a shotgun.

All Kookie's talkativeness left him. Now it was only the adults speaking—shouting, swearing, name-calling, threatening. Someone grabbed a wedge of handbills and threw them out the train window. They blew back down the car—a blizzard of paper—and individual sheets stuck to the windows, cheery with robins and candy canes and roses.

Then hands were grabbing Herman and Frank and Kookie and dragging them around and over the seats, propelling them toward the rear of the train. Women drew in their skirts and shielded their babies from these desperadoes in torn Sunday suits.

"We got tickets through to Bewick!" Frank Tate tried to tell them.

"You got one-way tickets to hell," said the car attendant.

Then they were out on the back platform of the train, where the backwash turned into a battering bluster of icy wind. Herman's hat blew off and bowled away down the track a hundred yards and more. The vibration through the platform hammered at the soles of their feet, made their teeth chatter.

"Not the boy," said Herman. "You can do what you like to us, but don't hurt the boy."

The distant landscape stood almost still: a tree, a rocky outcrop, a cloud. The foreground was a blur of rushing pebbles and grass and sagebush. Someone hit Herman with the butt of a handgun.

A wrought-iron railing surrounded the platform, in it a little picket gate that now the car attendant opened. "Jump!"

he said. Because of the motion of the train, the gate swung back on his fingers, adding pain to his bile.

"Where are we? We're nowhere!" said Tate, gripping the railing with both hands.

"Should feel at home, then," said the car attendant, his bruised fingers clutched between his thighs. "You gonna jump, or do we shoot you first and throw you off after?"

Herman made one last plea on Kookie's behalf—"*Of such is the Kingdom of God!*"—but Kookie made a rush at him and butted him in the chest: The words were more frightening than the guns or the wake of flickering track.

Scrambling up on the railing, holding on to the fancy ironwork around the platform's roof, Kookie stuck out his tongue at the car attendant: "Won't stay where we're not wanted!" His words were snatched away as he leaped outward—not onto the rails and chippings and ties, but out into the trackside grass.

Frank Tate walked out of the open gate like a man stepping into a swimming pool. And Herman scrambled upward toward martyrdom, snagged his jacket on the fancy roof edge, wrenched it free, and left the train spread-eagled, his back sprouting ragged cloth wings, for all the world as if he would fly to heaven under his own power.

His precious pocket Bible hit the rails and burst apart— a thousand tissuey pages fountaining upward and away on the turbulence behind the racing train.

144

10

COMMUNICATIONS

"We hold these Truths to be self-evident, that all Men are created equal, that they are endowed by their Creator with certain unalienable Rights, that among these are Life, Liberty, and the Pursuit of Happiness. . . ."

With an American flag worn diagonally across his body and with a large eagle feather in one hand, Everett Crew stood on the scaffolding over the foundations of the bank and declaimed the Declaration of Independence in its entirety to the first sunny sky of the year. Miss Loucien's class stood openmouthed, waiting for him to fall off the narrow plank, which bent and sprang under him, and his voice fell on them like apples from a tree. The little ones did not understand one word in three, but they knew it was some important mystery being paraded before them. They would remember it forever: that velvet coat bellying out with the wind, the flag crackling. The performance was too grand to be absurd. Even the older children, who had been told the words by someone some-where along the way, heard them as if for the first time, in Crew's strange, rich, rolling diction, powerful as a locomotive. Even the adults (who knew this was supposed to be a school lesson) stopped what they were doing and came out to watch.

My dear Hildy,

Today Mr. Crew gave us the Declaration of Independence from atop the scaffolding. Actually he gave it to the schoolchildren, but since it was outdoors, we gotten to hear. Sounded like I never heard it before. What I mean to say is, he found something to do with the words that made them new. I cannot rightly say what. Only that if I was Crew I could say what, and you would understand. Reckon if I was Crew, I could say all manner of things that need saying. But I am not.

Presently we fear for Habakkuk Warboys, who is gone missing. Maybe he is with Frank Tate and Herman, that Mormon boy. But that puts no one's mind at rest, because they are gone too. They set off to ride the RRR down country from Glasstown, selling the idea of Florence to their fellow passengers. But they never signaled from Bewick to say they got there safe. Half the Bible is out looking for him—Amos and Ruth and Ezra and Hosea—but Cissy says Kookie may have hidden out on the buckboard going to Glasstown, he so much wanted to go along. Just got to hope she is right and they are all together somewhere—wheresoever that might be.

Elsewise, Cecelia is in fine fettle, getting too long for her clothes, though they still fit her around, thanks be to Hunger. She sends her love. Last week she learned how to pluck a chicken. I never remember my schooling being so useful.

At school they have Mr. Crew most days giving out Shakespeare and such. He followed up the "Declaration" with "The Ancient Mariner," and I was very glad to be there. I wish you had been.

Hulbert Sissney let his pen rest so long on the last letter that a blot spread out from it, which swallowed up the Ancient Mariner like a black whirlpool. Reading his letter through, spreading his hand over it, he noticed the state of his nails, the ink stain on his middle finger. Even without the swagged wire of the telegraph company, he could hear his wife's words loud and clear, as she listened to some neighbor read out his letter to her: "Skip the poetry. Does he write about money? Is he broke yet?"

Hulbert crumpled the letter up and, balancing it on the back of one hand, tried to turn his hand over and catch the paper ball in his palm. After three tries, he batted it out through the open door. Later he would go up to the telegraph office and send a five-word telegram: AIN'T DEAD YET, HULBERT, CECELIA.

Down at the school-church, Everett Crew was teaching Tennyson's "Morte d'Arthur" line by line, sentence by sentence. He gave each child a line to say; then he had them pass the poem around the room, forward, backward, and in random order. Only when he came to Honey did she look back at him with large blue eyes and say nothing at all.

"Come now, child. No one's too young for Alfred, Lord Tennyson!"

Miss Loucien touched his sleeve and spoke in a murmur. "Honey's a darling, Everett, but I think God musta pushed home the stopper before the brains went in. We get by on smiles, Honey and me."

Undeterred, the actor repeated Honey's line, but she bent her head and did not look up again.

"Try Cissy," whispered the teacher. "She has a memory the like of yours when it comes to words."

So Everett Crew called on Cissy to stand up and recite as much as she could remember of "Morte d'Arthur."

> *"And slowly answered Arthur from the barge:*
> *'The old order changeth, yielding place to new,*
> *And God fulfils Himself in many ways. . . .*
> *If thou shouldst never see my face again,*
> *Pray for my soul. More things are wrought by*
> *   prayer*
> *Than this world dreams of. . . .'"*

Little by little, Cissy's head dropped forward until the poetry dribbled like curds down the front of her mother's outsized pinafore, and soaked away to a silence.

"Lift your head, child!" Crew exhorted her, and then Miss Loucien caught his eye and gave the smallest shake of her head. In the light from the window, she could see the gleam of tears clinging to Cissy's lashes, could recognize that

Cissy's normal voice was being strangled by sorrow. Watching her, Tibbie Boden also began to cry.

"You may sit down, Miss Sissney," said Crew in a voice of such unexpected softness that all eyes turned first on him and then on Cissy.

Instead, she looked up again, her thin face stretched out of shape like a piece of Mr. Lagerlöf's pastry. "Where are they?" she asked abjectly. "Where's Kookie? And Frank? And Herman?"

Just for a moment, Kookie thought he was dead. He could still see the sky, the clouds speeding by, the grass to either side of his head, the sawn ends of the railway ties. But he was not breathing, could not breathe. The universe seemed to be as empty of air as his lungs. Then, as he opened his mouth to call wordlessly for help, the wind found its way back into his chest. He could taste blood; he must have bitten through his tongue, or lip, or scattered all the teeth out of his head on impact with the ground. Also, he seemed to have landed on a cannonball.

Kookie pulled a squashed crab apple out of his back pocket and rubbed his hip. "Where are we?" he asked.

"Miles from nowhere," said Tate's voice, "and twice as far from anywhere." He was sitting nearby cradling his arm in his lap.

"Where's Herman?"

"Must be farther down the track. He came off later than us."

"Maybe they shot him," said Kookie, and immediately regretted the words. Words made a thing possible. He sat up too fast, and the sky spun around. Out of this whirlpool blue swam Herman, his white face a mass of red-and-white blotches. "Jumping jakies, what is it? Smallpox?" exclaimed Kookie. "I never knowed you could ketch something so fast!"

Herman, who had landed facedown in a clump of nettles, held one arm in the air so as to press the cool of his shirt-sleeve against his burning cheeks. He seemed to have parted company from his jacket, and it was very cold.

The upper sky seemed to be racing home, anticipating trouble, trying to stay ahead of disaster. The clouds swept overhead at dizzying speed, letting fall little streams of watery sunshine and then swilling away the puddles of brightness. The prairie around them was empty for as far as the eye could see.

"The thing is to stay by the tracks," said Tate, already several questions further on from Kookie's simple "where are we?" "If we try to strike off looking for signs of life, we'll just get lost past redemption."

"No man is ever lost past redemption," said Herman reflexly. "*Seek, and ye shall find. . . . In the day of my trouble I will call upon thee: for thou wilt answer me.*"

"Just how loud can you call?" said Tate irritably. His left hand hung down at an unnatural angle. Propping his forearm on his knees, he handed himself a twig with the right hand, but the fingers showed no interest in taking hold.

Kookie winced on his behalf. "That wrist's broke," he said, and tried to think of the kind of comforting thing his mother said when laborers came to her with lopped-off fingers, nails through their feet, or displaced kneecaps. "Just as well it's your left hand," he said.

"Why? I'm left-handed," said Tate.

Like cattle in a drove, the clouds herded across the sky.

"Do we walk back upline, or on downline to Florence? Which is closer?"

None of them knew.

"We could toss a coin?" suggested Kookie.

"Give me a coin, then," said Herman. Awkwardly, hampered by bruises, and not wanting to hurt the man, he reached into Frank's pocket and fumbled for a dime. It was odd to see the Mormon (who spurned all dealings with money) spin the coin high in the air and slap it down onto the back of his other hand.

"How d'you do that?" said Kookie admiringly.

"I wasn't always on the Lord's side, son. Heads it's upline. Tails it's downline."

"Ain't that like gambling?"

"The Lord has to have the opportunity to guide our steps, doesn't He? Tails it is." Herman spun the coin off the tip of his thumb, in Kookie's direction, and Kookie, not expecting it, muffed the catch so that the dime rolled away down a rabbit hole. Painfully he dragged himself to his feet.

Tate tried to do the same, but needed to rest one hand on the ground. To do that, he had to let go of the one he was nursing. With a gasp of frustration and agony, he let his knees flop wide and his head fall forward. "How far d'you reckon it is to anywhere, Herm?"

This was the vastness Florence had pitted itself against. Kookie had never really felt it before. Here were the huge distances that made a Florence-without-trains a Florence-without-hope. During the buckboard journey, hidden under the tarpaulin, he had dozed away the hours and hours of empty countryside that separated Florence from its nearest neighbor. Now it all lay between him and home. Not just Oklahoma but the whole continent of America was built on a superhuman scale—too large for people, too large anyway without their horses and trains.

"We could sit here and try to flag down the next train through?" suggested Kookie.

"We got no shelter."

"And it's cold," said Herman with feeling.

So they began to walk, downline toward Florence. At first Kookie expected it to come into view the moment they reached the horizon. But they never *did* reach the horizon. The line between sky and land occasionally puckered into a sneer of uneven ground or bared a few rocky teeth in a malicious grin, but when the hillocks were reached, the rocks put behind them, no grain silo came into view, no white water tower or Bison Creek, no black fumes off Jake Monterey's yard. The trackside was littered with timber scraps, giant metal staples, broken insulators, empty cable spools, rags of old burlap sacking—all left over from the recent rigging of the telegraph wires. It reminded him of the Montereys' backyard. At one moment Kookie's heart turned a backflip when he trod on something black that wriggled under his foot . . . but it was not a snake, only a length of discarded telegraph wire.

Kookie licked the blood off his lip. It was his nose that had bled, not his tongue. The geometric pattern of railway ties cut through the landscape like an infinite number of fallen dominoes; the looping telegraph wires scallop edged the sky. What a feat that had been, thought Kookie, to run wires down every yard of track. . . .

"Shame we don't have a ladder," he mused out loud. "Then we could shin up one of these poles and say we was coming."

The others were slow to answer; it made the conversation last longer that way. "Indeed we could," said Tate at last. "If we just had your father with us to do the Morse."

Away over to the left, a buzzard plunged to earth and snatched something small and wriggling out of the grass before flapping away out of sight, beyond the smirking horizon.

"Oh, I know Morse," said Kookie. "Paw came into school and taught us. The whole alphabet. It was dandy."

Herman, who was stepping from tie to tie along the track because of the thinness of his boot soles, stumbled into the gravel. "You mean you could send a message in Morse?"

"Oh no," said Kookie blithely, "'cause I don't do spelling. I just—" He broke off, wondering why they were staring at him, thinking they were disgusted by his inability to read and write after months of schooling. "Besides, I haven't got a Morse key."

Frank Tate looked like a man about to run in four directions at once. "It's just a matter of making and breaking a circuit, I'm sure of it!" he said, his feet dancing. "Damn and blast this wrist!"

153

"Language," said Kookie, embarrassed more for Herman than himself.

"Yes, yes, yes, yes!" said Herman, pulling off his shoes. "Language! Oh, Habakkuk, yes! Language! That's the key! Did it not occur to you, child? Tate and I, we *do* do spelling?"

"Speak for yourself," said Tate, but he was laughing as he said it.

It was hopeless. Herman trying to climb a telegraph pole was like a man at the county fair trying to climb a greasy pole and win a pig. Kookie tried to give him a leg up, but all of a sudden, the slight, wiry Mormon seemed to weigh as much as a white rhino. Then Kookie tried to stand on Herman's shoulders, but still he could not reach the rungs that started halfway up the pole. Tate crouched down, supporting himself only on his right hand, but no sooner did Herman stand on his bent back than Frank fell on his face and gouged his forehead open on the gravel.

At long last, Kookie, remembering the snowdrift, thought of piling up a mound of the gravel from under the train tracks. Then Herman stood on the gravel mound, Kookie stood on his shoulders, and his reaching fingers closed around the bottom rung.

"I can't pull myself up!" wailed Kookie, arms at full stretch.

Herman pulled off the shoes that were paddling on his collarbones. "Step onto my head!"

Then he was up, his feet walking up the splintery pole,

sweaty palms slippery on the metal rungs. (How could his hands sweat, when the rest of him was so cold?) "What next?" Kookie called down.

"Don't get yourself electrocuted," suggested Tate.

"Oh, I don't believe the charge is very great," said Herman. "These are not electric cables."

"What's next?" said Kookie again. "If I'm gonna mess up, I'd like to get it over with."

After two or three tries, they managed to fling up to him one end of the piece of off-cut cable he had found. Then he had to clamp the wire's end around the strung telegraph wire; it was too tough for his fingers, so he used his chattering teeth—feeling like a parrot with no beak trying to shell peanuts. A loose tooth creaked on its roots. The foot rung he was balancing on creaked in its timber socket. His mouth filled up with the taste of blood. Then it was back down the pole—dangling by one hand for a second, before dropping down and wrenching his ankle on the rail—hoping against hope that the wire he had attached would not simply detach and come snaking down on his head.

"Now we have to bury this end in the ground," said Herman.

"How do you know all this?" said Frank. "Was you a lineman in your ungodly days?"

"My grandpa was in the Civil War. They did wonders in the Civil War . . . leaving aside the fighting, I mean. Now, we need to bury this end good and deep in the ground—well down—deep as we can get—with a metal rod. It's styled a 'ground.'"

"A *metal rod*? You don't ask a lot, do you?" said Frank resentfully.

But then a railroad is made up of metal rods, once you start seeing things from the point of view of a desperate man. Between them, Herman and Kookie uprooted a rail spike and, with a couple of pieces of rusty scrap iron, excavated a rabbit hole to a depth of two feet. The spike stood there, like a wayside shrine to technology, listing farther and farther over to one side.

"Now we break the wire and touch the two ends together—make and break." A glimmer of sinful pride shone for a moment in Herman's eyes as he surveyed his "ground."

It took half an hour to fatigue the wire into breaking. And there was still a snag. "I just remembered," said Herman. "The ground's gotta be wet." The three looked at one another. Such a small obstacle, and yet there it stood, and nobody could quite put it into words.

"It wouldn't worry Fuller Monterey none," said Kookie. "He does it right in the school yard, up against the fence."

"When I was a kid," said Frank, blushing deeply, "we used to compete, me and my brothers, to see who could, you know, the furthest . . ."

"Two could step away while the third . . ." suggested Herman. But in the end they agreed that the Lord must be growing impatient with their shyness. And they shut their eyes, unbuttoned their trousers, and watered the ground at their feet as reverently as if they were pouring libations on the bizarre shrine. Then Kookie squatted down beside the two pieces of broken wire, an end in each hand.

"Send the town name first—Florence—and then your father's surname . . ."

"Pickard, you mean?"

"Warboys, I mean."

The two men stared down at the boy, willing him to succeed, gibbering with cold. "Well? What you waiting for?" said Tate.

What Kookie was awaiting was for the power of reading to fall on him out of the sky—a miraculous shower of literacy.

"Git on!" said Tate. "Why don't you do something? 'Florence.' F-L-O . . ."

And there it was—the secret code.

". . . R-E-N-C-E . . ."

Kookie knew the Morse for each letter; it was easy to send it singing away down the wire. "Keep it coming!" he urged.

"Warboys," said Herman.

"I mean keep the *letters* coming," said Kookie. "Words is no good to me!" When he got home, he vowed, he would learn to read. Then he would never again have to rely on two such ignoramuses.

Miss Loucien was telling a Choctaw legend about Frog and Coyote when the door crashed back and took a chunk out of the newly painted wall. The church hymn rack jumped off its peg and fell to the floor.

"*They're safe!*" It was Hulbert Sissney. "*Esther! Hosea!*

Nahum! Your brother's safe! Came in over the wire just now, and your father was sat right alongside. They're on the track! 'Bout halfway between here and Glasstown. Musta been put off the train! Pickard and Boden are riding up there now with some spare horses!"

The class erupted into uproar, with children asking to go and tell their folks, Cissy hugging her father, Tibbie Boden bursting into tears again.

"School's out," said Miss Loucien, and everyone made a rush for the Sunday-only double doors as the quickest way out. Honey, as usual, was the last to go.

"Shame," said Everett Crew, rising leisurely from his white-satined pew. "I was enjoying the story. Might I return tomorrow, ma'am, and hear how it turned out for the frog?"

"Our days would not be the same without your visits, Mr. Crew," said the teacher. "You are very generous with your time."

Crew put on his flat-crowned hat, then took it off again. "Might I make so bold as to suggest a celebratory drink, ma'am?"

"We have no saloon, Mr. Crew . . . and in any case, folks might look crooked at a schoolteacher who . . ."

Crew bowed and put on his hat. "I am gone."

The pin holding Miss Loucien's hair in place flew out, and her French twist subsided behind her as though in disappointment.

"One more thing, however . . ."

"Yes, Mr. Crew?"

"Might I suggest that you ask Lloyd Lentz to come and

deliver a talk about the science of sight and sound? It would give him a chance to check the children over. It is just that the little girl, Honey . . . I don't believe you will find she is stupid. Only that she is deaf."

When a coal train came through, the suction of its backwash was so strong that Kookie lost his crouching balance and tumbled over backward. The down wire was ripped out of his hands, and lashed to and fro for a few seconds before becoming detached from the overhead wire and dropping uselessly to the ground. A flock of passenger pigeons, disturbed from further along the wire, flew up in alarm and dropped white guano in his hair. At the same time, the thunderous vibrations of the train set the ground trembling, and the spike sticking up out of the ground keeled over and fell flat. "So help me," he gasped, "if I never see another train, it'll be three days too soon for my liking!"

"Is it enough, do you think? Did we get through?" asked Tate.

Kookie could reply only by way of a shrug. They sat down in a huddle. Though it hurt to press their bruised bones together, they needed the warmth. The day was dying around them. Herman, without his jacket and bowler, looked less like a pint of milk than an icicle.

"*I will lift up mine eyes unto the hills, from whence cometh my help,*" said Herman.

"Be a while, then," said Frank aloud to the flat, flat, endlessly flat prairie.

They sat so still and so silent that the prairie dogs came

out of their holes and sat gazing west, like worshipers doing homage to the setting sun. Bats, as indistinct as dust, teased at the corners of their vision.

"Are there any hostiles hereabouts?" Tate wondered aloud, as the last light faded. He was thinking of Indians. Herman was thinking of wildcats. Kookie was thinking of ghosts.

Only the ghosts materialized—palely huge and shapeless, mumbling their way over the grass as if smelling out the three stranded passengers. They came right up close, breathing hot, odd-smelling air into Kookie's face.

"Shoo. Shoo!" he told the steers. "Come back when you're milch cows."

"A milch cow is a walking restaurant," said Herman indistinctly, his jaws clamped tight by the cold. He was struggling to make a splint for Tate's wrist out of two boot soles and his own shirttails. Kookie, remembering his mother squelching plaster of paris between her long, callused fingers, teaching him and his classmates how to "daub it on good and thick," had to hide his face away in the dark. He did not want any mangy steer seeing a Warboys cry.

"I think we should pray," said Herman.

"You think we ain't been?" said Tate aggressively, and Kookie nodded his head in agreement.

It was three in the morning. "We oughtta light a fire," said Kookie.

"Why, you got matches on you? Is that something else

you been keeping to yourself?" Frank Tate's sweet temper was fraying on the jagged ends of his broken wristbone.

"I had a tinderbox once," said Herman, clearly tempted to regret its passing. "I traded it. I forget what for."

Kookie began to see that there was more to Herman than some religious separatist writing on walls and drinking milk. Here was a man with a past that included tinderboxes and coin flipping.

"When Lloyd Lentz came into school, he taught us how to light a fire," Kookie reminisced aloud.

They stared at him, Herman and Tate, hope surging despite themselves.

"You just pinch the rays of the sun through a spyglass and—poof!" Kookie broke off, deterred by the look on their faces. "What? Maybe it works with moonlight?" he said defensively. "You never know."

"And do you happen to *have* a spyglass about you, Habakkuk?"

"No, but—"

They did not speak much after that.

By four, they felt as if they had congealed together, three chunks of ice fused at the shoulder blades, as they sat back to back to back. A tumbleweed rolled up against them and scared their sluggish heartbeats into a three-part harmony of panic. Each awoke thinking some animal had pounced on them, and even when they were wide-awake, the tumbleweed still had an animal quality about it and would not be pushed away, snagging itself in their hair and clothes, wanting to be a fourth member of the group.

"So much for Samuel F. B. Morse," said Kookie disgustedly. "You can't never trust a man with letters 'stead of a middle name."

"It just couldn't be that you learned it wrong?" said Tate sharply, but Herman hushed him.

"Boy did his best, didn't he? Better'n we could do." His teeth clicked like a Morse key tapping out a message, and Kookie found himself trying to decipher it.

Could it be, though? Could it? That he had not learned it right? What would Miss Loucien think of him then? Or Mr. Lentz. What would his father—

The horses' breath was so hot against their cold faces, it was like standing near Lagerlöf's oven door when it opened. Kookie and Frank and Herman looked up into eyes as huge as puddles and full of moonlight. Hooves clattered over the railroad ties. As Pickard Warboys reined in, the riderless horses behind him fanned out, and their body warmth enveloped the boys on the ground.

"Coming home, fellers?" said Pickard Warboys.

Even Frank Tate, nursing his broken wrist, was quicker to his feet than Kookie. Kookie had not been expecting his father in person. Retribution. Where were his wits now— frozen to the inside of his skull? He could not think of a single sassy remark, one clever argument, no solitary excuse for skipping school and stowing away on the hearse bound for Glasstown.

"Sorry, Paw," he said, puzzled to find his lips as rigid as stirrup irons.

"Did you make that signal, boy?" asked Pickard, dismounting and lifting his son onto his own horse. Kookie tried to nod, but his neck was as stiff as a baseball bat. "Guess that redeems you, then," said Pickard.

As the warmth of the horse rose up through the seat of Kookie's pants, he found that thought returned with it. Turning to Herman (though his spine felt as rigid as a telegraph pole), he said, "Gosh sakes, Herm, you were right! No man *is* lost past redeeming!"

Inside three layers of horse blanket, Herman did not hear. With his face hidden, he was at last allowing himself to weep—for the loss of his pocket Bible and the boots he had sacrificed to the splinting of Tate's wrist.

It would take a whole pile of chicken eggs to buy him a new pair. Now he might never get to Salt Lake City.

11

FROM BAD TO WORSE

"Why did nobody tell me?" protested Miss Loucien. "Why did no one say?"

Honey's parents, a shy, reclusive couple, murmured that they had thought it plain from the way they always shouted at Honey. "Jumping jackrabbits, darlin's, my folks shouted at me louder'n that every waking moment of the day!" said Loucien. But in private she confided to Crew that she must have been "deaf, dumb, and blind, all three, not to have seen it before."

The truth was, the community of Florence was still too young for everyone to know their neighbors' private sorrows.

Apart from Honey getting a hearing trumpet, one other marvelous thing came of Lloyd Lentz's visit to the Academy. Tibbie Boden got spectacles. The eye-and-ear man tested every child, with jingling keys, soft whispers, and a big card strewn with letters. No one could read the letters, but Tibbie Boden could not even see the card.

Apparently, that wide-eyed, sky-blue vacancy, which made her look like a stranded mermaid staring out to sea, was nothing more than acute shortsightedness. Soon she was wearing lenses as thick as blobs of solder, and she gazed around her with the intensity of an astronomical telescope scanning the heavens. She was delighted with the novelty of seeing. Cissy was delighted, too . . . but more because Tibbie's angelic face looked now like an art gallery portrait scribbled on by vandals.

The next visitor to the school was Vokayatunga, who gave a talk to the children on the many uses of a bison. It was astonishing, the number of useful parts a bison owned. Apparently even its gallbladder could be ground up to make yellow paint. Peat Monterey came home full of this news. His father, too, was impressed.

Sadly, like Vokayatunga's glory days, the bison were long gone from the prairies of Oklahoma. But the boy's father decided to find out whether the same effect could be got from a horse's gallbladder. (Paint was in great demand around Florence that spring.) When the gall came out gall colored rather than yellow, Jake thought he'd heat it up, and then, when it curdled, he added linseed oil to make it coagulate again. The linseed oil spilled onto the stove, and the stove went up like a volcano, igniting the horsetails hanging from the roof. The burning tails wafted about for all the world as if they were still attached to animals, and the fire spread to the tarpaper on the roof.

That was pretty much the finish of Jake Monterey's business. He had never relished the work, but as his premises burned down, amid the stench of scorching hide and marrowbone, a new kind of despair settled on the man, blacker than the cinders raining down on his sons' home-cut hair. He took to muttering aloud to himself as he sat on the town horse trough. He took to painting Boden's ranch brand on fences and then throwing stones at it. He also dictated letters to Congress in Washington and the territorial capital, Guthrie, asking them to restore his land to him. Pickard Warboys wrote it all down for him, then, when Jake had gone, used the letters to light his stove: He was too embarrassed to ask Jake for the price of postage, knowing he did not have it.

People were very kind to the Montereys after the fire. They helped Jake build a sod house big enough for him and the boys, on an abandoned claim. Mrs. Warboys sent around soup better than anything Peat and Fuller had tasted in their lives.

But kindness served only to wound Monterey's pride and fuel his rage. He took it out on his boys, lashing out at them, making them do chores for anyone who offered "charity," and making them pray nightly for Gaff Boden to burn in hell.

So perhaps it was the strain of living with such a father that made Fuller Monterey do what he did next.

As Fuller saw it, Kookie came home Hero of the Hour for doing nothing but "sit on his backside by the railroad track." So Fuller began to cook up his own brew of gall. Now and then, the excitement of what he planned burst out of him in fistfuls of unexpected violence.

"Betcha I can stop the train right here in Florence," said Fuller, pinning Kookie's head against the school wall.

"Good for you, Fuller," said Kookie. His mother had

told him to "make allowances" and be charitable toward the poor unfortunate Montereys. Besides, Fuller had his elbow poised over Kookie's windpipe. "Need my help?"

"Don't need spit from you, Warboys," said Fuller. "You had your chance. You stewed it."

Peatie, for his part, looked uneasy, and dodged about behind his elder brother, fists tucked under his chin, his eyelids twitching shut involuntarily. "Stewed it, stewed it!" he echoed feebly, and ran in and kicked Kookie in the shins.

But the boast about stopping the train went clean out of Kookie's head when, having wormed his way free and into school, he found a wickerwork basket sitting on his satin seat.

"I begged and borrowed these from every unfortunate woman in town," said Miss Loucien. "One for each of you. So take care of them as if they was cribs with your baby brothers in them. They have to be returned after."

"After what, Miss Loucien?" asked Barney Mackinley.

"After the box supper, naturally," said the teacher. "Now, your task today is to fill that there container with something delectable: flowers, berries, mushrooms . . . I know, I know! It ain't the usual season for a picnic, and delicacies are scarce, but you'll just have to use some brain power. If you go out on the prairie, go in pairs. There's a pressing need to raise some money quick, and the Florence Town Committee have decided you can have the honor of raising it. Shame it ain't the cherry season—"

"It ain't the *anything* season, ma'am!" protested Sarah Waters.

The boys in the class were even more bewildered. "Us too?" they said. Box suppers usually involved girls and women packing goodies into baskets, and then the menfolk placing bids for each basket in turn.

"You bid money for a basket," Kookie explained to Cissy (who already knew), "and then you get to eat it 'longside the girl who packed it up."

"That's s'posed to be the best part," said Ollie West dubiously. "Me, I'd sooner go hungry than sit on a blanket with a gal."

"Looky, fellers," said Miss Loucien sharply. "I realize there's a long-held tradition that males were born to do nothing but eat the food put in front of them by females. But I'm breaking the pattern, see? I need supper boxes—lots of supper boxes. This here box supper is to raise money for a preacher."

Here was news indeed. Even though Florence would soon complete her long-awaited church, she still had no preacher to put in it. Sunday services were a self-help kind of affair. And, as the *Glasstown Daybreak* had joyfully and frequently pointed out, a town without a preacher is hardly worth calling a Christian town at all.

"How much does a preacher cost?" Marlene Bell wanted to know.

"Seems there's some young man straight out of theelogical college in Houston wants to come to Florence and preach to our 'mortal souls," Miss Loucien went on. "Now if we can raise him the fare, he's willing to risk starving when he gits here. Right? So we're having a box supper, like I say, to buy him a ticket on the stagecoach. And *every mother's son* is going to fill a box—right?—'cause that way we raise more. Proper working folk ain't got time to spare, so I figure Class Three can stir themselves off their fine satin seats and fill a few supper boxes. Now you got some objection to that, Fuller Monterey, or what? And where's Tibbie this morning?"

The class looked around at Tibbie Boden's empty desk.

"She got sick, ma'am," said Peatie instantly.

Miss Loucien looked him over suspiciously, but his elder brother chimed in: "It's true. We met up with one of the cowhands off the Boden place. He said to give you the message. Tibbie is ill today."

Miss Loucien was placated. "Poor sweetie. Remind me to mention her in prayers at going-home time."

"You gonna make up a basket, ma'am?" asked Fred Stamp, who had kept a torch burning in his heart for the schoolteacher right through the windiest days of winter.

"Oh, we'll see. . . ."

"Plenty people'd bid for it!" said Nahum Warboys, mentally calculating how he might raise some cash.

The teacher simply smiled and enquired what it took to get sixteen idle children off their backsides and out scavenging before midday.

Cissy could have had any number of partners. The question came at her from six directions:

"Your paw give us some vittles for the boxes, Cissy?"

"Can we come around your place and borrow some, Cissy?"

"Your paw won't miss a jar or two, would he, Ciss?"

In the days when her sharp-tongued mother had been around, Cissy knew, they would not even have dared ask. Something about that disgusted her and brought a lump to her throat, which she thought was rage. "Why don't you go up to Lagerlöf's and put the bite on him?" she told them, and her voice came out as hard and edgy as her mother's. Perhaps she was growing up, thought Cissy. Perhaps soon she would turn into her mother.

Still, Kookie was different. "Why don't we go ask your paw for some beans," he suggested, bold as brass. "Then we can go race turtles for the rest of the day." And Cissy agreed at once.

On their way down to the store, no one stopped them to demand why they were not in school. Florence had grown accustomed to its children roaming off in search of tin cans for target practice or animals' bones for anatomy, seeds for planting, or a scene to sketch. The stage was in, and they saw Sheriff Klemme taking mail from the driver.

"Never uses the telegraph office," said Kookie resentfully. "Says he has to keep his business private. What does he think? My paw can't keep a secret?" As a mischievous afterthought, he added, "I bet *he* makes a bid for Miss Loucien's basket this evening."

"Why? What do you think she'll put in it?" asked Cissy.

"Wouldn't matter if it was empty," said Kookie, man-of-the-world. "The sheriff would bid for it, just to sit by her on a blanket."

Cissy was deliciously shocked. "You reckon he loves Miss Loucien?"

"Sure as a fish likes bathing."

They passed Herman's chicken coop, its thirty birds pecking up worms from the bare, unpromising ground. "Whose basket are you gonna bid for, Kookie?" Cissy asked. Her diaphragm gave a small awkward twist that flicked her heart into the back of her throat.

"Tibbie Boden's, course," came the reply.

"But she's off sick!"

"Won't miss out on a box supper, will she? Not even if her neck's broke."

They were walking up the side of the general store. Suddenly, there was a noise like hail hitting the window beside Cissy's head; it was the window of the storeroom. From inside, her father's voice roared out like a bear in pain: *"Sodom and Gomorrah!"* Horrified, she stood on tiptoe to look in.

"The thieves! The sinners! The b—" shouted Hulbert at the empty room.

In the back room, a sack of coffee beans had been over-turned and spilled out across the floor like gravel. It was not only *like* gravel, most of it *was* gravel. Cissy and Kookie ran inside. They were in time to see Hulbert rip open another of the gunnysacks and shove in a hand. It might as well have been a hornet's nest for the noise he made. Pulling out a fistful of sugar, he pitched it at the wall. *"Why?"* yelled Hulbert.

Cissy dropped her basket on the ground and pushed Kookie's out of sight as well. This was not a man to ask for a handout, for a favor. Kookie backed out the door.

"What happened, Poppy?" asked Cissy, trying to take hold of her father's jacket. He pushed her out of the way.

"I been sabotaged, that's what. I been swindled! Robbed! Cheated!"

The supplies he had driven all the way to Glasstown for were ten percent coffee, ninety percent pebbles. The flour had been adulterated with sawdust, the sugar mixed with sand. Even the soap had been wetted so that the contents had begun to dissolve and then congeal again into a solid green mass.

Hulbert flung himself between sack and carton, but his weak legs betrayed him at last, and he fell sprawling against the table. His eye sockets were full of tears, eye sockets too deep dug by ill health and worry for the tears to climb out. "She was right. Your mother was right. It's hopeless," he said, sitting where he fell, slumped against a sack of gravelly coffee. "Worthless legs, worthless man." And his fist thumped over and over against the polluted flour sacks, so they coughed out little clouds of dirty yellow.

Cissy could find nothing to say; the mention of her mother seemed to stave in her rib cage. And this was Poppy, her Poppy, who had always found the sunny side to everything, who never gave way to spleen or complaints. Where was comfort to come from if this, her well of it, had run dry?

After a terrible wilderness of a minute, Hulbert Sissney looked up and became aware, for the first time, of his daughter

172

being out of school. "What is it, kitten?" he said, in a voice as flat as a skillet. "What you home for?"

"I—" She could not tell him. She could not say that she had come looking for a free handout of cookies or coffee or canned peaches. So she too backed out the door, leaving her father to take inventory of how much the cheats in Glasstown had stolen from him.

Kookie was of the opinion they should go at once and tell Sheriff Klemme that a crime had been committed. In fact he was so adamant that he walked straight into the lawyer's office without knocking.

Klemme snatched up the unopened letters from his desk and rammed them into a drawer. "You get out of here, boy, and don't come back till you've learned some manners!"

"Please, sir! We came to report a crime!" Cissy piped up. "Poppy's been robbed!"

The lawyer's face softened, and he beckoned Cissy forward. All the time she was explaining about the gravel, the sawdust, the sand, Klemme plucked and tugged at his side-whiskers, so that his cheeks made soft, wet noises against his teeth. As she finished, his face took on a blood-hound sadness, and he shook his head. "I'm afraid, my dear, it is a case of *caveat emptor*—let the buyer beware. A court of law would argue that the wrong lies all with your father, for not checking over the goods then and there, in Glasstown." He spread his small, square palms. "My hands are tied." Then he gave them a toffee each and told them to shut the door on their way out.

The toffees rolled about, one in the bottom of each

basket. It was a start, but not much of one. Cissy and Kookie walked as far as the creek, Kookie saying he would catch enough crawfish to fill both baskets. On the way they met up with Fuller, who had already filled his box—with cow chips. Marlene was collecting sheep wool off the thorn-bushes and fence wires. Honey, her prized ear trumpet slung across her back like a hunting horn, was slashing about in the bushes. Fred Stamp held out both hands to them as they passed; at first sight they appeared to be spotted with blood, but on closer inspection Cissy could see they were crawling with ladybugs. Ollie West had filled his box with lucky horseshoes from the scrap pile at the forge.

They found Kookie's brother Nahum already at the creek, picking the spines out of sticklebacks like a man seeding grapes. He told Kookie to go and find an idea of his own, and not to go disturbing the fish.

Cissy picked some of the spring flowers—the first to pierce the winter ground—but they wilted within the hour. Desiccated, shriveled, and colorless, they lay like dead wireworms in the bottom of her basket. It was almost as if someone had cheated her, too, substituting dead for live. Those dead flowers, and the thought of her father sitting alone in that storeroom, surrounded by gravel and trash, weighed almost too heavily for her to carry around.

Then she thought of the hives.

Miss Loucien had taught them about bees—how to tell them apart from wasps and hornets; how wasps ate up their papery mansions and died. Cissy remembered thinking the wasps were like the people of Florence gradually using up their savings, their health, their hopes. . . . "We can find some honeycombs!" she told Kookie. "I know where there's hives!"

So now did Kookie. The summer before, the Ponca Pirates had shown them crevices where anybody with a sharp stick could dig out a whole fistful of sweetness.

"Do we have time? Before the supper begins?" Cissy wondered.

"Better to be late than turn up with nothing at all," was Kookie's way of thinking. So they scrambled all the way up Golden Ridge—the highest piece of ground for miles around.

Of course the whole place looked different now that it was March and not high summer. The winter rain had filled up the water table, and the springs were beginning to fill, all around the base of the ridge; they had to wade over marshy ground. Then there were patches of spring flowers spread on the slopes, like Indian blankets; they masked the rocks that last summer had worn nothing but tonsures of scorched brown grass. The two children roamed about for a while. Lately, Cissy had been obliged to alter and start wearing a dress her mother had left behind. Its still overlong hems swept all manner of insects off the flowers.

"But whose blanket you gonna sit on if Tibbie *doesn't* come to the supper?" Cissy asked, giving a nonchalant swipe at a juniper bush.

"Yours, I guess."

Each time Cissy found a likely crevice, she poked it with a stick, but all that had so far emerged were some wood-borer beetles and the skull of a rabbit. "But you're still planning to marry Tibbie?" she said.

"Yep."

"What, even with the eyeglasses?" She could not help saying it, though it was unkind and dishonorable. Kookie gave her the withering look he had learned from his ever-charitable mother.

"I never unsay a thing once I've said it," he said grandly. "Behind the glasses, she is still the same lovely person."

"Oh!" It sounded so marvelously gallant, it gave Cissy real physical pain to hear it. She wondered whether, underneath her mother's dress, she was still the Cissy Sissney who had come to Florence a million years before, or whether she was little by little changing into her mother: sour, grudging. Jealous.

Kookie changed his mind about the honeycombs and began collecting crickets and grasshoppers instead—"They can race 'em, if they don't want to eat 'em"—and Cissy was left alone, trying to spot bees making a beeline for their hive. She would follow one for ten minutes, only to discover it was a hoverfly, or see it go where she could not follow, or lose sight of it against the grass.

"Fuller reckons he can stop the train." Kookie's voice came floating over the crest.

"How?" she called back.

"Use that chip on his shoulder to block the line is my guess!"

Bees bobbed about Cissy's ankles like ears of wheat, knocking the pollen in puffs off the small upturned faces of the primroses. Every now and then, she could hear Kookie's feet thump down as he pounced on naive young grasshoppers. Cissy thought of honey rolling golden off a spoon and licked her lips. Her eyes followed one bee back toward the big old oak that stood alone on the top of the hill. Straight as a train on rails the bee flew, until the tree's black shadow swallowed it up.

"You don't think he'd do anything crazy, do you? Fuller, I mean?"

"Like what?" *Thump.* "Gotcha!"

Cissy snapped off a dead twig and began to pick at a cleft in the trunk. "I don't know. Something."

"All by himself?"

"Him and Peatie."

"Nah!" *Thump.* "Dang it!"

Something brushed Cissy's cheek—a piece of bark, she thought. And then a dozen more pellets buffeted her face, and a noise started up around her head as loud as a ripsaw.

Hornets.

"Hornets, Kookie, help!"

They both ran like jackrabbits. They skidded down the steep parts on their heels, the shallow slopes on their toes. Crossing the marshy stretch lifting their knees up and outward, they felt the mud spatter their legs. They swung their baskets around their heads, sometimes hitting each other, sometimes hitting themselves. But the hornets might as well have been tied to their hairs' ends; there was no outrunning them. Cissy felt a sharpness under the jaw that hurt all the way from the tip of her chin to her eardrum. Another in her elbow was so intense, it could have been an arrowhead. They ran with their mouths shut, for fear of swallowing an insect—remembering the story Miss Loucien had told them of a friend whose tongue had choked him after he was stung in the mouth. They ran and they ran, till the March chill felt like mid-August and the air in their lungs felt like hot embers in the furnace of the RRR.

By the time the hornets finally gave up the chase, Cissy and Kookie had reached the railroad track about a mile downline of Florence. They began to walk back toward town, striding from tie to tie, Cissy all the time checking for trains behind her. Kookie was suave in his knowledge that nothing was due for another hour.

"How do you know that for sure?" asked Cissy, ready to be astonished, hoping Kookie's genius might take her mind off the pain in her face.

"At four thirty it's the upline cattle train. Five P.M. there's a downline timber-and-coal. Reg'lar as clockwork. My, but your face has gone fat!"

"But how can you tell what time it is *now*?" Cissy persisted, wrapping a hand around her jaw.

"Ah!" said Kookie coolly. "I just got a feel for things like time. To me, it just don't *feel* any later than three— What's that flag?" He peered ahead at something white, but it was barely visible against the white of the distant water tower.

"It isn't a flag. It's a petticoat hung up," said Sissy. "There's a pony, too—" She broke off with a gasp, and then they both began to run.

Alongside the marker flag, a figure lay across the track—

a small figure in a pale-blue dress. The skirt of the apron had been pulled up and back over the head, so that at first sight the body appeared decapitated. But as they ran, they saw the knees begin to rock to and fro, the back arch up away from the tie on which it lay. Tibbie Boden's hands were tied to one rail, her feet to the other, and with the apron swaddling her head, they were on top of her before they heard the smallest noise.

In fact, after three hours of screaming, her voice was almost gone. After three hours of struggling to break loose, her wrists were a mess of torn skin; her energy too, was all used up.

Only the faint vibration of an approaching train had raised her to one last demented fit of panic.

"I thought you said . . ." Cissy began.

"So? I was wrong, wasn't I?" Kookie went at the knots with his fingers, his teeth, the handle broken off his supper basket. But Tibbie had lain there far too long; her struggles had pulled the knots into such impacted lumps that no human hand would ever unfasten them.

And the four-thirty upline train was coming.

12

ALL JUMP UP

It was the oddest box supper anyone could remember: so unseasonable and so out of keeping with the town's mood.

Lloyd Lentz was playing sad Hebrew laments on his fiddle, and Hulbert Sissney was brewing coffee with a quiet ferocity, as if in defiance of the Glasstown thieves who had beggared him. Herman, in a pair of borrowed shoes too big for him, and still missing his pea jacket and bowler, felt obliged to point out to each new arrival that the *best* ministers were all in Salt Lake City and that this boy from Houston was unlikely to know the Lord's true nature. Monday Morning was peddling a tray of newly printed books around, asking apologetically for money he knew did not exist. He made an awkward salesman, though the books were handsome enough little volumes. Gaff Boden was asking after his daughter, who had left for school, on her pony, at the normal time, but who her classmates seemed to think was sick.

All the children of Class Three, except for Cissy, Habakkuk, and Peat, had returned with their boxes filled, and Sheriff Klemme (who had appointed himself auctioneer) opened each box in turn with a look of growing dismay.

"Don't open that, suh!" shrilled Fred Stamp. "'S full of ladybugs, suh!" And as Sheriff Klemme pushed the box sharply away, the creatures crackled about inside like seeds. He picked up another and rattled it.

"Them's white-footed mouses," said Barney Mackinley.

Klemme did not shake any more boxes after that.

Blankets had been laid out on ground overlooking the creek, though it was a gray evening and someone said they had seen a coachwhip snake "just hereabouts yesternight." The dew fell early and made everything damp. A prairie falcon cruised overhead like a vulture over a carcass, and the passenger pigeons were massing on the water tower, sensing a chance to be fed. Everyone said that Virgil Hobbs had lit the bonfire too early—it would eat up too much fuel—and besides, he had lit it with kerosene, so the smoke was black and smelly. It was not often that Sven Lagerlöf's doughnuts tasted of kerosene.

"Gotta do something! Gotta do something!" screamed Cissy under her breath, tearing at the ropes that fastened one wrist. (They both knew that shrieking and roaring out loud would only serve to make Tibbie's hell more noisy.) "Call someone to come, shouldn't we? Get someone to come and help!"

"There isn't time!" Kookie's head was down by the rail, his teeth chewing at the rope around the other wrist. His voice came out very high: a child's voice.

Buckled and broken, Tibbie's new spectacles lay on the

track, their lenses magnifying the gravel and grass. One of the lenses fell out into Kookie's palm as he snatched them up. He wrenched off one earpiece, to use it to pick at the knots. It might as well have been a hairpin for all the good it was.

"A burning glass!" said Cissy triumphantly. "You know? Like Mr. Lentz showed us?" They cracked heads as Kookie moved around to attempt it. Between them, Tibbie lay like a stunned deer, her great blue eyes traveling from one face to the other. All she said was, "Please. Please. Please. Please. Please. Please."

"Train's coming, Kookie!" Cissy could not help but say it, as the dim spot of brightness beneath the lens jumped and jogged over the tangle of hemp. Kookie moved the lens up and down, tilted it left and right, but the sunlight was simply too weak, or the lens was the wrong shape, because no black char mark bit into the fibers; no puff of smoke jumped up.

Through their knees, they could feel the ground tremble with the approach of the cattle train.

"Please. Please, Cissy. Please. Please. Please, Kookie. Please. Please."

Twenty feet away, the figure of Peat Monterey emerged from the bushes. He stood looking, just looking, his hands ajump beside his hips, like a gunslinger with no pistols, his bottom jaw slack from the rest of his head.

"You do this, you devil?" yelled Kookie.

Peat's small head rolled on its skinny neck. He shook it so hard, they could hear his big ears crackle. "Train'll stop. Fuller said. Train'll stop when it sees her. Fuller said."

182

"Why did you let him do it, you little pack rat? Why didn't you tell? Why didn't you get help? Go now! Quick! Go!"

But Peat continued to stand and gape at them, powerless to leave the spot where he had squatted for three hours, waiting for his brother to return and turn a nightmare back into a game. "Grabbed her on her way to school," he whined. "We shut her in the silo first! Then when we was let loose from school, Fuller says he's got a plan to stop the train thisaway! Thought he was kidding. Thought he was just fixing to scary-ate her, then let her go. But Fuller, he goes off." Peat flapped his hand helplessly in the direction his brother had gone, hours before. "Those ropes. You'll never budge them. I tried."

The distraction prevented Kookie keeping his hand still, focusing the lens. Then the sun went behind a cloud, and he pitched the useless lens away along the track, where it broke against the rail. He knew that wolves sometimes chewed through their own paws to get free of a trap; he wondered if he had it in him—had the time or the heart to do the same for Tibbie. Already his mouth seemed to be revolting against the idea, for his lips were lifting off his teeth of their own accord, trembling and flaring, and he could not understand why.

"Don't cry, Kookie!" hissed Cissy. "There isn't time. Get her pony and put it on the line. We got to make the train see us!"

But Kookie had lurched to his feet to run at Peat Monterey: the sight of him standing there—just standing— useless, senseless, mindless—put Kookie in mind of coyotes and vultures. He picked up a handful of gravel and pitched it at the boy. *"Fetch help, you rat-head skunk! You bunch of rubbish! Get someone!"*

At last, Peat took off, running awkwardly, in boots without laces, his arms flailing and his head ducking and his breath coming in loud, overlapping sobs.

Cissy untied the pony's reins from the track and pulled on them till the bit came clean out of the creature's mouth and it rolled its eyes in fear. With one hand she dragged it down-line—down the center of the track—while with the other she waved the petticoat Fuller had set up on a stick. It had been meant for a marker, to draw the train driver's attention to the girl on the track. But Cissy was perfectly certain it was not warning enough to a locomotive moving at forty miles an hour and fitted with a cowcatcher to clear its path of debris. If the engineer even saw Tibbie, it would be a second or two before he plowed into her, and not all the braking in the world would bring him to a stop in time. So waving the petticoat over her head and tugging the pony along behind her, Cissy Sissney walked toward the oncoming train.

Kookie turned from chasing Peat, saw her go, and was terrified: terrified of what she was doing, terrified of being left alone with Tibbie and a head empty of ideas. There was nothing, there was nothing, there was nothing to do but to go back and stand over Tibbie and promise her that the train would stop . . . right up until the very moment it did not. *"Train'll stop, Tibbie! Train'll stop, I swear!"* he called in his high babyish voice.

Then he saw the broken lens on the track: a milk-white raggedness of glass. It was so sharp that it cut him even in picking it up. It was so sharp it cut Tib's hand on his first wild slice at the ropes. He had to force himself to make tiny, rapid sawing movements so all that severed was the hemp. It was like chipping at an iceberg with a toothpick.

"Please, Kookie! Please. Please. Please. Please. Please don't let me die!"

Bob Eagle, engineer of the upline cattle train, peered ahead at the flicker of white cloth. He knew he was approaching Florence. He knew the kind of stunts they pulled in Florence. He knew there were villains living in Florence who would blast a man's brains out just to see a train come to a halt by their godforsaken shantytown. And he knew (as all the Red Rock engineers did) that his job was not worth a plug nickel if they persuaded him to apply the brake.

Cissy waved and bellowed and pointed, and the pony behind her reared up and pawed the air.

Bob Eagle rested his hand on the handle of the brake wheel. Were they using their kids now to do their dirty work? What kind of people sent their kids out onto the railroad track to stand in the path of a train? Everything they said in Glasstown about these people was true. They were unnatural, heartless vandals with not one scrap of moral conscience in their mischievous hearts.

Cissy could not keep hold of the pony. It skipped off the track and wrenched the bridle out of her hand, galloping off in a great curve, back toward the Boden place. Cissy came to a halt and, using both hands now, stood waving the petticoat in wide arcs over her head. The front of the engine's boiler, with its bolts and nameplate, looked like a face under its shag of gray smoke, the cowcatcher like the gappy teeth of a grinning mouth.

Bob Eagle leaned out of his cab. "Git! Git off the track! I'll run you down!" The child, too, was shouting at him, but her words were ground to dust by the pounding of the piston rods. Bob Eagle spun the brake handle once, lazily, like a roulette wheel. Up and down the cattle train, three hundred beef cattle swayed on their hooves at the lessening speed.

Sawing through rope with a shard of optical glass was like hacking through a mountain with a spoon. The razor-sharp jags had already worn smooth against the coarse hemp. Now it took ten little sawing motions to sever a single fiber. Kookie was Alexander the Great trying to slash through the Gordian knot with a butter knife.

A single flick of Bob Eagle's wrist: the brake handle spun a few more revolutions. There was a noise of friction on the line and the cattle began to blare. "I'm warning you! I'll run you down! You been warned!" he yelled at the little girl on the track, obliterating his own words with a blast of the whistle. The girl turned and began to run back up the track, looking over her shoulder, racing the train, pointing ahead. Perhaps, after all, there was some danger up ahead. Then Bob saw the other children. . . .

Tibbie Boden turned her head away from the train. "Please, Kookie. Please. Please. Please. Please. Please. Please."

"Citizens of Florence!" began Emile Klemme. "In my capacity as sheriff and doge of this town, I would just like to welcome you here this evening. . . . You will all have heard by now that we have the chance of a church minister, if we can just raise the money for his fare to come here."

"Couldn't we just swap him for Herman?" jeered Charlie Quex. "He wants for a fare, too!"

"Fare exchange is no robbery," said Monday Morning under his breath.

"What's he want to come here fer?" grumbled Virgil Hobbs. "What's anyone want to come here fer? Oughtta warn the boy off, not pay his fare for him. Be more Christian."

"So let's get right on down to business," said Doge Klemme, though a thunderous face belied the cheery words. "First the auction and then on to the dancing!" Out of the corner of his eye, he was watching Loucien Shades hurry across the picnic site toward the blanket where Everett Crew sat peeling an apple in a single spiral.

Everett Crew stood up in agreeable confusion as the schoolteacher bore down on him. "Miss Loucien—Mrs. Shades, I mean—might I induce you to share my blank—"

"Not now, Everett," said Miss Loucien. "I've just sent Gaff Boden back home, looking for Tibbie. But I was just

187

buying time. I figure something's happened to her. The Monterey boys said she was sick, but I reckon they're lying. They've got a hand in it. We gotta find her, Everett. She hasn't been at school all day. I'm scared outa my buskins. That Fuller can be a demon when he shuts off his brain. Reckon we got half an hour to find her before Gaff gets back and starts raising hell. Should we ask folks to help us look?"

"We can't just set off and scour the landscape," said the actor, cramming on his hat. "You leave Fuller to me. If he knows, I shall pry it out of him. Trust me." And they both slipped away, hidden by the smoke from the belching bonfire, Crew breaking into a run.

"What am I bid for this fine supper box that contains . . . contains . . ." Cautiously, Sheriff Klemme looked inside and seemed relieved. "Walnuts."

Sparks flew off the rail as Bob Eagle applied the brake. But his disgust at this latest ploy was so intense that he could see the track ahead only through red explosions of anger. He would slow his train, but he would not give them the satisfaction of snickering and jeering at him, these little saboteurs. He would scare them so badly, they would never want to see another locomotive so long as they lived. Where had they learned this little piece of melodrama? In the vaudeville halls? It was vile. It was childhood devilment turned to the devil's work.

The great wheels slowed but did not stop. Cissy turned around, smiling, breathless, to thank the engineer, but saw the great engine still rolling, at walking speed. The whistle was earsplitting; it made her duck and cover her head. She tried to take a stand, between train and Tibbie, but the great iron bow of the cowcatcher pushed into the hem of her dress and made her skip backward. She saw, with a violent shudder, that a dead rabbit was wrapped around one section of the great iron grid. Did the man not realize how far the front of his train reached out ahead of the engine block? "Stop! Stop! We can't get her free!" she yelled.

Faster and faster, Kookie sawed at the ropes, though his fingers were bleeding and he was filled with such a weariness. "This is a nightmare," he told himself. "I'm having a nightmare."

"Please. Please. Please. Plea—"

Clumsily, he covered Tibbie's mouth with one hand. Every one of these "pleases" had fallen into his head like wheat ears into a hopper, and his skull was bursting with them.

Cissy leaned her hands forward onto the cowcatcher, as if she were going to push against the might of the locomotive. *"Stop, mister! You got to! You just got to!"*

Bob Eagle had not the smallest doubt that the little girl lying on the line was fooling—that she was no more tied to the rails than the boy on the trackside was genuinely trying to cut the ropes. It was all a hoax to make him stop. Well, he would teach them not to play the fool on his stretch of line. He let the train cruise on at walking speed—at three, at two miles an hour. How soon, he wondered, before the little blonde leaped to her feet and made a run for it?

Cissy Sissney climbed up the cowcatcher. A torn length of hem caught on the leading edge of the cowcatcher and disappeared under the still-moving train, ripping an entire circle of cloth from the bottom of her dress. *"Stop, mister! For pity's sake stop! We can't get her loose!"*

Suddenly, Tibbie's hands came free. She gave a strange animal wail as she tried to move and found her shoulders frozen solid, her stomach muscles too cramped to lift her up. Kookie rolled her head and shoulders forward as if he were rolling up a carpet, but her legs were rigid, and the knots round her ankles meant that he could not raise her any further than a sitting position. Just for a moment, he hesitated, thinking the train was bound to stop now—still had ten feet in which to stop. Then he attacked the other ropes in a frenzy as the cowcatcher continued to slide over the track, jerking now, straining against the brakes. He had not realized before that there were adults ready to terrorize innocent little girls like Tibbie Boden—who would not so much as step down from their cabs to help the prettiest little girl in Oklahoma in her most desperate need. If Kookie had had a gun then, he would have shot Bob Eagle clean off his platform, and done a better job of it than Virgil Hobbs or Jake Monterey.

The cowcatcher was a great chevron cutting into the side of his vision. It was vast. Its leading edge touched Tibbie's outstretched hand, and she shrieked like a rabbit in a snare. But suddenly, when Kookie was least expecting it, the ropes around her ankles went slack and fell away. He took hold of one of her twiggy arms and pulled her off the track, her limbs still as stiff as jackstraws. Cissy Sissney jumped down from the cowcatcher, on top of Kookie.

"And don't you *ever* play that kinda game again!" bellowed the engineer as he trundled on by, his fist unwinding the brake handle so fast that it was a whirling blur.

As soon as she heard the shrill repeated whistle of the upline train, Loucien Shades guessed that it held the answer to the missing girl. She picked up her skirt and ran. Halfway to the track, she collided with Peat Monterey clumping along in his laceless boots, but he had no breath to explain what had happened. The color of his gills made her fear the very worst. As she reached the railroad track at the end of Main Street, she was in time to see the cattle train go lumbering by, picking up steam. Its engineer leaned out of his cab to shower her with abuse.

Picking her way downline, she did not know what she expected to find. As it was, she came across three children, as torn and crumpled and still as discarded dishrags. Their skin was clammy cold with shock, their eyes as dull as pebbles.

"It was just like in the play," said Kookie Warboys, waving a hand in the direction of the severed ropes. "Just like in Mr. Crew's play."

"No," said Cissy, her voice unnaturally high and sleepy. "No it wasn't. That was exciting. This was . . ." Her words petered out.

"Like being hit with a spade over and over," said Kookie, and this time his friend nodded her head in agreement.

Miss Loucien sat on the grass, cradling Tibbie Boden in her arms, rocking the child gently, gently. The girl let herself be rocked; she seemed to be nine parts asleep.

"Better hush this up, hadn't we, ma'am?" said Kookie, trying to anticipate his teacher's wishes. "Her paw would kill Fuller if he knew."

"No," said the teacher sharply. "I was wrong. If I hadn't hushed you all the last time, this couldn'ta happened. It's my fault."

Within a matter of moments, Everett Crew also arrived, at a run, hopping between steps, favoring his injured leg. Kookie began to explain (though the very task of talking seemed like some high mountain range he had to overcome).

"No need, son," said Crew, dropping down beside them. "I wrung it out of Fuller." He did not rage. He did not ask questions. He simply sat, one arm around Kookie, one around Cissy. "Well, look now," he murmured at one point. "We're a picnic all on our own here, aren't we?"

"What am I bid for this boxful of white-footed mice?" asked Sheriff Klemme.

"Fried or poached?" someone called out.

"I'll pay you two bits to take 'em outa here!" called another.

Doge Klemme winced and directed a reproachful look at little Barney Mackinley, who had collected them.

"Them's cat food!" said Barney in self-defense. "Ain't nobody got a cat? Cats need a box supper too, don't they?"

He tried to withdraw the mice from sale, saying he would keep them himself, but his mother clubbed him about the ears and told him he could take them back out where he found them, plus a mile to ensure they stayed away from her garden.

The next auction lot was the box of ladybugs. Fred Stamp sprang at once to their defense. "Ladybugs eats aphids!" he said. "Miss Loucien told us! Miss Loucien says ladybugs is the gardener's best buddy!" The picnickers gave a hum that showed they were impressed. A man with fruit trees bought the ladybugs for a dollar. Nahum's sticklebacks fetched only fifty cents. Vokayatunga bought himself a box full of long quill feathers, to make himself a dream catcher.

The Ponca Pirates had collected empty turtle shells and filled them with pebbles, as musical instruments. They were deemed "charming" (though inedible). Quite wrongly, people assumed the Poncas were supporting their local church because they were all good Christians.

"Holly leaves?" said Sheriff Klemme, looking into the next box.

"Miss Loucien says you can use them to make black tea!" Sarah Waters piped up. The picnickers crooned with surprise, and several of the ladies wanted to experiment.

The wild turkey eggs went for two dollars, and Ollie's horseshoes sold to an Irishman to nail up over his door. The same man bid for a carton of cinnabar when he was told how it could be ground up to make vermilion paint. (Miss Loucien had said so.)

Honey's supper box of juniper berries was greeted with guffaws by the men, shocked tut-tutting by the ladies. "But Mith Louthien thayth you can uthe 'em to make a nithe dwink!" said the little girl, startled by the reaction. "I thought people'd like a nithe dwink." (It was bought by Virgil Hobbs, who was very partial to a drop of homemade gin.)

Partway through this, the schoolteacher herself returned to the picnic ground in company with Everett Crew and some very grubby children, including the missing Tibbie Boden. Crew came and asked to borrow the sheriff's keys.

"Certainly not!" said Klemme, covering his keychain with one hand.

"Just give me the key to your back room, then! I need to lock up Fuller Monterey for his own safety. You can deal with him after."

Kookie Warboys came forward with the remnants of a smashed basket full of dead grasshoppers and set it down on the auctioneer's table. "You mince 'em up with Juneberries," he said somberly. "Make Injun fruitcake. Miss Loucien taught us."

Cissy went and sat down beside her father, who looked her over with raised eyebrows. Her mother (thought Cissy) would have seen only the strip torn from her hem.

"You been in a fight, kitten?" Hulbert asked. She shook her head. "Where's your supper box, then? What did you find for the doge to auction?"

Again Cissy shook her head. So much to explain. Too

194

many words. "Couldn't find any honeycomb," she said, and a tear crawled down her dirty face like a bee looking for nectar.

Hulbert Sissney pulled out the copy of the *Glasstown Daybreak* that he had been sitting on in place of a blanket. He began absently to tear it up. "I'm sorry, kitten, but we're bust," he said in his singsong, matter-of-fact voice. "Kaput. Finished. I just bid a dollar for some pickled peaches. Hope you like pickled peaches. It was my last dollar."

"You still have that ten dollars in Mr. Guthrie's bank, Poppy!"

"Took that out last month. Used it to buy gravel and sand and soap slime, in place of merchandise. I'm sorry."

Cissy moved closer, pressing herself up against him. "Ma will be pleased, in any case," she said.

He apologized again. Cissy did not want her own father apologizing to her. She wished he would stop. She did not any longer care where she lived. "I just want to see Ma again," she said.

Hulbert took off his hat and filled it with the torn newspaper squares. "You take this up to the sheriff. Can't be the only kid without a supper box to sell."

So Cissy took it and laid the hat down in front of Emile Klemme, who smiled a watery smile at her and sighed even more deeply. "Tell me," he said, loudly talking down his nose in his most refined lawyer's voice, "and what, pray, can be done with a hatful of newspaper, Cecelia?"

"I—" said Cissy, too tired to think, too depressed to care.

195

Her teacher's voice came to her rescue, however, ringing out over the heads of the picnickers. "Don't talk foolish, Emile! You must be the only person in Oklahoma who doesn't know the use of a square of newsprint! You wipe your behind on it, of course!"

The laughter was long and loud. It broke off only when a fight began between Gaff Boden and Jake Monterey, the two men scuffling for a moment, then tumbling down toward the creek, locked in a vicious brawl.

Boden had just discovered what had been done to his daughter, and with Fuller safely locked up in the sheriff's office, there was no one to hit but the villain's father. Nate Rimm, Monday Morning, and Frank Tate became embroiled in the fight as they struggled to pull the two men apart. Sheriff Klemme pulled out his pistol and fired it into the air. Little Honey, her cheeks sparkling as brightly as her hair with sugar from Sven Lagerlöf's doughnuts, put her hearing trumpet to her ear and asked what the crossness was all about.

"Something 'bout the danged train," said Fred Stamp. "Ain't it always?"

Honey gave her doughnut to her mother to hold and went to where Loucien Shades stood watching the fight. Nothing of the noisy day had impinged on Honey's silent, thoughtful world. Her smile was as bright as ever, her eyes serene.

In an effort to incite a party mood, Lloyd Lentz led off with a square dance call to get people dancing:

"All jump up, and when you come down,
Swing your honey 'round and 'round.
Swing your honey, then do-si-do,
Send her on 'round to another beau!
All jump up, and when you come down
Swing your honey 'round and . . ."

"Teacher," Honey said, slipping her sticky hand inside Miss Loucien's. "If we wan' people to thee Florenthe, why don' we juth bwing 'em and thow 'em?"

"And how would we show them Florence, Honey?" asked the teacher into the ear trumpet, the copper horn hiding her smile.

"Ith eathy. We juth wait for a fu' train one day," said Honey. "Den we . . . bowwow it."

13

THE GREAT TRAIN ROBBERY

If Jake Monterey had said it, people would probably have thrown rocks at him or locked him up alongside his son. Coming from Honey, it took on the color of innocence. Sheriff Klemme was busy threatening Jake and Gaff about what would happen for breaching the peace; he was not there to say, "Train stealing is a felony." The new church minister was still in Texas; he was not there to remind them, "Thou shalt not steal."

Besides, as Honey put it, they were only going to *borrow* the RRR.

Sheriff Klemme was gone some time. Meanwhile, Miss Loucien took over the auction. Honey stood at her side, holding on to the teacher's skirts with one hand and her hearing trumpet with the other.

As if by magic, Miss Loucien produced, from underneath the table, more boxes to auction. "Ah! A pair of boots!" she said, looking inside one. "And what's this in with it? Bless me: a Bible. Dog-eared, but I daresay the words inside are in much the same kind of order. What am I bid?"

No hands went up, but thirty faces turned in Herman's direction. The young man looked embarrassed, but the crowd, in a neighborly mood now, urged him to seize the moment.

"Bid eggs, Herm!"

"Bid chickens!"

"Well, now I come to think of it, I'm needing feathers for a new pillow," said Miss Loucien, as if the thought had just occurred to her.

And so Herman got back what he had lost, and if his pride squirmed for a moment at the thought of someone feeling sorry for him, he cheered up when he realized it was just one more example of God's wonder working.

Little by little, the notion of borrowing the train mysteriously spread around the picnic site, like the chicken feathers that Herman brought in a holey sack to pay for his supper box. The feathers blew in among the blankets and, with them, a new color and excitement. Night came down like a shutter, and the black smoke from the fire could no longer be seen, only the sparks spiraling upward into the darkness, like inspiration.

Only for Hulbert Sissney was the darkness unrelieved. The idea of stealing a train held no excitement for him: he would not be in Florence to see it. He was finished, bankrupt.

Clambering painfully to his feet, he made a sudden, resolute plunge in the direction of Samuel T. Guthrie, who was squatting by the bonfire with a stick in one hand. "Forgive me talking business on a party night . . ." Hulbert began in a rush.

"Sit down with me, won't you, Mr. Sissney?"

Hulbert sat. What he needed to say was so hard that it

was like pulling his own teeth out of his head. "Could you see your way clear to advancing me a loan, Mr. Guthrie, sir? I'm all finished. Busted. But I'll be able to pay you back when I sell the shop! I just got to get the girl back to her mother somehow—she's eating her heart out—and the stagecoach company won't take shirt buttons in payment."

Samuel T. Guthrie used the stick to retrieve a potato out of the embers of the bonfire, rolling it toward himself with schoolboyish glee. Taking out a large, white handkerchief, he picked up the potato and squeezed it until the cooked center burst out through the slit skin, in a mound of snowy whiteness. "How much did you have in mind, Mr. Sissney?"

"Eight dollars. Twelve maybe. You'll get it back when I sell up!"

Samuel T. Guthrie took out the wrap of goat cheese he had just bought in the auction and introduced it to the potato tenderly, lovingly. The cheese eased itself into the potato, as though onto the white satin of Frank Tate's furnishings. "I'll do better than that, Mr. Sissney. I shall advance you one hundred dollars. Stock up. Paint your storefront. Run some special offers."

Hulbert Sissney picked up the charred stick and went to the bonfire himself now. He hunkered down and raked around for a potato. "Business been good to you, then, Mr. Guthrie?" he enquired. His voice was casual, though it did tremble somewhat.

"Business is always good in banking, Mr. Sissney. Even in Florence. It will get better yet, you mark my words."

Hulbert's face reddened in the heat from the fire. "But why would you want to lend so much as a plug nickel to the likes of me, Mr. Guthrie?"

A dollop of creamy whey fell onto the banker's shoe. With a corner of his tartan blanket, he wiped it off and polished up the shine. "The first week we got here, you trusted me, Mr. Sissney. Trust. It is a critical factor in banking. Well, in any line of business, when you think about it. When people heard about your ten dollars, they came to me with their fifty cents and their annuities and their farming accounts and their wedding savings. . . . Trust, you see. A critical factor in friendship, also, I find. One of these days, Mr. Sissney, I am going to be a rich man, in a three-story bank with marble floors and paintings on the ceiling. I would like it just fine if you were still in the vicinity and would drop in some days—on your way between the many branches of your store—to take a cup of coffee in my third-floor office. Consider it, and tell me if the thought appeals."

Hulbert Sissney produced a jar of pickled peaches and offered one to the banker, who placed one peach half on top of the goat cheese. Together they regarded this, like art connoisseurs admiring a Caravaggio. "It's a date, Mr. Guthrie. Each time I drop in, we shall eat peaches and cheese together. I may make it a special line in my chain of stores. Specialty de la mayson, as they say in Paree. And thank you, Mr. Guthrie."

"Pray don't mention it, Mr. Sissney."

The bonfire settled itself, like an old dog. A chill wind blew smoke into Cissy's face where she sat hugging her knees, watching her father and the banker share their picnic supper. They were happy. Despite everything, they were laughing! She had no idea why, but the tension that, all day, had been winding her back muscles into tighter and tighter coils, suddenly relented. She was so tired, she thought she might just rest her stung face down on her knees and sleep. Just here. Where the dreams might be peach sweet and lit by rising sparks. . . .

"Ma's taken Tibbie home to sleep at our place," announced Kookie, pounding up behind her, balancing two doughnuts on his bandaged fingertips. "Sheriff Klemme's locked up Fuller for his own safety, case Gaff Boden tries to rip his head off. And Gaff's challenged Jake Monterey to a gunfight for letting Fuller do it in the first place! No joshing! But Everett Crew says they gotta postpone killing each other till after the train robbery, 'cause everybody's gonna be too busy to bury them. Miss Loucien says we gotta all pull together, but not to tell the sheriff, 'cause law officers shouldn't be party to lawbreaking, though Sheriff Klemme'll be glad enough when we done it. My brother Amos reckons he's gonna emigrate 'cause in the lottery he won a photograph of some actress in England called Lillie Langtry and now he's in love. And Barney's white-footed mice have just got loose an' invaded the bran tub 'cause Ezra filled it up with licorice shoelaces. Nahum don't care, 'cause he's just persuaded Miss Loucien to teach him how to waltz and now

202

he thinks he's all kinds of a beau. . . . Wanna dance?"

Cissy piled up the various items of news inside her head and rested Kookie's question on top, like half a pickled peach.

"Wouldn't mind," she said.

They did not rush anything. There was too much to prepare, if Honey's plan was to work, and besides, they judged that Florence would look its prettiest in the May sunshine. Houses were whitewashed and flowers were transplanted from the prairie, to mask any holes chewed in the timber by wood-borer beetles or rotted away by splashing winter rain. Jake Monterey was persuaded to groom his cows and sweep the dirty streets, though mostly he spent his time practicing his quick draw in readiness for the gunfight he and Gaff Boden had promised each other.

At the next meeting of the FTCC, nothing was said about "borrowing" the train. This was done so that if Sheriff Klemme was ever called into a court of law, he could swear, with his hand on a Bible, to knowing nothing about it. Naturally Klemme was aware of *something* in the offing but could persuade no one to tell him what or when. "You just rest easy, sugar," the schoolteacher would say, patting his cheek, and the sheriff would color deeply—whether with pleasure or frustrated curiosity it was difficult to tell.

Every day the weather grew sunnier and the prairie around Florence more rainbow colored under spring flowers. Still the RRR tore through as fast as the bend in the line allowed, but any passenger glancing out at this place stranded between Somewhere and Somewhere Else now saw Nowhere putting on a brave face, wearing a clownish, greasepaint grin.

On the night of May 3, Pickard Warboys, Monday Morning, Everett Crew, Frank Tate, and Nathaniel Rimm led out the best horseflesh they could muster and mounted up.

"You sure you want to be doing this, Mr. Rimm?" said Pickard under his breath. "It's your daddy's train, and he won't care much for it."

"My father doesn't like anything I do, Pickard," replied Nate. "It's the one thing that counts in my favor as a human being. It's Crew here I find baffling. Are you in the habit of fighting other men's causes, Everett?"

"Who, me?" said the actor, tying back his long hair, using his string tie. "Put it down to boredom, my dear. Or literary pretensions: Perhaps I shall write a book about it one of these days. But Pickard's right about your father, Nathaniel. Best keep your face covered when it comes to the actual—er—borrowing."

Despite the hour, there were women there to see them off. Loucien Shades wanted to go along—"Wouldn't it kinda ease the passengers' minds, to see a female?"—but the men would not hear of it. What if there was shooting? Fisticuffs? Besides, she did not own a horse. Mrs. Warboys tended to her husband as though he were sick, stroking the hair out of his eyes, introducing him to his packed supper, buttoning his jacket. Sickness and injury she was good at dealing with;

recklessness she did not understand, so she did not mention the purpose of his journey.

There was a frosty ring around the full moon, making it look like the headlamp of a great locomotive cannoning through the sky, blaring out silence, clanging on the vast black bell of night. The only sound was the squeaking of its well-oiled couplings: night noises of the prairie.

For four hours they rode downline, till the sound of dogs barking signaled that they had reached the outskirts of Bewick, next station down the line. They passed some sod huts and a couple of tents. Newcomers were still arriving here, expanding the size and prosperity of a settlement blessed because it owned a working railroad station. A boot-and-shoe factory stood two stories high, hard up against the track, with gantries for lowering crates directly into the freight cars. A tannery laid its distinctive smell over the reek of latrines and cow-chip stoves. This was what Florence ought to have been by now. This was what Florence could still be, given use of the railroad.

Bewick station was pretty, with a row of newly planted prairie sage at either end of the platform. In the half-light of dawn, they looked like snowy-haired children holding hands. On the prairie side of the track opposite the station platform, the town's litter—empty bottles, fruit cans, broken wheels, fuel drums—had accumulated into a dump. Even in the dark, this rubbish heap murmured with flies.

Dismounting, Nathaniel, Monday, Crew, and Pickard gave their reins into the hands of Frank Tate, who at once set off on the return journey. They saw the glimmer of his thin, pale face as he turned once in the saddle and looked back. He could probably no longer make them out against the dark mass of the rubbish dump.

Peter Bull, on his first journey of the day, left Guthrie for Glasstown while it was still dark. No more than a handful of passengers slumped in the cars, large boots propped up on the seats, large hats tipped forward over weathered faces. Traveling salesmen with thin-soled shoes and large carpet-bags sat white faced, empty eyed, eating peanuts. One, with a batch of cloth samples, sat reading them, like a baby reading a cloth book, learning his stock. There were also a few heading north for the fair in Glasstown.

At Hennessey, they picked up a couple of sisters on their way to see a lawyer in Glasstown, a family returning from a funeral, a school inspector, a government clerk, and, of course, a few more making for the fair.

The car attendant was at his most whining. He had arrived at five, only to find a new assistant waiting for him—fifteen, and still wet behind the ears. The kid said he was a new employee of the RRR who had been sent for training. "You mean I gotta teach you? Nobody tells me these things! Why does nobody tell me these things?" wailed the car attendant. "Ain't it bad enough with the fair an' all?"

It was the day before the big annual fair in Glasstown. As the train steamed northwest out of Guthrie, it would fill up more and more at every stop, with people heading for the festivities.

The idea of large numbers of passengers irritated the engineer, Peter Bull. Bull prided himself on reaching the railhead in Glasstown on the dot of time. But thanks to the wretched fair, there would be families with squalling children and baby carriages, silly women who could not shut a train door without trapping their skirts, and bunkhouse louts trying to ride north without buying a ticket.

At least the Florence gangsters had fallen quiet lately, the engineer mused. Maybe they were all dead. To Peter's way of thinking, Florentines were like prairie dogs: You just had to stop up their holes and wait for them to starve—end of problem.

Bewick came into view. Every time he saw it, the place seemed to have grown: phenomenal how these land-rush towns had turned from an idea on a map into sprawling acres of church spires, warehouses, shops, homes, gardens with picket fences . . .

Peter Bull heaved a sigh. The platform ahead was aswarm with passengers. A great interference to the smooth running of a railroad: passengers. He wound the brake handle as delicately as a fly fisherman winding in a line. Usually, he aimed to leave the last car overhanging the platform. (It was entertaining to watch passengers trying to scramble down into mud and nettles.) But such tricks would take up too much time today. So he brought the train to a perfect stop, hooked his fingers over the whistle cord, and gave a long, loud blast to hurry the passengers aboard.

Leaning outward from his platform, holding on by one hand, he shouted at an old man having difficulty with the steps: "Git on or git off, but git movin'! . . . What the—?"

At the same moment he saw his fireman tumble from the far side of the platform, he felt a crack on his knuckles that made him lose his grip on the handrail and topple into a newly planted row of prairie sage . His bottom set of teeth fell out into the soil and were instantly lost. Cussing and jumping up, he saw that his cab was full of strangers, and that the strangers were letting off the brake! His brake!

"Why won't it go? I took off the brake! Why won't it go? Do something, Crew!" said one of the strangers, panicking.

"I believe you have to let out the throttle, too," said some old guy in a duster coat with long gray hair, who was heaving on the throttle. Bull's throttle!

"Of course! Of course! I'm a fool! I'm a fool!" said the one on the brake handle.

There was some black man, too, throwing coal, piece by piece, into the furnace with his bare hands. Bull's coal! Bull's furnace!

Rage overcame discretion, and Peter Bull began pulling himself up the ladder again. "Let my coal be, you—" His head and shoulders reared up in the cab opening, as the train jerked violently into motion. Doors along the train banged shut, but no one was left behind: The RRR was notorious for rushing its departures.

Peter Bull reached in and made a grab for the shovel but could not quite reach it. It was only when he was confronted by a face with a bandanna pulled up across it that the word "bandit" went through his head for the first time.

"The engineer's back aboard!" yelled the black man.

"Well, throw him off again!"

"But we're moving! He might break his neck!"

Bull took advantage of their indecision to grab the whistle cord and haul on it. He must alert the station to what was happening! A gush of hot steam burst downward into the cab and scattered everyone to separate corners of the metal platform, and the noise made them all draw their heads between their collarbones.

But the station staff at Bewick were accustomed to Peter Bull's heavy, impatient hand on the whistle. They did not so much as look toward the cab of the departing train. Peter Bull made a second grab for the shovel, and this time he had it.

"Well, then, I'll just have to shoot him, won't I?" The one with the long gray hair screwed on a flat, low-crowned hat with silver cord tips hanging down the back and twirled a large and villainous mustache. Flaring his top lip off immaculate teeth, he leveled a Colt .45 at the engineer's chest. It was Peter Bull's worst nightmare: a gang of Panhandle bandits was stealing his beloved train, and his legs had just turned to jelly. The shovel clattered to the floor. "Eat coal, buster," drawled the bandit.

Bull turned to jump voluntarily from the cab, despite the flickering speed with which the shoulders flashed past. But the black bandit caught him by the suspenders and sent him sprawling facedown on the coal tender, and sat on his head, saying: "Now, now, sir: Unless you carry insurance, I believe you'd be better advised staying here with us. We mean you no harm."

After that, he was in no position to know what was going

on, except that there were feet crunching over the coal beside his head. One or more of the train robbers was climbing over the coal tender to reach the coaches. Now, presumably, they would systematically rob and murder their way down the train, stealing everything, from the pocket watches in first class to the mailbags in the caboose. "They left the gun with me, Mr. Bull, so don't get any ideas," said the black man sitting on his head.

"*Mmnurph,*" said Peter Bull.

"Ladies and gentlemen," said Everett Crew, removing his stage hat and duster coat, brushing the coal dust self-consciously off his trousers. "Might I be allowed the privilege of introducing myself to you? My name is . . . of no importance. But I am here to announce that the Red Rock Railroad morning train will be making an unscheduled stop today, courtesy of the people of Florence, where you are invited most cordially to partake of a little light refreshment and attend a small—ah—cultural function in your honor—at no cost to your good selves, I hasten to add. My friends here undertake to have you in Glasstown in plenty of time for the fair, or any other appointment you might have. . . ."

The car attendant, hearing the sound of a voice as loud as his own, quickened his swaying stride through second class and into first. "Make yourself useful, boy," he remarked over his shoulder to his staggering, stumbling new assistant, "and get me the shotgun from the caboose. I smell trouble."

In the front coach he saw a man addressing his passengers in Shakespearean tones. The word "Florence" still hung in the air like a soap bubble, just asking to be popped.

"Oh Mikey," said Pickard Warboys under his breath. "He didn't take long to find us. Watch yourself, Everett."

"What's this?" enquired the attendant in tones larded with sarcasm and menace. "Do I spy *Florentines*?"

"Indeed you do, sir!" agreed the spokesman, advancing down the train toward him, hand outstretched in greeting. "And do I have the pleasure of addressing that renowned employee of the RRR with whom my associates have become acquainted a priori?"

The attendant hesitated for a moment too long, wasted valuable time glancing over his shoulder to see if his shotgun was coming—where was that stupid boy?—so the actor's hand closed around his own.

"Is this the gentleman we have to thank for the reputation of the Glasstown–Guthrie line? So delighted to meet you!" The voice boomed out, as if reciting "The Charge of the Light Brigade"—as though this *were* the charge of the Light Brigade. Words to the right of him, words to the left of him, volleyed and thundered. The sheer volume drove the attendant back down the train. "Is this the gentleman who throws his fellow man off the tail of speeding trains? The one who maroons fare-paying passengers in the midst of the wilderness? The one who destroyed the Holy Bible of a Christian believer, in his very face? The one who beat a pacifist? Who smashed the working hand of a master craftsman? Who *de-fen-e-stra-ted a child*?" (This was not the Charge of the Light Brigade: It was the Last Trump. The carriage rang with righteous wrath.)

211

"Shame!" cried a woman, clutching her child close.

"Incredible!" barked the school inspector.

"Who would've thought?" exclaimed a Texas rancher.

"He didn't!" gasped a Mexican Catholic nun, kicking her luggage farther under her seat.

The attendant looked at the faces of the passengers and promptly retreated to second class. Only when he had put two closing doors between him and the train robbers did he begin bawling, "But they're Florentines, for Abe's sake! *Floo-ren-tines*!" And *still* the fool of an assistant did not come with the shotgun! He would have to go himself and get it.

When the attendant finally reached the caboose, there the boy stood, holding the shotgun as though it were a stick of celery he had just dug up.

"Have I gotta do everything myself, you one-handled jug?" demanded the attendant, advancing into the luggage car and snatching the weapon. "Gimme that before I tear off yer other ear!"

"Don't know what you gonna do with an empty gun, suh," said the boy, ducking a blow and squirming out of the car.

"'Tain't empty. I keep it loaded for just this kinda . . ."

But by the time the car attendant had discovered that his shotgun had been emptied, Amos Warboys—assistant—had clanged shut the barred gate of the caboose and padlocked it with a flick of the wrist.

The RRR was in the hands of the Great Train Robbers of Florence.

———

"They're coming, Mith Louthien! They're coming!" Honey, who had been posted as lookout, thumped her hand on the wall of the schoolhouse.

Faces turned to each other, ajump with uncertainty. No one knew yet whether or not the ambush had taken place, whether or not it had been successful.

"Now you all remember what I told you," said the teacher, as the oldest children rose to their feet. "You remember to take your manners out and dust 'em. You have to behave so nice, they'll want to buy you 'fore they leave." She lined them up and looked them over: Sunday clothes outgrown, hand-me-downs too big, bodies surviving on rabbit stew and grasshopper cake. "Well *I'd* buy every last one of you, if I had the ante," she said, hands on hips, and the Grasshopper Cake Brigade filed out into the sunshine to meet the RRR . . . or to watch it steam on by.

Aboard the train, Nate Rimm, in the cab of the RRR, had no way of knowing whether his fellow bandits had taken the train. He had the throttle wide open and the brake fully off.

"So fast?" said Monday, still sitting on the engineer's head. The train seemed to have picked up a rolling motion.

"I don't want to give the passengers too long to consider whether they like us or not."

The prairie seemed so unremittingly flat that the incline was not obvious. But the train knew. It had been gathering speed for several miles now. The pile of coal on

213

which Monday and the driver lay gave a tremor and settled flatter in the tender. Peter Bull's mouth rose to the surface, and he used it to shout, *"Brake! Brake! For Jude's sake, brake!"*

Suddenly the wheels on one side spun clear of the track, with a hysterical, ungoverned shriek from the pistons. The coal heap shifted in all directions, and Monday and the engineer were rolled apart. Peter Bull made a grab for the gun, and Rimm, instead of winding on the brake handle, went to help Monday Morning. He could barely tell the two apart, they were so smothered in coal dust. Beyond them, the cars of the RRR teetered like spectators trying to see past each other. Bull was strong and desperate: He threw a punch at Rimm, which fell short of breaking his nose but snagged the bandanna so that it slipped down.

"You!" cried Bull, and his remaining top teeth flashed startlingly white in the blackened face. He was so surprised to see his employer's son that he allowed himself to be overpowered. "Where you taking my train, Mr. Nathaniel?"

"We are simply stopping it in Florence for a while," shouted Rimm above the noise of the vibrating train. His feet were being bounced clean off the platform; he felt like a pea on a drum.

"Never stop in time," said Peter Bull, smugly doom laden. "Ken see that danged water tower from here. You'll come off at the bend. Kill us all." And he grinned at them both, like a chimney sweep at a wedding.

Inside the train, only one passenger was kicking up a fuss. A big, beef-fed gun salesman objected to having his journey interrupted, and got out an eight-gauge shotgun to prove he meant what he said. "Who do I have to shoot to get to Glasstown on time?" he enquired of the carriage at large.

"Ah, set down and be still," said a homely woman with a wicker cage on her knee. "Where's your sense of adventure?"

"Yeah!" agreed the fairgoers. "These folk asked you real nice."

"People got children, señor! Put the gun away!"

Pickard Warboys (who had no gun and would not have used one if he had) held stone still—frozen—until enough passengers had ganged up on the man with the eight-gauge. Only then did he dare to set off at a run, through the cars, in search of his boy Amos. Father and son approached each other triumphant, arms raised above their heads. But the train (which seemed to have picked up enormous speed) gave a sudden, violent lurch, and Amos missed his footing. As he picked himself up, he chanced to look out the window. "That's Golden Ridge!" he said. "Why ain't we stopping?"

Crew, too, came jumping down the train calling, "What's Rimm doing? Are we going on through? What about the bend?"

The all-too-familiar sight of the water tower flashed by, as did the faces of a dozen gaping children. Within the same split second, the wheels began to skid as the brake was applied. The cars accordioned. The gun salesman was thrown backward into his seat, and the eight-gauge shotgun went off with a noise like Armageddon. Shotgun pellets buried themselves in the ceiling, but at the heart of the blast a hole as big as a fist appeared, and beyond it the sky. To the passengers, and to the Florentine train robbers gaping up at it, it looked like a comet passing through a storm of asteroids.

14

FAIR FLORENCE

The RRR went through Florence amid a shower of sparks and the shriek of skidding wheels. The faces of the watching crowd followed it, all turning to see the caboose receding into the distance toward the bend in the line. Fifty hearts shrank with disappointment. Fifty hearts expanded again, as the caboose did not disappear around the bend but stopped and, after a minute, began moving toward them again. The RRR was backing up!

The first passenger to climb down was a homely woman carrying a turkey in a wicker cage. The train door was opened for her by a young man in full mourner's dress: black suit, black crepe scarf tied around a black top hat. She was greeted by a young girl with honey-blond hair and indistinct speech, who presented her with a dazzling smile and a bunch of prairie flowers. The funereal young man offered to carry her turkey. For a moment, she suspected him (seeing how thin he was) of wanting to cook and eat it. But then she smelled the delicious savor of baking bread mixed with roasting beef, and allowed her turkey to be put inside a shed for safekeeping. Clearly Florence had plenty to eat.

Each visitor—men and women alike—received a bunch of flowers and an escort, saying: "Welcome to Florence Fair: My name is so-and-so and I am your escort for today. Please tell me if I can help you in any way." Some of the younger children could not remember so much script:

"Hi," they said. "I'm Joe."

A few times, where nerves took a hand, it did not come out in quite the right order: "Welcome to Fair Florence! You're my escort for today. . . ."

Some of the older children, at the awkward, tongue-tied age, could manage only an embarrassed grunt. But no one was spared. Every child old enough to walk and speak had been recruited into Miss Loucien's army of guides, steering the visitors between the highlights of Florence Fair.

At the north end of Main Street, one of the bandits off the train, now changed into a velvet coat and holding a large dried sunflower, was declaiming loudly, *"What a piece of work is a man! How noble in reason! how infinite in faculty! in form and moving how express and admirable! in action, how like an angel! in apprehension how like a god! the beauty of the world . . . !"*

The visitors moved through the streets like explorers through a ravine, cautious at first, running their eyes over the buildings, peering into alleyways between the houses. But all they saw there were smiling faces . . . and a great many notices, beautifully executed:

Hear the Choir of the Florence Academy

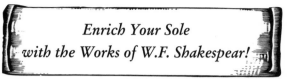

Enrich Your Sole
with the Works of W.F. Shakespear!

**JOIN WITH US ON A LANTURN-SLIDE TOUR
OF THIS GREAT CONTENENT OF OURS
(BACK OF GENERAL STORE)**

SEE THE FLORENCE ILLUMI-NATIONS
CURTESY OF MR. FUDD, ESQUIRE.

HAVE YOUR EYES TESTED. EARS FREE!

**A FEW LAND PLOTS REMAIN!
INQUIRE AT SHERRIFF'S OFFICE**

**ONE DAY ONLY:
Have your hair cut free
by CHARLES QUEX of Paris**

Every door was decorated with bunches of newsprint curled into springy cockades to signify that it stood open to visitors.

So those from the train with an interest in furniture nosed their way into Frank Tate's workshop, and although it was a little dismaying to be shown a marquetry-inlaid cabinet by a young man in mourning dress, no one thought to question him.

"What does the F stand for?" one visitor asked of his young escort.

"F?" said Kookie.

"The F in W. F. Shakespear."

"Couldn't say, sorry," Kookie told him. "I never met the man to ask him."

Once they had shown their charges all the way around the town, Class Three broke away and formed ranks in the schoolhouse to begin singing a "repertory of well-loved songs." They did "O Susannah," "Turkey in the Straw," "Sweet Betsy from Pike," and "Soapsuds over the Fence."

Meanwhile, in the back room of the general store, Hulbert Sissney had hung sacking over the windows for darkness, and a continuous slide show was in progress. It comprised a botanist's collection of orchids, a zebra, some hide ships docked in San Francisco, the winners of four Kentucky Derbies, views of the Alamo battle site, and some exotic dancers at the Folies-Bergère. Hulbert thought it gave a rather misleading impression of America, but nobody seemed to mind. There was a free glass of the oculist's renowned "temperance punch" for those who wanted it.

One businessman off the train found his way into the newspaper offices. "I see you publish books," he said.

With ferocious pride, Monday Morning showed him the fourteen books he had typeset with his own hands—the plates, the inking and binding processes, the finished volumes. "The paper is low-grade, but our aim is to make these books available to ordinary working people at an affordable price!"

The eyes behind the thick spectacles fell eagerly on a copy of Neville Crupper's *History of the Cherokee Strip*, and he examined every aspect of it: the binding, the blocking, the endpapers, the font. "What royalties are you paying the author?" he asked.

Across the room, Monday's partner gave a snicker of laughter. "Royalties? You think we could sell for a dollar fifty a copy if we paid royalties?"

The visitor continued to thumb through the pages, then put one hand in his pocket, as if the temptation to buy Crupper's *Cherokee Strip* were just too much to resist. "And what do you think Crupper would say to you printing his books?"

This time it was the printer's turn to laugh. "Crupper? He's long dead, isn't he? Anyway, he should be gratified to see his work nicely turned out and getting a wider readership. I know I would be if I ever wrote a book. Wouldn't you?"

The gentleman did not answer but returned the book. When he drew his fingers from his vest pocket, it was only to pass them a calling card that read:

NEVILLE T. CRUPPER
147 Geary Street
San Francisco

In the churchyard, the Florence Academy Choir took a bow and then trooped inside the schoolhouse, ready to prove that Florence took seriously the education of its young people.

One man and several women, charmed by their little hosts, ranged themselves along the open windows, drinking lemonade from Charlie Quex's barbershop. They marveled at the caliber of the furniture, until they realized that this was also the church. "Even so . . . white satin!" they could be heard whispering.

The schoolmistress, statuesque in a dress of yellow and blue stripes, had seated herself among the children and was telling them a story.

"Now for a few years, everything went just dandy. But then First Woman and First Man began to spat. Everything she did, he found fault with. Pretty soon, she couldn't take any more nagging, and she went off East toward Sun Land. Then First Man remembered soon enough about the good times! Oh yes. He missed her so much, he couldn't get up the energy to do anything much except sit and feel sorry for hisself. . . ." (Miss Loucien broke off here to pass a handkerchief to Cissy, who seemed to be finding the story a little too close to home.) "Well, Mr. Sun looked down outa the sky, and he was real sad to see First Man so miserable. Mr. Sun decided to take steps to put things right between husband and wife. He leaned right down outa Heaven and he planted a row of big fat Juneberries bang in front of the lady's feet. You know what? She was crying too much to see them! Next thing is, the Sun's planting blackberries in the hedges either side of First Woman's path. But still she's too busy thinking and regretting

222

and crying. She doesn't notice a blue-blamed thing. Well, Sun tries plums and Sun tries grapes—black and green ones both— but still he can't stop the woman from walking away from home. So last of all, he leans down and plants a great red patch of juicy strawberries. First Woman has never so much as seen strawberries—well, nobody has, on accounta Sun's only just invented them for the purpose. Well, this time First Woman does stop, and she bends down and she reaches out and she picks and she tastes one. And having tasted one, well, there's nothing to do but to eat another and another. Each sweet, luscious, delicious, blushing red strawberry seemed to be full of sweet thoughts about her husband, dang him. He might be a wretch and a waster and have a mouth three sizes too big for him and no brains, but she'd gotten kinda used to him. And she knew just the look that would come on his face if ever she set down a bowl of these new scarlet berries on the table in place of his usual grasshopper cake. . . ."

Not until the story finished did the spectators drift away from the schoolhouse windows.

"How do you think it's going, Miss Loucien?" asked Kookie.

There was an instant clamor to know. "Do they like us, miss?"

"Did we do good, miss?"

Then the door opened, and it was the man who had been watching through one of the windows. "Griffin's the name. Might I be so bold as to satisfy my curiosity on a few trifling points?" he asked politely.

223

"Indeed, Mr. Griffin! Come right on in and join us," said Miss Loucien.

"That story of yours . . ." said Mr. Griffin. "Do you often draw on the culture of the—ah—tribal peoples?"

"Sure, honey! We've shared hundreds, haven't we, folks?" Class Three was quick to agree: thousands.

"And you find no—ah—*conflict* between these stories and—ah—Christian teachings?"

Miss Loucien looked blank, wondering if the Bible had something different to say about the creation of strawberries. She set her head on one side. "Reckon God made us all, didn't he?" she said.

"Oh indeed. Most indubitably."

"Including the Choctaw and the Ponca?"

"Ah—y-e-e-s."

"So anysoever stories that are in their heads—God musta put them there. Right?"

"I—er—" For a moment, the visitor's eyes wandered up and down the Choceapolis Miss Loucien, taking in her restyled dress, her fall of red hair tumbling like lava from Mount Vesuvius. The eyes came to rest on her block-heeled boots. "Would you permit me to catechize your pupils, madam?" he asked with a charming smile.

"They ain't Jewish," she replied, with a big throaty laugh, "but if it's legal and they got no objections, you do just as you see fit, honey."

The gentleman with the half-moon glasses eased himself between the children on the white satin pews. "Tell me, child. What is your favorite lesson here in school?"

"Horse grooming, suh," said Peat Monterey.

"Horse . . . And can you tell me the sum of ten, fifteen, and twenty?"

"Nope."

"The gentleman is talking cattle, Peatie," Miss Loucien interjected in a low, encouraging voice. "Ten steers, fifteen heifers, and twenty calves."

"Well, why didn't he say?" said Peatie. "That's forty-five head. You a rancher, mister?" But Mr. Griffin was not a rancher.

"And you, young man, will you spell the word 'lighthouse' for me?"

"Spell it? I never even seen one," said Ollie West. "You from the seaboard, mister?" But Mr. Griffin was not from the seaboard.

"Can any of you tell me the Ten Commandments?" he asked.

The teacher gave an audible sigh of relief as eager voices called out:

"Thou shall not kill!"

"Thou shan't not steal!"

"Thou shalt love the Lord thy God!"

"Thou shan't gamble on a Sunday!"

"Thou shalt not play suzyfandangle with thy neighbor's piece of home comfort. . . . Hey, are you our new preacher, mister?" But Mr. Griffin was not the new preacher.

"We generally ask our visitors to share with us some

special gift of theirs," said Miss Loucien, looking a little flustered. "Won't you do us that honor, honey?"

But Mr. Griffin had no gift to share, such as Morse code or setting a broken bone. As he said, "I am not sure what skill a mere school inspector might share, but I do want to thank you and your children for today. It has been a real—ah—*education*."

Peter Bull was taken to the sheriff's office and locked up alongside Fuller Monterey. Mrs. Warboys took one look at him, caked from head to foot in coal dust, and called for a zinc bathtub, hot water, and soap. For an hour she soaped and scrubbed him. Then Charlie Quex came and cut his hair and Lloyd Lentz came and cleaned the wax out of his ears free of charge. He put up a fight at first, cussing and throwing his fists around. But since they had taken away his clothes, there was nowhere modest for him to be but in the zinc bathtub. And as kettle after kettle of hot water was poured over him, his resolve to escape grew waterlogged. Meekly he submitted to Mrs. Warboys's scrubbing and pummeling and first aid, to her cooking, to her sympathetic crooning, to her singing. He concentrated, instead, on thinking what he would tell his wife when he got home smelling of carbolic soap and talcum.

The weather smiled on Florence Fair. Frank Tate's two-man rowing boat—the only satin-lined rowboat on the whole Bison Creek—was kept busy for two solid hours, cruising the wider reaches, powered by Ruth Warboys dressed as a Venetian gondolier.

At the end of Everett Crew's final dramatic recital, Lloyd Lentz began to play "The Hatikvah" on the fiddle, sweet and soulful.

Miss Loucien put a hand on the sheriff's arm. "Speak to them, Emile. Before they go. Speak to them."

But the arm she touched was rigid. Emile Klemme said nothing, neither in his role as doge of Florence nor sheriff nor sweet-tongued lawyer.

"Hope we didn't offend you, Emile, by keeping you in the dark. But we didn't want anyone to be able to say you were party to it—you being an officer of the law. *Won't* you speak to them, honey? Tell them how they can help? Please?"

But Emile Klemme's tongue seemed to have cleaved to the roof of his mouth, for he turned back toward his office without a word. "I have letters to write," he said, casting a watery smile in the teacher's direction.

All of a sudden, rain put an end to everything. There was a cloudburst overhead; the visitors put their free copies of the *Morning Star* over their heads and ran for the train. Their hosts ran with them. There was laughter and the hurried exchange of names, waves, handshakes, even kisses. Then the doors were banging shut, the Florentines stepping back to a safe distance.

Peter Bull had at last been given back his overalls and his freedom. Like a dog allowed back into its kennel, he purged his locomotive's cab of any trace of strangers, cleaning the shovel, flushing through the whistle, letting off steam. It was he who let off the hand brake.

As the RRR moved slowly out of Florence, its passengers looked out of windows opaque with condensation. Lloyd Lentz played a Hungarian rhapsody, until the wet strings of his fiddle grated and broke: a strange noise, like a heart bursting its springs.

Flapping open their specially printed, commemorative copies of the *Florence Morning Star*, the passengers read:

AN <u>APPEAL</u> ON BEHALF
OF FLORENCE, OKLAHOMA

Have you enjoyed yourselves today? We earnestly hope it.

Come back next year, and it will be gone.

Have you seen things you like here? Met congenial folk?

We rejoice at it. Come back next winter, and they will be gone.

The town you have seen today has been shunned by the Red Rock Railroad.

Because of this, the citizens of Florence are at the end of their resources.

Their hopes and dreams can come to nothing so long as the town repines without a railroad.

We brought you here today to show you a town worth saving. For the sake of Florence, we intruded on your time, imposed upon your patience.

If, however, you were to speak kindly of us

after today—if you were to tell your friends and kin that here is a town that deserves as much chance as her sister towns up and down the Glasstown–Guthrie line—then might Florence, Oklahoma, yet be saved from the fate that over-shadows her.

These things we respectfully ask you to grace with consideration on your homeward journey, for the which we wish you **GODSPEED**.

Nathaniel Rimm, EDITOR

15

SHOWDOWN AT
TEN FORTY-FIVE

The days that followed were like the days after a birthday. The ordinariness of everything piled up like a thundercloud over the fields, the gardens, the workshops.

"I blame myself," said Loucien Shades. "That inspector of schools thought I was training up heathens and fools."

"No, no," said Monday Morning, head in hands. "If anyone's to blame it's me. I am the fool of all fools."

"Ah, don't torment yourself," grunted his partner. "How were we to know Crupper was still alive, let alone riding the railroad around Oklahoma Territory?" Even so, Nate Rimm's voice was full of self-disgust: He too held himself to blame for the failure of Florence Fair.

For fail it surely must have. Nearly a week had come and gone, and still the RRR thundered through Florence with never a sign of wanting to renew its acquaintance.

When copies of the *Glasstown Daybreak* arrived aboard the stage, the Florentines discovered the true reason. Filling an entire page, and printed in twenty-eight-point capital letters, a notice under the triple-R emblem read:

THIS COMPANY WISHES TO ASSURE ITS LOYAL CUSTOMERS THAT NEVER UNDER ANY CIRCUMSTANCES OR FOR ANY INDUCEMENT WILL ANY OF ITS TRAINS STOP FOR THE CONVENIENCE, BENEFIT, OR COMFORT OF THE SQUATTER TOWN OF FLORENCE, OKLAHOMA.

TO THIS I HAVE SET MY HAND, IN THE PRESENCE OF AN ATTORNEY-AT-LAW, AND FROM THIS, YOU MAY REST EASY, I DO NOT MEAN TO DEPART!

SIGNED: *Clifford J. Rimm*
PRESIDENT OF THE RED ROCK RAILROAD COMPANY

Nate Rimm looked like the man who shot the albatross. The fact that his own father was personally responsible for the ruin of this town's hopes weighed on him so heavily that he took an axe to the elegant sign over his door and began to pack away his printing press.

"What is this?" said Monday Morning. "Sardanapalus destroying his most beloved objects? I was under the impression there were two of us in this enterprise."

"I'm broke," said Rimm. "Besides, I can't look these people in the face anymore. I encouraged them to stay, when rightly I should have been helping them pack up. I can't stay and I can't go home. I'll have to find somewhere I can make a living at least. If you want to come along with me . . . Where are you going?"

Monday paused in the doorway only to pick up his

notebook. "I am going to cover the news story of the day for the *Morning Star*, naturally. Someone has to." And he was gone.

The up-and-coming news story of the day had reduced Class Three to a mixture of frenzy and tears. Fuller Monterey (freed from jail) was roaming about the schoolroom slapping the walls and anyone who came within reach. His younger brother sat slumped in abject misery, clutching a vest that belonged to his father, and weeping bitterly. Tibbie Boden was not even present: Mrs. Warboys had taken her to the telegraph office to make sure the poor child saw nothing of the day's business.

It was the day of the showdown—the gunfight between Jake Monterey and Gaff Boden, two enemies whose hatred had grown so all-consuming, nothing but blood could satisfy it.

"Do something, Emile!" the teacher had said to the sheriff. "Put them both in jail till they cool off!" But even she knew that nothing would cool the incandescent hatred each man felt for the other. Nothing but blood would do that.

"Let us go out and watch, miss!" said Ollie West, and the teacher gave him such a clout that the lice in his hair slid down his collar.

"I seen enough gunfights to last me a lifetime, young man! If the male species came fitted with brains, they'd think better of spreading God's miraculous creation all over Main Street!" But that only set Peatie crying even harder. She flung herself down beside him, lifted her skirts, and blew his nose

232

for him on the hem of her petticoat. Class Three knew they were free to do as they liked, and many of them slipped away, then and there, unable to resist the shocking lure of Main Street.

Gaff Boden arrived on horseback from his ranch at half past ten. He was wearing a fob watch strung across his belly and his Sunday hat, and he had a rifle stowed in his saddle. Jake Monterey came on foot from the direction of the Waldorf Hotel. It was plain he had been drinking (although the Waldorf claimed to be temperance), and he was armed with Virgil's Colt .45.

From nowhere, Everett Crew stepped out in between them, hands upraised, still trying to talk them out of a rendezvous that could only end in tragedy. But all Jake Monterey could see was the rifle behind Boden's knee.

"See that? Always the unfair advantage!" he jibed. "You gonna let him use that? Look, you all! Bear me out! See? He's got a rifle. S'pose yer gonna sit up there on that horse and pick me off, is that it, Boden?"

Boden protested that he did not own a handgun, so Monterey would have to find himself a rifle.

"Someone give the bug a pistol!" bawled Monterey, reeling backward unsteadily on his heels.

Up in the loft of the livery stable, the ghouls of Class Three squirmed at the thought that two grown men could be reduced to this. Monterey began trying to pull Boden out of the saddle, prying the stirrups free of his boots, dragging on his leg. Boden pushed him away with the butt of the rifle, but one of his boots came half off in Monterey's hands. The horse took fright and began to turn around and around on the spot. Everett Crew snatched the reins.

"Well, if you're completely set on killing each other in front of your children," he hissed furiously, "at least give them something better than farce to remember you by!"

At that, the undignified tussle broke off, and Boden climbed down from his horse. A second pistol was produced, and the two men retreated to either end of Main Street. Up in the livery loft, the children of Class Three craned their necks but could no longer see either duelist. All they could hear was Jake Monterey's voice, whining and shrill, complaining about the pocket watch on Boden's watch chain. ". . . means to shelter his soft parts from my bullet, that's what that timepiece is fer!"

From the doorway of the schoolhouse, Fuller's voice threatened Boden: "You kill my paw and so help me, I'll come after you and fix you good!"

"Do something, Kookie!" Cissy whispered in her friend's ear, but Kookie's cleverness did not extend to miracles, and it would take nothing less than a miracle now to keep someone from getting killed.

Ollie West suddenly changed his mind about wanting to watch and shinned down the loft ladder. They could hear his boots banging as he ran, trying to get as far away as possible from Main Street.

Virgil Hobbs, raised in the Rockies, counted himself an expert on gunfights. He reminisced about the times when he had seen "three or four shootings in one afternoon." It was he who told Boden and Monterey how far apart to stand, reminded them to "keep shooting till yer chamber's empty." And when the upline freight train went by ten minutes early, Hobbs said, "Shame. We coulda used it for the signal if we'da been ready."

Then even Virgil Hobbs withdrew, and the whistle of the receding train howled up the street like some jackal scenting carrion. The very next thing that would happen would be when one of the men reached for his gun . . .

Another howl—thinner, reedier than the train whistle—came keening up the street, jolted by Ollie West's heavy-footed run. *"Come quick! Come quick!"* A dozen figures stepped out of a dozen doorways to keep him from running into the line of fire, for Ollie had plainly forgotten all about the gunfight. High over his head he wagged a buckled wafer of metal that had once been a cone or funnel.

It was Honey's hearing trumpet.

"She wouldn'ta heard it! She wouldn'ta heard it coming!" Ollie bawled, as if loudness were still needed for Honey's sake.

Miss Loucien emerged from the schoolhouse and ran to him, snatching the flattened trumpet out of his hands. "Where did you find it?" she asked. Monterey and Boden came running, same as everyone else, their petty melodrama eclipsed by a far greater tragedy. *"Where did you find it?"* Miss Loucien asked again.

"On the railway track! It mowed her down, miss! It must've! She didn't hear it coming, and it ran her down! *They killed Honey, Miss Loucien! They killed Honey!"*

16

KILLING TRAINS

There was not a trace of little Honey on the tracks. But then she had been so small, so light—like a golden puff-ball—that the RRR with its great cowcatcher could have swept her away without even feeling the jolt.

In an instant, the gunfight was forgotten, and with it whole months of petty wrangling, needling feud. Only room for one hatred now: a hatred so huge that it filled up the settlement like smoke from a brushfire, boiling between the houses, making the heart pound, the eyes water; making it hard to breathe. And everyone in its path was swallowed up. Hatred. The railroad had killed Honey. Now the railroad must be killed.

Its low-lying lines squirming across the prairie took on the dimensions now of a rattlesnake, to be pried off the grass and beaten to death with a stick. Suddenly everyone was running. Suddenly their hands were full of hoes, spades, wheel rimmers, door lathes, scaffolding from the half-finished bank. Hulbert Sissney grabbed up the window pole he had brought all the way from Arkansas and broke it trying to pry up a length of rail. It snapped off piece by piece until it was no more than a truncheon in his fist. Virgil Hobbs bent the tines of a pitchfork all the way over, and still the rail would not lift. Then Kookie Warboys came, dragging the blacksmith's metal hammer down from the forge. It was as large as he was, so he looked as if he were dancing some morose dance, dragging it through the dirt. His teacher took it from him and made to swing it, but it was too heavy even for her. The exertion was so great that the Indian choker burst from around her neck and fell to the ground.

The actor Crew took the hammer out of her hands. "I thought you were the one who wanted to hold this town together." He spoke it quietly and urgently in her ear.

Then Gaff Boden pulled the sledgehammer out of his grasp, and it continued on its way. It was as if Anger itself were being passed from hand to hand.

For the women, with their hoes and rakes and trowels, here was a new kind of gardening—in reverse—uprooting plate bolts and tie spikes, as the prairie rabbits had uprooted their potatoes and carrots.

Cold reason was at work, as well as rage. They attacked the line just south of the bend, so that the noon train would have no time to see the danger and apply its brakes. It would simply plow off the tracks and into the prairie, deprived of what it needed to keep going—just as Florence had been deprived this long, lonely year.

Each mind could see it—each mind reveled in the imagined destruction—the slow, sideways roll of the great locomotive as, pistons flailing, its wheels touched dirt and it pecked and went down, smashing its funnel, bleeding its steam and fire into the grass like a great vanquished dragon turned belly up and tumbling. How far would it plow on, flaying the turf, scorching the nettle beds, plucking down telegraph poles and wires like a whale fouled with harpoons and ships' rigging? And the carriages: would they smash free, like the separate vertebrae of a broken spine? Or hold fast and go chain dancing out across the prairie, clinging to the crashing train?

"*Stop!*"

It was Herman—face as white as milk, hands as thin and pale as Bible paper. "Don't do this," he said. He stood aloof, hands atwitch, hair shaggy, boots too big. Once so distinctive, in bowler hat and pea jacket, he had become simply another Florentine bum. When Virgil Hobbs threw a plate bolt at him, the impact raised a tuft of dust from Herman's clothing. But he persisted. "This is wrong! People will get hurt. Your quarrel's not with the passengers."

A sneering jeer erupted from the crowd hysterical with grief and frustration; the misery of a year's failure had been concentrated into one tragedy.

"They killed Honey!" yelled Jake Monterey.

"Don't you think you should find out first whether . . ." A shower of pebbles from several different hands forced Herman to turn his back. He began to walk away, upline.

"He'll warn the train! He'll flag it down!" shrieked the thin baker's wife, her cold hands full of railroad gravel.

"Bull won't stop for the likes of him," replied Mr. Fudd with a sneer. "He's one of us. Trains don't stop for

Florentines." And no one went after Herman; they were too intent on destroying the track: their violent toil an antidote to mental anguish.

Frank Tate slung a rope around one leg of the water tower and fastened it to the axle of his hearse. Then he stood at the horses' heads, exhorting them to pull, to strain in their traces. *"Timber!"* he cried. There was glee as well as spleen in his face as the leg detached and the water tower slowly toppled.

It smashed like a cup, its white planking looking as fragile as rice straw, and the residue of stale water inside, quilted with green algae, slopped out like bile among the feet of the wreckers. Despite the recklessness of the deed, the danger to those toiling in the tower's shadow, they only cheered Tate's effort. Violence had made them indifferent to danger, and they simply gathered up the smashed planks to make a bonfire over the wooden ties of the track.

"Herman's right!" said Tibbie Boden.

Hearing the news, she too had run down to the railway track from the telegraph office. But she did not go out onto the track. Ever since her ordeal at the hands of Fuller, she had been unable even to cross the railway line, such was her terror. Now she stood on the stoop outside the printing office, with Mrs. Warboys plucking at her sleeve, begging her to come away. But Tibbie stood her ground. "They're our people! The ones who came to the fair!"

Cissy, down on her knees, gouging at the earth to expose the plate bolts, suddenly saw the same picture as was in

Tibbie's head. It flashed on her inner eyes as sharply and fleetingly as a lantern slide. It was the woman with the turkey in a wicker cage. Another lantern slide, another face: the Mexican nun joining in the singing of "Soapsuds Over the Fence." The women sitting on the windowsills of the classroom. Did Cissy really want to see them flung out, like chicken feed from a bucket, just to be revenged on the Red Rock Runner?

"Kookie," she said to her friend. "What about the people on board?"

Kookie was busy trying to turn a tie on its side—a slab of wood that weighed five times as much as he did. Here was David about to kill Goliath. His mouth was set in a ferocious grimace of effort and malice.

"You saw that engineer," he puffed. "On picnic day! Tibbie tied to the line, and he wasn't even going to stop! He was ready to run clean over us!"

Cissy's gorge rose at the memory of it. Her hair bristled on her head. Even so. "This is Peter Bull, not that other one. Your maw scrubbed him in her bath!"

Kookie gave up his struggle with the tie, uttering a great gasp of strain and frustration. His Goliath came armor plated and wooden souled. It must die, all the same. This was the day when the Philistines must be destroyed.

"Kookie! How is this gonna solve anything?" Cissy was still willing to be convinced.

"They killed Honey, Ciss! Don't you care?" he yelled back at her. "They killed Honey!"

A pair of hands closed around Cissy's shoulders. It was the actor. Behind him, clinging to his jacket, stood Tibbie Boden. Crew's face was completely impassive now—deadpan almost alongside the grimacing of the wreckers. He saved exaggeration for the stage, gestures and posturing for when he was putting on an act. Now that he was in deadly earnest, his face was a virtual blank. "You reason with the children," he told Cissy. "I'll do what I can with the rest." He spoke as if he were talking to an adult.

Cissy and Tibbie joined hands. They looked toward Miss Loucien: fount of wisdom, tower of strength. But she, like red-haired Boudicca, was in full battle cry, her face barely recognizable where the red dust of digging had settled on streaming tears and congealed into a terra-cotta mask.

Cissy thought of the author Mr. Crupper, with his thick spectacles; the woman with the small children. She could picture them, dozing, shoulders joggled by the motion of the train, foreheads pressed white against the dirty coach windows. She thought of Mr. Griffin, the school inspector; the farmhands on their way to the fair . . .

A dozen boys went by, carrying a length of railway track, like pallbearers carrying a coffin. One was Nahum Warboys. Cissy ran up to him and heaved on the back of his dungarees. The yellow dust rag with which they had been patched tore under her hand. He looked around, startled. "There'll be children on board!" said Cissy.

Not waiting for a reaction, she ran to her father, who was down on his hands and knees, gouging up gravel with the stub of his broken window pole, teeth gritted, grunting out the words: "*That's* for pebbles. *That's* for sand. *That's* for wet soap!"

"Gonna be children on board, Poppy! You remember all those folks who came here. Be some of them, maybe. Ma, maybe."

Tibbie, following her lead, ran to Miss Loucien and began swatting at the blue and yellow behind. "All those people! We told 'em: 'Godspeed.' Didn't say we'd kill 'em!"

Kookie stood up to catch his breath, and a punch from Cissy Sissney sent him back down onto the seat of his pants. His nose began to bleed. He stared up at her in astonishment.

"*Trains don't die. It's the people on 'em!*" yelled Cissy.

Kookie put his hand to his nose. The palm filled up with blood. When he flicked it away in disgust, bright red drops fanned out and splashed on the gravel, on the grass. He was not fond of blood; it had always made him queasy. Through the pain in his nose and the squeamish queasiness, he heard Cissy's words like echoes in a cave: "*Trains don't die. Trains don't die. Trains don't die. It's the people . . .*"

For the first time, Loucien Shades remembered that she was the Florence schoolmistress, with seventeen children in her care. She looked around her and saw them, like small, indistinct figures at the wrong end of binoculars. Little by little, her head cleared. She clawed the dust off her cheeks. Only then was she able to see that Class Three was . . . withdrawing, child by child, from the wrecking party, that they were being persuaded away from Pandemonium. Soon they stood like captured pawns on the edge of a chessboard, watching their elders and betters vandalizing the railroad.

As dogged as a pupil reciting tables, Tibbie Boden kept up her barrage of words, never letting go of the teacher's skirt. "We told 'em 'Godspeed.' We never said we'd kill 'em. We told 'em 'Godspeed.' . . ."

When at long last silence settled, it was a silence so profound that a blackbird on the top of the silo began singing. The track lay like the epicenter of an explosion: five lengths of rail gone, a fire burning under the uprooted ties. One by one, heads turned toward the bend around which the RRR would come at noon, cradling ranchers and bakers, gunsmiths and nuns, fathers and boys, car attendants, turkeys, and grocers. Maybe not the same ones who had come to Florence Fair, drunk Lloyd Lentz's punch, squinted at slides of zebras, had their hair cut for free . . . but people just like them. And children, of course. There were bound to be children. There might even be a little girl with hair the color of honey.

Once again, in the mind's eye of sixty or seventy souls, the RRR careered off its rails and tumbled into the fuel heap of cattle dung, bursting its boiler, spilling its coal tender, breaking its articulated spine at every coupling.

"Sweet Jesus. What have we done?" said Monday Morning.

They tied ropes to each end of a loose rail and dragged it across the loosened gravel and dirt, hoping to harrow it, smooth it back into place. The men divided into teams of six and brought the other rails back on the run. But the ends had been so chewed and mangled that the rails refused to lie end to end. Monday Morning, who had coopered many a wagon wheel, swung his hammer on and on and on, but the tracks still looked mangled—like an assortment of swords half beaten into plowshares.

Mrs. Warboys organized the women into finding red items of clothing and taking them upline, to flag down the train. At least they would *try* to flag down the train, though they knew that Peter Bull would not stop if all the Pilgrim mothers and fathers were standing on the line.

Miss Loucien organized her children into scooping up bucketfuls of the scattered gravel and filling in the track bed again, so that the rails would not sag as the train went over them. It was futile; the hole was huge and there was no time. The replaced rails ran down into a great dip, then climbed back out; a six-inch gap separated them from the undamaged track—quite enough to derail a locomotive.

"Great God," said Charlie Quex. "What've we done?"

"Should I go and telegraph Glasstown?" said Pickard.

"It's too late," said the sheriff. "They'll have left Glasstown long ago."

"Anyway, they'd hang us all for 'tempted murder, if we said what we'd done," said Virgil, and spat to vent pent-up emotions.

"They'll hang us anyway," said Cissy's father. "If anybody dies."

They wondered now where the energy had come from to

do such damage: They could barely lift hand or foot or voice now, they were so weighed down by clammy dread. Poor little Honey. It was not much of a memorial: a train crash, Oklahoma's first rail disaster. Poor Honey. No one had so much as thought to tell her parents (who farmed a quarter three miles along the creek) that their daughter was dead.

The only noise was the clanging of Monday's hammer and his sobbing breath as he tried desperately to pound the rail rims back into shape. The six-inch gap still yawned. The dip beneath them still sagged downward, like Florence's hopes.

"If you're up there, Mr. Shades," prayed Miss Loucien, "look down on us and don't let this happen."

Nathaniel Rimm contemplated his great career: a failure and a traitor to his father's company, a misguided champion to these poor benighted people, a publisher who paid no royalties, a man with nothing to show for a year's hard labor but bankruptcy and a worn-out printing press.

"The printing press!" he shouted aloud. "The bed of the press!"

Monday Morning lurched to his feet; he was plainly exhausted. Nate took one look at him and knew he would not be able to help carry the press. But eleven other men looked expectantly at Rimm, scenting a plan. They ran with him to the printing office. They heaved the printing press off its base; they squeezed and bumped their way out of the narrow door again. Monday Morning was there, by then, to say, "I need this piece here—no, that one's a better length—quick!"

Soon the press lay on the ground like a carcass stripped by coyotes, and the heavy bars that made up its frame were being lugged to the trackside. Backward letters lay scattered about on the ground—dying words of a printing machine.

"Train's coming!"

The segments they inserted into the six-inch gap looked like a rotten tooth in a smile, but they fitted. More parts from the machine were squeezed under the rails to help them hold up when the train passed over them. As he pushed them home, Monday Morning felt the rail begin to throb with the approach of the RRR: His fingers were still under the rail when the RRR came around the bend, whistle blaring.

Peter Bull was hunched like a gargoyle over the throttle. Instinctively the crowds stepped back. Monday Morning rolled backward, head tucked between his knees. The locomotive hit the repaired track, and loose gravel sprayed outward, biting into Monday's back. The train listed slightly to the left. The pistons chattered, a pair of wheels lifted clear of the line. A shower of sparks burst from the makeshift repair. Vibration dislodged the bars under the rail.

In his cab, Peter Bull felt the tremor; his face said so. He saw the wreckage of the water tower, all swept away into a heap on his left. He darted a look at the gathered, dirt-stained, immobile crowd.

But that was all he had time to do.

Then the RRR was through Florence and rattling on down the track, its cars skipping one by one over the repaired rails, breaking their rhythmic clatter but continuing on their way in safety. The gaping crowd stood and stared after it. Even if they had seen, at the flickering windows, the faces of Mr. Griffin, Mr. Crupper, or the lady with the turkey, none would have had the strength to lift a hand in salutation.

As it was, the windows were mere empty rectangles of dirty glass. Neither strangers nor acquaintances peered out at Florence through the haloes of their wet breath. The RRR, from end to end, was entirely empty.

A small hand squirmed its way into Miss Loucien's limply hanging fist. "What happen', mith?" said a small, unmodulated voice.

"Nothing," said the teacher. "Thank God, nothing." Then the pupils of her lilac eyes expanded and shrank, within the duration of a heartbeat. She looked down at Honey, who was sucking the thumb of her other hand and regarding the crowd with mild curiosity. Her small face was dirty with the train tracks of tears long since cried and long since dried.

"Where did you spring from, hon?" said Miss Loucien. "Your ear trumpet . . ." She was afraid of being unable to make her voice come out loud enough for Honey to hear.

Honey looked at her feet, ashamed. "Wath my fault," she said. "'Cauthe I didn' know my Ten Commandmenth. When the 'thpector came into thchool. Wath my fault the train didn' thtop. Tho I put my nice 'rumpet on the line. For the train to cruth. Went to cry after. In my private plathe. But Mr. Herman found me and brung me back."

Miss Loucien looked around her. Sure enough, Herman

was standing in the shadow of the silo, like a bottle of milk on a step. "You put your ear trumpet on the railway line?" asked the teacher, as if in a dream.

"Yeth. 'Cauthe I was bad, and didn' know my Ten Commandmenth. My ma thayth you have to pay for thinning."

"Thinning?" said the teacher, mesmerized by the working of the little rosebud mouth.

"Sinning," said Lloyd Lentz, who had been deciphering the speech of the deaf for many years. "She said 'sinning,' Mrs. Shades. I believe Honey sacrificed her trumpet to the railway, because she thought she had let us down."

"Dear God," said Miss Loucien. "Let us down? How can you let people down who've sunk as low as us?"

17

THE TRAITOR

"Who's been using my key?" said Pickard Warboys, in puzzlement rather than anger. "Someone been in my office, using my Morse?"

But if anyone was about to own up, they were kept from it by the sound of hooves. Riders—strangers—were coming down Main Street from the north.

It had been an odd morning altogether, what with the aftershock of the previous day, long hours of work to restore the track to wholeness, the unspoken agreement to pretend nothing had happened. There had been oddly few freight trains—some problem with the rolling stock, perhaps, or some seasonal glitch in the demand for timber, coal, beef. Not only did trains not *stop* in Florence, they seemed to be shunning the place altogether.

Right now, the only noise to break the prairie silence was the sound of these horses' hooves clopping down Main Street. The sunlight glinting on a badge was as sharp as a hatpin. It coaxed people out of their houses to stand and stare. It was a U.S. marshal and his deputy.

So they were not, after all, to escape justice. Somehow,

news had gotten out of the attempted derailment.

The horses continued on down the street, as far as the railroad tracks, and picked their way mincingly over the straight and gleaming rails, their riders leaning sideways out of their saddles, clearly checking for sabotage. Did the marks of the rakes still show? Were there still sheared rivets lying amid the gravel to betray the crime that had almost happened? Those watching held their breath in suspense.

Emile Klemme had come sharply out of his office, and shut the door behind him, before the marshal introduced himself.

"Sheriff, I am Federal Marshal Haggar," said the rider wearing the badge. He was a lardy, bulging man. His flesh bulged softly through the buttons of his shirt, over the belt of his trousers. Even his forearms bulged out of his riding gloves, his head out of his hat. His words, too, oozed out of him like melting lard. "What happened to the water tower?" he asked, though patently he already knew. His look of disappointment said it all. His scene of the crime had been willfully cleaned up, his evidence tampered with.

"Fell down," said Virgil Hobbs. "Mighty big winds we get around these parts."

Marshal Haggar shot Virgil a look of malicious contempt. "You Pickard Warboys?"

Pickard, startled at hearing his name, let go of his wife's arm. "No. I am. Why?"

The marshal referred to his notebook. "Un'erstand you tampered with telegraphic equipment a while back. Caused damage to the overhead wires. Cut into them. That right?"

Pickard stood openmouthed. He began to protest his innocence: "My son was stranded in the middle of nowhere. He—"

But the marshal seemed to accept this as a confession of guilt. "A man's responsible for what his fry get up to. According to the information I've been given, there's a fine of fifty dollars outstanding on yuh. Daresay you'll be hearin' from yer employers about when to vacate yer premises." He turned back to Klemme. "Un'erstand you had a killing here yesterday. I'm here to apprehend the killer."

"No, no," Mrs. Warboys began, "you don't understand..." But her husband took her elbow and steered her to the edge of the crowd. Florence's only hope now lay in a solidarity of silence: Everyone must keep mum. Sheriff Klemme looked agitated past endurance. His fellow members of the FTCC pitied him, torn as he must be between his honest nature and loyalty to his neighbors and friends.

Meanwhile, Marshal Haggar referred to his notebook again. "Gaffrey Boden or Jake Monterey. Which of them ain't dead?" A startled murmur swept along the street. Boden? Monterey? "Word is there was a gunfight hereabouts. The law don't look kindly on gunfighting no more. It's clamping down," said Marshal Haggar, and his fat top lip clamped down, as if to demonstrate the rigor of the law. "These here ain't frontier days no more. Frontier law don't apply." His small eyes darted around the assembled faces, accusing them, in a general way, of mischief.

"There's obviously been a mistake—" Klemme started to say, without conviction.

"Amos! Ride and fetch Gaff Boden from his ranch," Pickard told his oldest son.

"No need. I was in the forge getting my horse shod." Gaff came sauntering down the road and stood in front of the marshal. "Something wrong, officer?"

A great holler went up for Jake Monterey to show himself, too, and he emerged from the baker's shop, eating a doughnut.

"There's been no duel here, marshal," said Nate Rimm, wiping inky hands on an inky rag: He did not want his hands to betray his nervousness. "You must have been misinformed."

The marshal and his deputy were unconvinced. They clearly suspected collusion. "How do I know these bucks are who they say they are? You folks know it's a crime to cover up a felony?"

"Check the graveyard," he was told. "Nobody has died here. We settle our differences amicably here in Florence. Ask the sheriff."

And when Sheriff Klemme vouched for Boden being Boden, Monterey being Monterey, there was nothing the marshal could do but turn his horse around and ride out of town. "I heard about you Florentines!" he called darkly, by way of a parting shot.

The people in the street did not disperse. Their dizzying relief at their narrow escape did not last long. They sympathized with Pickard about the crippling fine.

"It's not the fine, so much," said Pickard, his face ashen with shock. "I just ain't got that. You can't pay what you ain't got. No. I'm out of a job, that's what. Out of a job. Out of a home. And there's no one going to let me operate a telegraph office between here and Alaska. Tampering, huh! Tampering!"

"So," said Hulbert Sissney, from the door of his shop. "Who's the traitor?"

No one was shocked by the word: Everyone had been holding it in their mouths like a hot stone, all the while the marshal was in town.

"When we gave out the handbills," said Herman, "they knew we were going to be on the train. They were expecting us."

"Someone snitched to the marshal about our gunfight," said Monterey to Boden. They shared their mutual outrage like a cigarette, passing it between them. Someone had informed on them to the law. Someone had tried to get the survivor of the fight locked up, even hanged. Someone had told of the town's attempt to derail the train. While they had worked to repair the railroad, some traitor had used Pickard's Morse box to summon a federal marshal down from Glasstown.

But who?

Could it be Herman, the disapproving Mormon? No! Herman had been thrown bodily off a speeding train, in the cause of promoting Florence. Could it be that Nathaniel Rimm had, all along, been in the employ of his peevish father—a stalking-horse, biding his time until the town committed a sin for which it could be evicted en masse? Never! No one could read a single edition of the *Morning Star* and think the traitor was Rimm. Could it be the banker, trying to boost the value of his real estate by clearing the town? Could it be Lloyd Lentz, because he was not of the Christian faith? Every man moved a little away from his neighbor. Who? Who was the Judas in their Garden of Gethsemane? Who was the Benedict Arnold in their war? An outsider, surely, and that left only . . .

"I saw Everett Crew come out of the telegraph office yesterday," said Sheriff Klemme, a terrible saddened solemnity clouding his sober features.

It was like a weather vane moving around. Everett Crew turned, in the space of a single sentence, from prized guest to snake in the grass, from local celebrity to prime Enemy of the People.

"Everett Crew sold us down the river! Everett Crew sent for the federal agents!" Amos and Ezra Warboys came clattering into the schoolhouse and set it chattering like a chicken coop. The children dropped their slates. The teacher stood, pastel chalk raised, in the process of demonstrating how to sketch from life a human head.

The head was Crew's.

Crew rose from the high stool where he had been sitting as artists' model. His face fell into a disbelieving grin. He began to shake his head—"No, no"—and then, when he saw the mood of the boys, and the baying mob behind them, slid off the stool and moved backward through the side door. Hand moving automatically to his injured leg, he began to run. The mob streamed through the classroom, some of them jumping over the pews to reach him quicker, grinding their dirty boots on the white satin, breaking slates with a noise like pistol shots.

"Let's get him!" said Kookie to the Ponca Pirates, and then again to Cissy: "Let's get him!"

But Cissy did not get up. Something kept her from getting up; some fatigue or recollection of the day before. She put one arm around Honey and the other around Tibbie Boden, and sat tight.

The hue and cry chased Crew clear around the building and up Main Street, where he dodged through the swinging door of Charlie Quex's barbershop: "Keep them off me, Charlie!"

Charlie's only answer was to swing at him, two-handed, with an enamel basin. Crew ducked and kept running— through the shop and out the back. The mob followed after, breaking the barber's chair and cracking a mirror in their haste, spilling a vat of Quex's Patent Lemonade as they chased Crew out through Charlie's living quarters at the back of the shop. And all the while, the reasons that damned Crew for a traitor piled up in their heads.

"We shot him, so he wanted to get back at us!" shouted Marlene Bell. "That's why he did it!"

"He's an actor. Course he could pretend nice!" said Fred Stamp.

Back in the schoolhouse, Loucien Shades did not move. She did not join in the chase. She simply stood, chalk in hand, looking at the likeness on the paper in front of her. As the shouting faded into the distance, toward the railway track, she went to her coffin-bed, with its array of integral drawers and cubbyholes, and drew out her pearl-handled pistol. Checking to see it was loaded, she took aim and fired.

Even Honey jerked in her seat at the noise. All three girls got up and fled. The pastel portrait of Everett Crew's head was thrown backward, along with the church lectern on which it was resting. It skidded across the schoolroom floor, a single sheet of paper with a scorched black hole directly through the large, brown eye.

The mob caught up with Crew down by the silo, where he shut himself in and bolted the door on the inside. They could hear his breath rasping as he sank to the floor behind the locked door. The boys and some of the men began to beat on the metal walls of the silo with sticks and tools.

"Ken get him outa there soon enough with an axe," said Taffy Jones.

"Let's lynch him!" Fuller's voice was high pitched and whooping—the voice he used when he was out of control. "Let's string him up!"

"Ah, for gosh sakes." Hulbert Sissney sounded weary past all redemption. "Let's just put him on a stage outa here."

"Let's throw him under the train!" cackled Virgil Hobbs.

And they might have done it, too. But as Taffy bent and

buckled the silo door with a pickaxe, the *wang-wang*ing of the rails heralded the late passage of the noon downline passenger train. As on two hundred other days, all eyes were drawn to the great grinning grid of the cowcatcher coming around the bend.

There was Peter Bull, his face a mask of soot and distaste. There was the anvil-shaped pall of steam, the screaming whistle, the golden pistons pumping. There were the cars, heeling over one by one as they rounded the bend.

Then the giant wheels were being overtaken by their own steam, the pistons pausing like grasshopper legs before a great leap. There were the cars shuffling into one another, softly rebounding. The Red Rock Railroad locomotive had drawn to a halt.

"Florence and Bison Creek!" called a voice from inside, and every door flew open.

18

PASSENGERS

First to step down from the train was a young man with a guitar and a Gladstone bag. Heat had plastered his hair to his head, but for half a dozen blond curls, like parings from a bar of butter. As he touched ground, he sank to his knees and lifted up his hands in prayers of thanksgiving. Florence's church minister had at last arrived.

Another passenger descended, and promptly tripped over him. Picking herself up, and lifting the pince-nez that hung around her neck, she peered around her at the crowd of gaping, disheveled Florentines. "May March," she said, lighting on Gaff Boden as the most respectably dressed. She extended a hand, the wrist arched at a most refined angle, and repeated, "May March. I understand that you require a qualified schoolmistress. To whom should I present myself in this regard?"

"But we have a schoolmarm," chirped Kookie, overhearing. "We have Miss Loucien. Don't we, Cissy? We have a school—"

But Cissy was not listening. She had just seen, embraced in steam from the locomotive, like a ghost wreathed in mists, her own dear mother.

Hildy was wearing a bonnet and coat of her mother's; it had made her momentarily hard to recognize. But now both Cissy and her father were running, Hulbert flinging his game leg clumsily out ahead of him in a crablike sprint, Cissy hitching up her hand-me-down dress. Hildy, meanwhile, stood taking stock of the changes that had befallen the town since her leaving.

"The bank's still not up, then" was the first thing she said, unsmiling, pinch-faced, sallow.

"You came back!" cried Cissy, crashing up against her mother, burying her face among the loops and buttons and clasps of her mother's old-fashioned clothing. The shape of the pocket Bible was still there, hard as a snuffbox, hidden in her underwear.

For all his haste, Hulbert Sissney stopped short of embracing his wife. Her face did not invite it. There was an awkwardness among the three of them: the same old awkwardness. "Is your mother well?" he asked, like a polite stranger.

Hildy ignored the question. "Read in the *Tribune* about the boycott," she said, shooting a glance at Cissy, defensive, almost resentful. "Leastways a neighbor read it out to us, knowing we had . . . kin down this way. Had to come back, didn't I? Or you two would just let the opportunity slip: I know you."

"Boycott?" said Hulbert foolishly. His brain was not fully in gear. He had just noticed how the streaks of gray in his wife's hair had disappeared—stained with boot polish. His thoughts were all taken up wondering whether it had been done for him, to please him. "What boycott?"

The passengers who had attended Florence Fair had made their feelings plain in a dozen letters, a stack of telegrams, and several personal visits to the offices of the Red Rock Railroad. A manufacturer of umbrellas had been so impressed by his sister's description of the town that he was eager to open a factory there. As he told "Red Rock" Rimm, he naturally needed the guarantee of a railroad station.

But every polite letter, every genteel approach, every impassioned plea, had been met with a terse rejection. "Red Rock" Rimm had set his face against Florence, he said, and the passenger was not born who could make him turn around.

When his solemn declaration appeared in the *Glasstown Daybreak*, the passengers were enraged. They did not like to read that their wishes and opinions counted for nothing. They had drawn up a petition, only to see it ignored. Now they declared an ultimatum: Either "Red Rock" stopped his trains at Florence or they would not buy another ticket, dispatch another load, invest another cent in the three Rs.

"To hell with them!" he had told his shareholders at the annual general meeting, and ostentatiously ripped up the petition. "I fired my own son over this business!" he boasted. "Do you think I'm gonna let a bunch of picnickers and a roll of toilet paper change my mind?"

He had expected the shareholders to applaud his

courageous stand. But they only looked back coldly, rustled their papers, and talked together in low voices during coffee.

News of the boycott had been picked up by the national press—a national press read in Washington and on the eastern seaboard. Public opinion was all on the side of the Florentines, plucky, suffering little frontiersmen who were risking their all to establish the territory of Oklahoma. Were they to be trampled flat by one man and his greedy pride?

Soon, "Red Rock" Rimm had been leaned on by so many people, from such great distances, that he felt like a man being pelted by asteroids from outer space.

Up in his cab, Peter Bull sat, eyes front, his bottom lip folded almost over the tip of his nose. Allowing just enough time for the minister, the schoolmistress, the triumphant campaigners, the new settlers, the news reporters to get down from his train, he heaved on his whistle cord and unwound the brake handle, never once looking around, never once acknowledging the greetings shouted up at him—"Hi, Peter!" "Thanks, Peter!" "Good to see you again, Peter!" Memory filled his head with the smell of carbolic soap and talcum. He wiped it away with the back of a coal-blackened hand.

The heady excitement, the arrival of so many new faces, the spread of the good news, had set a holiday mood. Children and adults alike sauntered through the sunshine, down to the creek or up Golden Ridge, chattering, laughing, looking back at the tracks from time to time, still hardly able to believe the train had stopped. The new minister, feeling that perhaps he ought to say a word or two, perched on a rock and suggested a prayer. It was a popular idea.

"O Lord, let us give thanks this day for the railroad!" intoned the young man in a swooping voice obviously kept specially for the purpose. "For is not the word of God very like unto the railroad tracks? Keeping Christian folk on the straight and narrow? But let us remember, too, brethren, how the great iron horse, with its smoky nostrils and its burning fiery furnace, is also like unto a morsel of hell! It speaks to us, in its whistle, of wicked, far-off cities full of sin and of greed and of ambition! Let us recall, O Lord, that fine song 'The Iron Horse,' and give us strength to brace ourselves against all the sin and evil and temptations that will come to this town aboard the railroads. . . ."

He struck a chord on his guitar and was clearly threatening to sing "The Iron Horse" at any moment, when he noticed that his "congregation" was scowling at him. Some were even drifting off. Mr. Fudd the toolmaker put a fatherly hand on the youth's shoulder and gave it a squeeze. "That there ain't our all-time favorite song, Reverend."

The new minister blushed scarlet. "But I—"

"Don't worry 'bout it, son. You'da had to be here, this last year, to understand."

Inside his silo, Crew was forgotten. He tried to unbolt the door, but the blows of the pickaxe had buckled the metal latch, and he was well and truly kenneled inside. So he climbed the metal rungs to the platform overhead and sat watching the RRR steam away across the landscape, the people of Florence celebrating their redemption.

"How all occasions do inform against me," he said to himself, softly, bitterly, under his breath. He could see the livid red flag of Loucien Shades's hair unloosed, could see Sheriff Klemme offering her his arm solicitously, passing her a handkerchief to dry her tears, steering her away from the noisy celebrations. "It is not nor it cannot come to good," muttered Crew, though the quotation did not exist that could do justice to the feelings inside him.

"I wish you would not distress yourself so, Mrs. Shades . . . Loucien!" Sheriff Klemme transferred his hand from her elbow to her waist. "You must know that since you came to Florence, you have come to mean more to us than simply a schoolteacher!" Even so, he did not reject her resignation. Miss Loucien had quit the moment she heard tell of the teacher newly arrived.

"I don't have a qualification to my name, Emile honey," she had said. "Class Three deserves better. I'm glad they've got theirselves a proper schoolmarm. Don't know where it leaves me, though. I don't exactly got savings to fall back on." Fright and unhappiness vied for possession of her face. "Nowhere to go and no money to get there, that's me." Miss Loucien looked ten years older since the train had come to a halt.

"Mrs. Shades . . . Loucien." Sheriff Klemme steered her aside from the path, into the shade of a large, mossy rock. Bison Creek bubbled past a few feet below, dark with trout.

Passenger pigeons were crooning to themselves on the ledges overhead. "There is really no need for you to go anywhere."

"I got to earn a living, hon." She frowned, preoccupied, barely listening. Some grief greater than either unemployment and homelessness seemed to have stolen all her energy.

Sheriff Klemme, by contrast, was exultant. "But that's what I've been saying, Loucien—my dear. Only a widow or an unattached lady needs to struggle alone and lonesome in this life! No friend of mine would ever want for a roof over her head or food on the table."

Loucien Shades was startled out of her gloomy train of thought. "Emile! Are you proposing to me?"

Klemme's face was a bubble rising toward the surface, a trout mouthing after bread. A bee buffeted the distinguished gray of his temples and he flapped at it irritably. Whether he had been going to propose more formally—whether he had been going to propose at all—he was prevented from going on by a squeal and a giggle. A sprinkling of pebbles from overhead made them both look up. They were in time to see Marlene Bell scramble to her feet, both hands full of strawberries, and call out as she ran along the rocks: *"Miss Loucien's marrying the sheriff! Listen up, everybody! Miss Loucien and the sheriff are getting hitched!"*

Emile Klemme was annoyed. He called after Marlene to come back. But Miss Loucien only laughed and laid a hand on his arm. "I came here to be a mail-order bride, honey. Cain't pretend it was my first ambition in life, but a woman's gotta eat. . . . I liked myself better for teaching school instead.

264

But now that's gone, and that skunk Cr—" She broke off and began again. "You've been a good friend to me since I got here, Emile. I think . . . if you think . . ." She looked around her at the verdant little spot, the distant shine of the silo roof. "I think I'd be honored to marry you."

19

CHANGING NAMES

Two telegrams arrived in Florence the day before the wedding. The first was from the Bright Lights Theater Company, and it was for Everett Crew. His brother had completed a successful winter season in the East and was once again touring. He was eager for Everett to rejoin the company.

Everett had been transferred from the silo to the town jail while it was decided whether or not to lynch him. If they did, the new minister might get agitated. Besides, it was generally held that Crew's treachery, for all he had *meant* to deliver Florence into the hands of her enemies, had not succeeded.

So the FTCC decided not to lynch him but to ship him out. He could catch the noon train south while the rest of the town was at the wedding. That way no one would have to look at his perfidious face ever again. They felt they could afford to be lenient.

They could afford to be all kinds of things they had never been before, because Florence had won.

Nathaniel Rimm was oddly discontented without knowing why. All day long he sat staring out the printing office window, a copy of Mark Twain's *Roughing It* open but unread on his lap. The gentle, metallic chink of Monday Morning typesetting the special celebration issue of the *Morning Star* was no more than the clinking of ice in a drink. He barely noticed when it stopped—only when Monday came back in at the door. "Where have you been?"

"I went to catch Klemme before he departed for his honeymoon."

"You'll see him at the wedding tomorrow, won't you?"

"Oh, this was legal business." He seemed both embarrassed and exultant, but Nate Rimm was not a man to pry, so he did not. After a time, Monday could not keep his news to himself another moment. "I have been changing my name!" he exclaimed.

The book fell between Rimm's knees. "Oh!"

"A name's the jug they pour you into. I just changed the shape of the jug."

"So . . . who are you now?"

The typesetter hesitated, partly out of shyness, partly because it would be the first time he had spoken his new name. "Sunday," he said at last. "I changed my name to Sunday Morning."

It was then that Nathaniel Rimm knew what had been gnawing away at his peace of mind all day. He pumped his partner's hand up and down in congratulation. "Monday—Sunday, I mean—hold the front page. I have to write a new editorial!"

AN OLIVE BRANCH

Your editor has a boon to ask of the people of Florence.

Mr. Clifford T. Rimm, president of the Red Rock Railroad Company, has become—against his will—chief benefactor of this community. In our hour of victory, may we not extend the hand of friendship and be reconciled?

"Red Rock" Rimm (as we have come to speak of him) is a man both proud and obstinate. I can vouch for this, through lifelong acquaintance. But then can we say any different of ourselves? We too have proved proud and obstinate, and should not condemn such qualities in another.

At the beginning of May, Mr. Clifford T. Rimm swore an oath in the presence of an attorney-at-law that he would never allow his trains to stop at the town of Florence. Shall we gloat that we have forced him to break that oath? Shall we triumph over him like David over Goliath? Shall we make of him a pledge breaker?

I say we have it in our power to do better—to meet pride with good grace, to disarm hatred with an olive branch of peace. . . .

". . . You want to change the name of the *town*?" cried Sunday Morning, reading over Nate Rimm's shoulder.

"Why not? 'A rose by any other name,' et cetera . . . We

didn't choose the name 'Florence.' Some railway clerk in Guthrie chose it. Why not 'Red's Crossing' or 'Saturday' or 'Bison Creek' or 'Ethel'?"

"Ethel?"

"Well, maybe not Ethel . . . But something—anything!—as a peace offering to my father. To show him we understand the importance to a man of his sworn word! To help him keep his pride."

Sunday Morning puckered his brow. It was many years since he had promised himself: If ever he found himself a true place in the world, he would change his name. That had been a kind of oath. His mind began, of its own accord, to play with words. "How about 'Olive'? Then one day they will end up calling this the Olive Branch Line!" Nate looked quite foolishly grateful. Sunday laid an understanding hand on his shoulder. He, too, had been estranged from his family for too long, and knew the importance of a father and son staying in touch. "I must get over to the telegraph office. Inform my wife that she is married to a different name. You still have to convince the rest of the town about that name, of course." He paused in the doorway. "I may tell her it's time. My wife, I mean. Time to come here, I mean. A wedding in town is inclined to make a lonesome man lonelier. Should I? Do you think I should?"

"High time," said his partner. "I'm looking forward very much to meeting all the other Mornings." And Sunday beamed with pleasure.

—•—

In the room behind the general store, Cissy and Hulbert Sissney sat across the table from one another while Hildy stood at the window, holding up a lantern slide of a zebra. She had found it as she cleaned, flicking outrage around the house with all the same old vigor and energy. "It's some stripy brand of an animal. Never saw the like! 'Tain't natural. What's it doing here?"

"Oh, that," said Hulbert, winking at his daughter. "That there's a horse in pajamas. A new line. Pajamas for horses. They reckon soon all the cowboys will be wanting them. So I ordered a hundred pair."

Cissy laughed, despite herself—despite the feeling that she had had all day of something amiss, something vital left undone. Her mother's voice came baying after her as, suddenly, she knocked over her chair and ran outdoors: *"That's right. Break the furniture. Go gallivanting off when the supper's all but on the table! Thanking you very much, miss! Is that what they teach you at that school of yours? And what happened to the hem of my dress, that's what I want to know?"*

Cissy ran all the way to the telegraph office—and then felt foolish and took her hand off the door handle. In the upper windows of the house, pieces of Miss Loucien's wedding dress (which Mrs. Warboys had offered to make) loomed whitely, like ghosts. Cissy was just turning away when Mrs. Warboys came to the door and turned the sign to "Closed." She at once greeted Cissy and asked her in. "Stay for supper, sweetheart? Eight can always stretch to nine. How's your dear ma? Musta missed you something fearful while she was away visiting." Dear Mrs. Warboys.

"I just need Kookie," said Cissy. "I need him."

Kookie emerged, looking so clever he could have charged for it. Cissy felt better just for seeing him. "I been thinking," she said.

"Is that why yer hair's mumping up like that?"

"I been thinking all day," said Cissy, smoothing her hair absentmindedly. "And it's not true. Mr. Crew's not the traitor."

Kookie's face closed down like a window sash at the mention of Everett Crew. "Supper's on the table. I gotta go."

Cissy caught hold of his sleeve. "I keep remembering things! How he tried to stop the gunfight. How he thought up the idea of the handbills. How he was at the fair!"

"Just putting on a show. He's ferever putting on a show. That's what his kind does."

"But he helped to hijack the train! He *knew* about Florence Fair: Why didn't he warn 'Red Rock' Rimm about the fair? He had plenty of time!"

"Wasn't ready to show his hand. . . . Just 'cause he said once you had a good memory. Just 'cause you took a fancy to him, don't mean to say he ain't a snake. Your trouble is, Cissy, you're sen-tee-men-tal. All girls are." He said it with perfect certainty, eyes half shut, chin tilted upward, arms crossed.

Cissy gave a gasp of anger and stamped on the toe of his boot. *"And your trouble is, Habakkuk Warboys, you think you know it all, so you stopped thinking altogether, years back!"*

Their raised voices brought Pickard Warboys to the

271

door, fork in hand. He was astonished to see his son hopping about on one foot, throwing cusses at the storekeeper's girl, who, with tears streaming down her face, was cupping handfuls of water out of the horse trough and pitching them at Habakkuk. The telegraphist was just intervening when the tink of the Morse machine alerted him to a new incoming message. Wiping his mouth on his sleeve, he went to transcribe it, pleading for quiet, as the rest of his family burst from the table and the baby began to cry.

It was a telegram for Sheriff Klemme, short and to the point: ARRIVING TOMORROW. DEPART ARKANSAS CITY 5 A.M. LETITIA, JANE, AND EM. Wedding guests, presumably. Relations.

There would be a lot more telegrams like this, Pickard mused: people announcing their arrival in Florence: Sunday Morning's wife and children, Mr. Fudd's sister, more mail-order brides, perhaps, more settlers. . . . It was just a pity he would not be there to receive them. Unless the telegraph company relented, Pickard would be out on the street with his wife and eight children. The townspeople had all chipped in a dollar to pay his fifty-dollar fine, and he loved them all for it with a hot, smarting passion. But surely nothing could save his job or keep a roof over his head.

Pickard collared Kookie and told him to deliver the telegraph to the sheriff—"And quick, too, you little savage!"

Miss Loucien had no guests arriving by train for her wedding. But she did not lack for people to fill her side of the church.

The previous night she had spent at the bakery, as a guest

of the Lagerlöfs: "You can hardly get out of bed, and dress, in the same place as you are getting married," said Harriet Lagerlöf delightedly. (She and her husband could at last stop reproaching themselves because Sven had broken Miss Loucien's heart.)

Arriving at the church aboard Frank Tate's hearse, Loucien Shades took one look inside and said, "Dan-*dee*-dy, Frank! I got more friends than Noah had animals!"

The room that normally served as Class Three's class-room had been transformed, with tansy and daisies. On a table by the door, where once Class Three had learned to bone a goose and clean a rifle, stood the wedding presents—jars of jam, hand-stitched carpet slippers, a lantern slide of the Eiffel Tower, a first edition of Crupper's *History of the Cherokee Strip*. There were two pairs of crocheted gloves, an almond-cream wedding cake, a table lamp. The banker, Mr. Guthrie, had ordered in three dozen oysters, all the way from Houston. The bride's hair flickered maple-leaf-red against the white of her dress, as if with strength of emotion.

The young minister arrived from the Waldorf Hotel, scratching and pale from a sleepless night among the bed-bugs. Nervous, he kept reading through the wedding service; this would be the first he had ever conducted. Only one thing was missing to make the day perfect.

"Anybody seen the groom?" called Gaff Boden. There was a ripple of laughter.

"Maybe Sunday's got him changing his name to Wednesday!"

"Maybe them white-footed mice have come back and

they're chasing him around town!"

"Maybe he wants to stay and make sure Everett Crew gits on that train!"

The bride's smile slipped.

The children in the congregation were restless. They could see no reason why this marriage was necessary, why they had to have a new teacher at all, why things could not go on just the same for Class Three. Besides, the bride's nervousness was starting to infect them, like horses in a lightning storm. From opposite ends of the same coffin-pew, Kookie and Cissy avoided looking at each other. Kookie knelt up to watch the door.

"I saw some people sitting on his stoop when we passed," offered Charlie Quex. "Woman and two kids."

"That'll be the guests who telegraphed," said Pickard. "I'd best go and show them the way to the church."

"Maybe Crew killed the sheriff in a jealous rage!" said Kookie, and his mother smacked the back of his thigh.

Just then, the door opened. The woman who looked inside was embarrassed to find herself the target of fifty pairs of eyes. "I beg your pardon," she said in a church whisper, "but is there a Mr. Emile Klemme here? I went to his address, but there seemed to be no one . . ." Around the folds of her skirts, two small children pushed their way into church like sheep breaking through a hedge.

"Is Daddy here, Mommy?" asked the girl.

The congregation did not answer the woman's question. It simply went on looking. Unnerved by these blank and staring faces, she struggled to explain herself. "I'm Mrs. Klemme, you see. His wife? Came in on the early train. From Arkansas City? I thought . . . I mean this is Florence, isn't it?"

The church hall—the very building, or so it seemed— gave a great groan, as if its timbers would spring apart, its roof beams tumble.

"Dang train," was all the bride said.

It was a common story among the new prairie towns. A man told his family to wait until he could send for them, until he had established himself, until he had saved up a little money, until he had built a home for them all. But finding he liked the single life, finding he could pass for a bachelor again, finding some prairie face prettier than the one he had married, the man put off sending for his family. Finally, he put off even thinking about them.

"I got Emile's address from the railroad company. I'm sure I have it right!" said Mrs. Klemme, more and more flustered by the thought that she was delaying a wedding service. She fumbled in her purse for a tattered piece of paper bearing the triple-R letterhead.

"Your husband has dealings with the railroad?" Gaff Boden asked, taking the letter from her and looking it over.

"Oh yes! Many years now. He used to do all its legal work. A great personal friend of the chairman there, Mr. Rimm. . . ."

Emile Klemme, forewarned by his wife's telegraph, and fore-seeing public disgrace, had fled aboard the Watonga stage-coach. Florence's doge was gone, its sheriff, its legal man, its chairman of the FTCC. Its bridegroom.

Mrs. Warboys hurried Mrs. Klemme and the children away to somewhere quiet, somewhere private, where she could break the bad news.

The church stirred, awash with whispers:

". . . did he think he could get away with it?"

". . . *that's* why he always sent his mail by the stage . . ."

". . . poor woman . . ."

". . . kinder if he'd died . . ."

". . . ought to be horsewhipped!"

"Back in the Rockies we tarred and feathered a man . . ."

"I . . . think we done that actor man a terrible wrong . . ."

The bride stood stock-still, immobile, her face toward the cross on the wall, her bouquet of wildflowers dangling in one hand. Pickard Warboys suddenly thought to get her a chair. The noise of the feet squeaking across the floor made everybody start. But Miss Loucien did not choose to sit down.

Kookie got up and moved along the pew, tripping over his brothers' and sisters' feet, making them, like ten in a bed, move up so that he could sit down beside Cissy. "You were right," he blurted. His spiky hair made him look as if horror had stood it on end. "Klemme made out it was Crew, and we all believed him. The sheriff was the traitor all along!" He had never learned the art of keeping his voice down.

The young minister, cheeks red with panic, scampered to the lectern like a squirrel bolting up a tree. Someone had to break the spell, and with all the recklessness of youth, he took it upon himself to do it.

"What has just happened here," he said, his voice breaking like a schoolboy's, "what has just happened, I know you are all thinking, is a shameful, diabolical thing. Miss Loucien . . . though I don't know her myself, of course . . . is clearly a fine woman—one who deserves no such slight! One who deserves—ah—" His fist struck the lectern before the young reverend discovered that he did not know what to say. "And I say . . ." he said, racking his brain for something chivalrous, "and I say that this town is full of men who would be honored to—ah—*do better* by her!"

There was a startled silence. Still jarred by the awfulness of what had happened, the congregation misunderstood.

Amos Warboys was the first to his feet, but his brother Ezra was not far behind. "I'll marry you, miss!"

Soon all the boys in Class Three had risen from their seats, from six-year-olds to sixteen-year-olds. "I will, miss!" "I'll marry you!"

Frank Tate, his top hat under his arm, its crepe band bleached almost white by the prairie sun, wore his most solemn expression, as he too rose to his feet. Cantankerous old Virgil Hobbs jumped onto his pew.

Kookie glanced sideways at Cissy who, gulping down her own selfish feelings, nodded, granting him permission to stand up. Peatie Monterey went to do the same but was pinned down by his elder brother with a "Don't be 'diculous; she's a grown woman; she don't wanna marry a tadpole." Then Fuller licked the palms of both hands, flattened his hair, and stood to attention. His father, too, got to his feet at the selfsame moment; eyeing each other, father and son pushed out their chests like pouter pigeons competing for a mate.

Honey, too, stood up, being only five and hazy about the qualifications for a bridegroom.

When Hulbert Sissney, caught up in the excitement of the moment, put his hands on his knees and began awkwardly to rise, his wife tugged him back down. "Sit down, Hulbert! What are you thinking of? You already got a wife!" There was a look of pure fear on her face.

Mr. Guthrie, the banker, and Nathaniel Rimm and Sunday Morning also rose to their feet—if not to propose, then to express the strength of their regret. The young minister was reduced to silent wonder at the affection this woman had inspired. He felt excluded by it and wondered for the first time how he would manage to teach these people anything they did not already know about neighborly love.

Away across the prairie, the approaching Red Rock Runner sounded its whistle, as if it too were willing to make amends.

Miss Loucien turned and saw her array of bridegrooms and tears appeared, like condensation, on her cheeks. She gave a big barking sob of laughter. "Gosh sakes. I never knew there was so many eligible men in Florence! Thank you. Reckon the Queen of Sheba never had a better choice of men . . ." She tossed her bouquet to Honey, who caught it within the horn of her shiny new hearing trumpet: a cornucopia of prettiness. "But I won't put any one of you to the trouble of a wedding today," said Loucien Shades. "It's only right that this thing has happened. I shouldn'ta been here in the first place. Marrying ain't a thing you ought to do to keep a roof over your head, or food in your belly. There's only one reason for marrying, and that's love. There's only one man I loved hereabouts. And it wasn't Emile Klemme. That's why I won't be spilling tears for what's happened. I deserved it." She paused to dry the tears she was so sure she was not crying.

"Hildy! You bring my newspaper?" hissed Hulbert.

Hildy gaped at him. "You wanna read the newspaper? In church?"

But Hulbert had already turned to Cissy. "Find me some paper, kitten. A piece of paper!"

The whisper traveled along the satin-lined pews like dominoes felling each other until it reached Herman. He looked toward the Sissneys and pulled out his pocket Bible. It passed from hand to hand, back along the same route. Hulbert snatched the pencil from behind his ear. Those nearby gave a whisper of horror as he tore out the Bible's flyleaf, brittle as the rice paper on a macaroon, and, licking the pencil lead repeatedly, wrote a handful of words. Then, pressing it into his daughter's hand, he told her: "My legs ain't fast enough. You take it, kitten. Quick. Get this to Everett Crew. Before the train goes."

Miss Loucien was saying, "It does me good to see how many kind gentlemanly souls I'm acquainted with." She picked up the youngest of her bridegrooms in her arms, little Honey. "I thank you all for the kind offers. But I guess I'll just go home—I mean . . ." She looked around her at the room that had served for nearly a year as her home and church and workplace, all three. "I guess I'll just get my things together and make room for a proper teacher." She glanced across at the newcomer, who was sitting in a severe, undecorated bonnet near the door. The children all looked around, too, and then back at her, like condemned prisoners pleading for a reprieve. "You're very lucky, fellers, in Miss May March. Nothing in the world so useful as a proper, qualified schoolmarm. So you take care of this one, you hear? She's got even better things to tell you than I did. . . ."

Cissy ran, and Kookie, bound to her by curiosity, came charging after her. "Where are we going?" he asked.

"To stop the train!"

"Why? I mean, why *this* time?"

Cissy unfolded the brittle note as she ran and glanced down at the seven words scrawled on it:

KLEMME RUMBLED. WEDDING OFF. SHE LOVES YOU.

"How should I know?" said Cissy with a shrug. "Cain't read, can I?"

They ran past the half-built bank and the livery stable. They passed the telegraph office, where the Morse machine was tapping merrily away. They jumped the horse trough and skirted tools lying outside the forge. They ran around the empty silo that would soon be filling with the grain of

280

Olive's first harvest. They passed the big new sign gleaming with wet paint: Herman's finest work. It read:

OLIVE TOWN STATION
(FORMERLY FLORENCE)
GLASSTOWN–GUTHRIE LINE,
RED ROCK RAILROAD COMPANY

The train stood embroiled in its own steam, roaring with pent-up energy, its doors banging like artillery.

"Stop the train!" shouted Cissy, but the noise swallowed up her words.

"Stop the train!" bawled Kookie. He leaped aboard the caboose with its open platform, its little filigree railing. "If you know what's good for you, don't go *anywhere*," he told the car attendant.

Cissy, for her part, ran along the outside of the train, jumping up on tiptoe to peer through each coach window. Peter Bull leaned out from his platform and tugged on the whistle cord.

At last Cissy found him. She saw the white duster coat hanging down from the luggage rack. He was sitting in the corner of a coach, reading a book. His face was still bruised from the pounding they had given him on the day he was locked up. One sleeve of his velvet jacket had been wrenched half out at the seam.

Cissy banged on the window, but Crew did not look up.

Another passenger did—a woman in a beaded vest. Cissy mimed for her to open the window. The window was stiff. It would not open more than a crack. The train was already starting to move as Cissy poked the scrap of brittle paper through the gap, pointing with her other hand at Crew.

Crew glanced up at the woman, at the window, at the page torn from Herman's Bible. Then Crew got up and ran, against the motion of the train, while Cissy ran alongside him, on the track edge.

Everett Crew and Kookie came off the back of the train like rats off a sinking ship, like squirrels off a felled tree, like pigs out of a burst barrel, squealing just as loud. Somewhere a dog began to bark, disturbed by the vibration of the accelerating train. Soon only the *wang-wang*ing of the track remained, like a heart beating with irrepressible joy.

20

MARRIAGE LINES

No one liked the new regime under Miss May March, except perhaps the parents. As Herman painted out the old name and painted in the new—OLIVE ACADEMY FOR THE EDUCATION OF YOUNG PERSONS—it was as if he were painting over past joys. The children of Class Three watched him working, through the windows, as they recited aloud their alphabet, their tables, their prayers, their verbal declensions. That was how the days passed now, in learning to read, write, add, recite, and sit still.

Kookie founded the SEOCT (Society for the Emancipation of Olive's Children from Tyranny) but it did no good: They still had to learn their numbers, their letters, their books of the Bible, their states of the Union . . .

Their new copybooks contained lists as straight and long as railway lines.

Unlike Class Three, Herman formed his letters with loving enthusiasm. For , in return for his overpainting every "Florence" sign with the name "Olive," the Olive Town Committee of Citizens had agreed to supply a ticket all the way to Salt Lake City. He worked like a man earning his ticket to heaven.

When it was time for Herman to leave, Frank Tate presented him with four large cages so that he could take with him the chickens he had bred during his time in Florence. "'Tain't cabinet work," Frank said, dissatisfied with the quality of his handiwork, "but there wasn't enough time, and they're only chickens. Mormon chickens, but chickens, all the same." Shyness stopped them actually shaking hands, but their shadows on the ground were linked by the shadow of a single telegraph wire.

The vacant lot would not stay vacant for long. Not only the umbrella manufacturer but a lens grinder, a stationer, and a toy maker were planning to open businesses on Main Street. A bathhouse was soon to open, and a builder had already begun putting up housing for workers who would come to Olive looking for work with one of the manufacturers. Then there were the rail yards, of course, for the cleaning and refurbishment of railway rolling stock.

When Sheriff Klemme's secret life was looked into, his desk pried open, his mail read, it was found that he had been in weekly communication with "Red Rock" Rimm. The only reason he had not kept the train theft from happening was that the townspeople had kept him in the dark for his own good.

His law proved as unsound as his character. Deliberately or otherwise, he had misinformed Marshal Haggar. Pickard Warboys could not be held responsible for the damage his son had done to the telegraph wires. The fifty-dollar fine was repaid and there was no more talk of him losing his job.

Klemme had also been quite wrong in awarding Jake Monterey's land to Gaff Boden. When they checked with the courts, they were told Boden's claim (processed by Klemme) was faulty; they would have to *share* the plot of land.

The two men looked at each other and were in perfect agreement for the first time in their lives. They would sooner share a bath with a rattlesnake than a ranch with each other.

"No matter," said Monterey casually. "Boden can keep it. I'll settle for Bible restitution."

His boys stared at him. The OTCC stared, too. It was the biggest word they had ever heard Jake Monterey utter.

"Well? What'ya gawping at? That skunk Klemme owes me. The Good Book says a man who wrongs another man ought to pay seven pounds of goods in restitution. Herman told me that one time." The smashed-open drawer hung from the desk like a lolling tongue. Monterey pointed at its contents. "So! If nobody objects, I'll take Klemme's sheriff badge and his gun and his keys to the lockup. I'm gonna be sheriff of Olive, that's what!"

All eyes rested on the open drawer, its bundles of secretive notes, its photograph of the abandoned wife and children. The townsfolk had been taken in once by a man's outward respectability. Jake Monterey? Well, he looked like a crow's nest fallen out of a tree, he smelled of home-made whiskey, and he talked aloud to himself in public. No, no one could think of one good reason why Jake should not be sheriff.

———❖———

"I'm gonna be sheriff one day," Kookie whispered to Cissy, as they sat, hands on heads, waiting for roll to be called. "I'll lock up Miss May March and pass a law 'gainst reading an' 'rithmetic."

Cissy gave this some thought. "'Rithmetic, anyway," she said.

Miss March rapped on her desk with a ruler. "Fuller Monterey, when you have quite finished picking your teeth with your pen nib, I have something to say." She drew out a letter from among her books. "I received a letter by yesterday's mail. It is addressed to you all, but some might have difficulty in reading it." (Here she broke off to eye them accusingly.) "So stand up, please, Cecelia Sissney, and read it out to us—with good diction, if you please."

The postmark on the letter said Saratoga.

Deer Class 3,

The werld dont seem hardly to have stood stil sinse the weeding. I hop you are all been good childen for Miss May. You lissen up good, cos she ken teech you wot you need to no in life.

As for me I am erning an precareous living with darlin Everett and the rest. In the plays I play the heroeen's muther mostly. Sumtimes qweens. Qweens you say? Wot Miss Loucien? But qweens is OK cos im happy as enny qween.

286

Yool see wen we visit on toor. As you ken tel, my darlin Everett has bin teeching me to reed and rite. I sinseerly hop Miss May is doin likewhys for you. Its mor yoosful than plukking pijuns even.

Your everluvvin Loucien Crew (Mrs.)

AUTHOR'S NOTE

Although this novel is based on true events, I used the astonishing history of Enid, Oklahoma, only as a jumping-off point for a work of fiction. You won't find Florence or its neighboring towns on the map. You won't find the Red Rock Runner rusting in any siding. But I hope the finished story is true to the character, resourcefulness, and downright bravery of the original land runners.

Geraldine McCaughrean
Berkshire, England

ABOUT THE AUTHOR

GERALDINE McCAUGHREAN is the winner of England's most prestigious children's book award, the Carnegie Medal, for *A Pack of Lies*. She is also the author of many other prize-winning books for young readers, including *The Pirate's Son*, *Gold Dust*, and *Forever X*, which was short-listed for the Carnegie Medal. She made her debut on the HarperCollins list with *The Stones Are Hatching*, which *Publishers Weekly* called an "evocative and profound fantasy" in a starred review. Her most recent book, *The Kite Rider*, was an ALA Notable Book, an ALA Best Book for Young Adults, and a Nestlé Smarties Book Prize Bronze Medal winner, and was chosen for the Carnegie Medal shortlist.

She received a degree in education at Christ Church College, Canterbury, and now writes full-time. Ms. McCaughrean and her family live in Berkshire, England.

www.geraldinemccaughrean.co.uk